HER

PERFECT

FAMILY

ALSO BY
TERESA DRISCOLL

HER

PERFECT

FAMILY

TERESA DRISCOLL

Published by Thomas & Mercer, Seattle

www.apub.com

Amazon, the Amazon logo, and Thomas & Mercer are trademarks of Amazon.com, Inc., or its affiliates.

ISBN-13: 9781542028752
ISBN-10: 1542028752

Cover design by The Brewster Project

Printed in the United States of America

HER

PERFECT

FAMILY

PROLOGUE

Pink

The daughter looks at her outfit. And suddenly, at this eleventh hour, she realises the colour is all wrong.

A shaft of sunlight has broken through the crack in the curtains. On its hanger on the wardrobe door last night, the dress looked fine. This morning, in this new and unforgiving beam of light, the pink is all at once . . . *too pink*.

In the shop mirror a month back it had seemed softer somehow. Her mother loved it immediately – there were tears. Hugs. The daughter sighs at the memory but is wondering now if there was some trick; if the shop mirror was smoked and they had not realised just how bright the dress would look in daylight. In sunlight. In *today's* light.

She sits up to see her reflection in the mirror across the room. She pinches her cheeks and tries to imagine how the addition of make-up might help. But no. There is no lipstick in the world that can fix this.

She gets out of bed and moves to her wardrobe, the bubble of panic in her stomach growing as she holds the dress on its hanger against her frame. She does not want to disappoint her mother;

they had such a very lovely day choosing this dress. But it looks so wrong now that she fears today's photograph will haunt her forever.

She imagines the picture, framed on the piano at home – the dress forever too pink.

And now her phone buzzes on the dressing table. A notification of yet another direct message. *He is not who he says he is . . .*

She feels the familiar shiver of unease. She badly needs to make this stop but simply has no time today. She throws the phone on to the bed and looks back at her reflection. It's decided. *Sorry Mummy.*

She will not wear the pink. She will wear the lemon dress instead . . .

Navy

The mother looks at her outfit. And suddenly, at this eleventh hour, she worries about her daughter.

She stares at the dress and jacket hanging against the shiny white of the hotel's wardrobe door and thinks of her beautiful girl, getting ready all alone at her flat.

She takes in the sensible navy of her ensemble. Somehow in the cold light of this bright and breezy Wednesday, it looks too conservative. Too 'mother of the bride'? She turns away; doesn't care.

Today is Gemma's day. She imagines standing alongside her beautiful girl in that gorgeous pink dress and feels the punch of pride that has swollen her heart and yes, her head too, ever since the results came in.

A first. Did I remember to tell you? My daughter Gemma: she has . . . a first.

She did not go to university herself and has never even been to a graduation ceremony. She turns to her husband who still sleeps, envying his calm. He's from a world where everyone goes to university and doesn't understand her nerves.

She thinks of the cathedral and the choir and her special girl in that *very special* pink dress.

She imagines it will be the best day of her life.

This mother who cannot know in this moment that it is to be the very worst.

CHAPTER 1

THE MOTHER

When the trumpets start up, the volume is a shock. A child near the back of the cathedral starts to laugh and we turn our heads, stifling our own smiles.

It is indeed surreal, all this pomp and this pageantry. And yes – loud. It is *very loud*.

I turn back to the front, my ears adjusting, as the university hierarchy file in to take up their seats in the choir stalls. They're all in different colours. Rich purple and yellow and red. Different headgear too. Some have velvet caps with gold tassels. Some have fur on their gowns. Others not.

I imagine those in the know understand all these sartorial signals of intellectual pecking order. Which colour for which university each professor attended. I have no idea. I'm simply wondering how uncomfortable all those hats must be.

I smooth the navy dress across my knee and watch as the trumpeters finish at last and we hear the audience's collective clearing of throats and blowing of noses as the chancellor steps up to the microphone. I feel myself smile again and for a moment am enchanted and proud and exhilarated by the warmth of the welcome.

I listen. I beam. I listen some more. And then – much too quickly, I'm embarrassed to become rather bored. The chancellor, a tall woman with enormous red glasses, goes on much too long and soon I am thinking – *yes, yes, we know all this. Do please get on with it.* I steal a glance at the programme on my lap. Gemma is page four and I am wondering – how long per page?

There is more coughing and shuffling of chairs. A child crying. The scraping of wood on stone floor as a parent apparently decides to take the weeping child out. I turn to watch them near the back of the cathedral. The child, on his father's hip, looks no more than eighteen months and I wonder if it is a second marriage. Or just a big age gap? And how on earth do divorced people manage occasions like this? We were only offered two tickets.

I turn back to the front. Maidstead is the smallest cathedral not just in the south-west but in the country – only just scraping its official status. I like that you can see front to back from my vantage point. For some reason we are in the VIP seats directly in front of the choir stall. No idea how we ended up here but it's a happy mistake. A great view. There are narrow corridors with stone arches beyond the choir stalls and I can see glimpses of university staff with clipboards.

For a moment I think I recognise someone in the distance – Helen's sister. Mandy. Or is it Molly. For the life of me I can't remember but it suddenly occurs to me that maybe *she* organised our seats? Mandy (or Molly?) is the sister of one of my book-group friends, Helen. When Gemma expressed an interest in this uni, Helen very kindly passed on some tips. Her sister's in the comms department. Gave us some general pointers on the most popular accommodation for freshers – that sort of thing. Nice woman. We've met her very briefly at a couple of uni events – on nodding terms, no more. Would she have done this for us? I doubt it . . .

But now I am frowning. Reconsidering. I have been going on and on about the ceremony at book club, worrying about the seating, so maybe Helen *did* put in a word. It's the sort of thing she'd do. I glance at my bag, thinking of my phone. I should message Helen later. Yes. If her sister wangled these seats on the quiet, we should at least thank her . . .

And now the chancellor is telling us that our sons and daughters, lined up in these anterooms off the rear corridors, are presently graduands – the technical term until they miraculously transform into bona-fide graduates once their certificates are in their happy hands.

I turn to Ed, who sits alongside me, his shoulders still tight – no longer quite the ball of fury he was when we first took our seats, but he's still cross with me. I touch his arm and whisper again that I'm sorry about the bad atmosphere in the car.

He finds a small smile but as payback will not look at me. But I can tell, even from his profile, he's softening; that I am *almost* forgiven. Good.

It wasn't my fault – the row. Well, not row; we don't really have rows. I'm lucky that way. It was just that I wanted to leave the hotel nice and early as we were supposed to meet Gemma at the 'dressing tents' to see her in her gown and do some photographs ahead of the cathedral. But Ed, who's a great deal more relaxed than me about timings, wanted a full English. *Stop catastrophising Rachel.*

And then a lorry with gas canisters decided to burst a tyre – and my bubble – right in front of us on a major roundabout on the way into the city centre. Of course, I blamed Ed. I didn't say anything out loud – I just let out this huff. Looked away. But the problem with Ed is sometimes he just won't leave things . . .

Spit it out, Rachel. You really saying this is my fault? This lorry? I'm fine.

You're not fine. You can't even look at me.

Leave it, Ed.

I didn't rise to it. The thing is I absolutely can't stand arguments and there's no way we need all that. Not today. I just messaged Gemma – devastated to miss the dressing tent. She said no worries, then texted something rather odd: *Don't be upset when you see me, Mum. Promise?*

And now she's had to turn off her phone and I'm in limbo. Puzzled. How could I be upset with her – today of all days?

Suddenly there's applause and I'm pulled back into the moment to see that the chancellor is *at last* wrapping up. I clap. Ed claps. Someone else, an alumni, steps forward to take up their position to our far left to hand over the certificates. Someone off the telly but not A-list famous. I will have to look them up in the programme. Gemma did tell me.

And now – hurrah – the first glimpse of *the graduands* – appearing in a line through a stone arch off to the right, behind the choir stalls. My goodness – what a logistical feat this is. Gemma told me the briefing was a right palaver.

I clap and smile at the first batch as if I know them. There are hoots and whistles from some of the parents and I love that this is more relaxed than I expected. I can feel tears pricking my eyes. It's all so huge. And then? Name after name after name and my palms are sore already. I realise that I cannot possibly keep up this level of enthusiasm. I simply can't love all these strangers quite this much. I glance down. Good Lord. We are still on *page . . . one.*

I reduce the quality of my clapping and distract myself by taking in the very different shoes that all the girls have chosen. Some spectacularly high. Gemma has this phobia about tripping in public and has chosen wedges. *I need to have something solid to walk on, Mum.* I suggested kitten heels, but she was not having that. Reckoned it would make her legs look stumpy in the photographs.

I think back again to that day we chose her dress. A gorgeous sunny day. Lunch at the café by the river. I feel a sigh leave my body as I picture her in the mirror. That gorgeous shade of pink.

I feel tears coming once again, imagining the moment her name is called. I turn to Ed and he winks. Good. I am properly forgiven. I stretch out my hand and he squeezes it.

It takes fifteen minutes per page and finally we are on to the fourth.

I take in a deep breath, counting the names. One more batch of six. Then her group.

I am this ridiculous ball of emotion. Suddenly there are all these scenes swirling around my brain. The day they put her in my arms. That picture on the fridge of her in a paddling pool with Ed spraying cold water on to her. I think of the day she got the offer to come here. The scream of delight from her room when she logged on to get the 'yes' even before we picked up her A-level results.

And now a pause. Her batch next. I find that I am holding my breath. I trace the names with my finger. Walk, applause. Walk, applause. And then at last.

Gemma Hartley . . .

I see her appear at the back of the choir stall in her gown and her mortar board with her long dark hair loose over her shoulders. I take in the neutral shoes and the slightly tanned legs. And then there is this little punch of shock as she walks forward.

Not the glimpse of gorgeous pink beneath the black of the gown as she moves. I feel myself frowning. I turn to Ed, but he hasn't noticed.

It's the wrong dress. I don't understand. The dress is pale lemon.

Ed is calling out – '*Hurrah! Well done Gemma*' – and everyone is applauding.

I am clapping too and smiling now, trying to cover up the puzzlement.

Gemma recognises her father's voice and turns to spot us. She looks down at her dress and then up at me with this sort of worried look on her face.

I just smile. I don't understand . . . but I deliberately turn the smile up to a beam.

Then she turns towards the guy holding out her certificate so that we are looking at her back as she reaches out her right hand to take her prize.

There is this noise from behind the trumpeters. A sort of thud as if someone has dropped something heavy, like a large music book, at the back of the choir stall.

It startles poor Gemma and the very thing she has feared all her life – at sports days and presentations and the like – happens right this moment. She stumbles.

My hand is immediately up to my mouth. She is flat on the floor and everyone sort of leans forward.

I am all at once mortified for her and also overwhelmed with love for her. I want to be beside her telling her that it doesn't matter. That no one will care. *Just get up and smile. No one will care.* A part of me wants to run to her but I know it will make things worse; magnify her embarrassment.

There's a beat as we all wait for her to get up so that we can cheer her on; signal that it really doesn't matter. But the beat is too long. I stand now, worrying that she may have fainted. Or banged her head?

Two professors sitting nearer have now moved also. All at once they are crouching beside her. Next there is shouting.

'*A doctor. We need a doctor.*'

I am aware only that I am suddenly pushing. Ed too. I *push, push, push* past the three people seated in my way and reach the aisle just as they say it . . .

'She's been *shot.*'

Next come ugly, unimaginable words. A bubble of bile suddenly surrounding me.

'An ambulance. We need an ambulance. She's been *shot* . . .'

And now slow motion. People screaming. *Run. Run.*

There is a chaotic surge of bodies – parents and students and ushers too. A starburst of panic blocking my way as everyone rushes to the various doors.

I have to shoulder people aside. No longer pushing – shoving. *Get out of my way. Out of my way. It's my daughter . . . I need to get to my daughter.*

When finally I near the huddle around Gemma, a woman is barking instructions. *Give me some room. I'm a doctor and I need something to press against the wound. That shawl. Give me your shawl.*

Someone's handing the doctor a green shawl as I crouch down to stroke my daughter's hair.

'Gemma. It's Mummy. I'm right here, darling. Right here . . .'

She's head down, utterly still, and I try again to push the hair back so I can see her face as I take it in – the wrong dress.

This dress covered in blood that is seeping into a large and terrifying pool on the stone floor beneath her.

Not the pink dress – not even a lemon dress any more.

Dark red.

Everything blood red now.

CHAPTER 2

THE PRIVATE INVESTIGATOR

'Do you want a flake, sweetheart?' Matthew Hill holds out a five-pound note to the ice-cream seller as his daughter Amelie frowns. It's a simple enough question but Matthew's learned that nothing in life is simple with a child of Amelie's disposition. She tilts her head as if world peace is on the line.

'Quick, quick, lovely. Chocolate flake – yes? There are lots of people waiting.' The ice-cream van's on the high street and Matthew is shocked by the queue behind him and the crowds in general. He'd quite forgotten it's graduation season. Would never have come into the centre of Maidstead if he'd remembered.

Amelie is off nursery with a stomach ache that miraculously disappeared once a stay at home was confirmed. She's starting proper school soon and they wonder if that's worrying her. She used to love nursery so Matthew and Sally are 'going with the flow', hoping it's not to be a new fad.

Amelie's good at fads.

'Yes to the flake,' Sal adds suddenly. 'I'll have it if she doesn't want it.'

And then, just as the man takes the money, there's suddenly shouting and some kind of commotion off to their right.

'Run. *Run.*' A male voice, loud and desperate, from the midst of a small group running from the narrow street that leads to the cathedral. 'There's a gunman. There's a gunman in the cathedral.'

The speed of the ensuing panic is extraordinary. Very soon there's a lot of screaming. More people are running from the alleyway. People on the high street start running too. Matthew feels the familiar shot of adrenaline as he turns to grasp Sally by the shoulders.

'Right. You need to take Amelie out of the city centre. Fast as you can. Jog so you don't fall. Go to the Asda car park on the outskirts. I'll meet you there.'

The look of horror on Sally's face is like a physical blow. 'You're not coming?'

'I'll be right behind you. I just need to see if I can help first.'

'No, Matthew, no. You come with us. You come with us *now.*'

'There's no time, Sally. Just go. I'll follow you, I promise. Soon as I can.'

A terrible expression sweeps across his wife's face. He can't quite read it and just watches as she pauses for a beat before grabbing Amelie's hand and starting to flee. He stares at their backs – Amelie crying over the lost ice cream – as Sally scoops their daughter on to her hip and jogs just as he instructed. A strong and steady pace down the high street.

Then Matthew turns to push against the tide of people running away from the cathedral.

As he forges forward, he puts his phone up to his ear and speed dials the only person he can think of. He prays for the sound of sirens. Prays that he won't be needed after all.

DI Melanie Sanders picks up immediately. 'What is it, Matt? Emergency here.'

'I'm on Maidstead High Street. People screaming there's a gun-man in the cathedral.'

'*That's* my emergency. What are you doing there?'

'Never mind. I'm not hearing sirens yet . . . Why no sirens?'

'Traffic. They're on their way but it'll be a few minutes, Matt. I just got the call. I'm on my way too.'

'And armed support? What's the ETA for armed support, Mel?'

A pause.

'*How long Mel?*

'Ten minutes minimum.'

Matthew increases his pace. As he reaches the green in front of the cathedral, there is the shock of a crush outside the main door. Some people are running away but others are standing still, faces terrified, calling out the names of loved ones.

'Move away from the doors,' he shouts. 'Everyone away from the doors.' He presses the phone back to his ear. 'I'll do what I can, Mel. But it's chaos here.'

'Not on your own, Matt . . .'

He hangs up and runs around the west side of the cathedral, avoiding the throng.

There's a man in a high-vis jacket – some kind of usher or maybe security – looking completely overwhelmed, standing by temporary fencing, designed presumably to keep the graduation visitors to the front lawn, but which is now making the crisis worse – restricting the flow of people.

'Get these fences down now so we can get everyone away faster.' Matthew kicks one of the temporary barriers over by way of demonstration. The man in the yellow jacket copies him. As the fence is reduced – crash after crash after crash – people start to step and leap over the barriers, which slowly improves the flow.

'Are all the doors open?' Matthew barks.

The man frowns – can't hear him over the screaming.

'Are all the doors open?' Matthew now shouts and the man shakes his head.

'We locked some to check tickets.'

'Get them all open now. All of them, you hear me – fast as you can? What's my best way in? I can't get through these crowds.'

'Tower at the back. There's a door by a laburnum tree. It was supposed to be left open for the staff to leave.'

Suddenly another man, grey-haired and face desperate, holds on to Matthew's shoulder. 'Are you in charge? Our kids are in there. The students. Some of them are still in rooms at the back. We can't get to them. How do we get to them?'

'I'm on it. Move away from the crush, sir. Help get this fence down. And get more doors open. Can you do that for me?'

The man nods. Matthew then jumps a fence on the ground himself and runs around the back of the cathedral towards the laburnum. Sure enough there is a small oak door with a large, black iron handle. Open.

Inside, Matthew moves fast through a narrow stone corridor to find himself to the side of the choir stall. This end of the cathedral is almost empty but there's still a large crush of people at the main door, trying to get out.

There's a lot of shouting. Some men are urging the women and children to leave but others are screaming to know where the students are.

'Where are our children? Are they out? Who's getting them out?'

In front of him, Matthew sees a small throng of people crouched down around a young woman on the ground in a pool of blood. Instinctively, he looks up, trying to work out where the shot would have come from. There is an upper gallery with carved shapes in the stone balcony. He watches. No shadows. No sign of movement. But the gunman could still be up there.

He realises what easy targets they are: sitting ducks. He thinks of Amelie and Sally and feels this terrible lurch. No choice. No sign of any uniforms yet . . .

He moves out into the open central area and joins the small group surrounding the shot girl. A woman is rolling her over, testing a pulse and doing compressions while instructing someone else to hold the girl's neck in place. The woman's voice is steady and firm – must be a doctor or nurse at least. Good. It may be a while before an ambulance is allowed through.

At last he hears sirens but not close yet.

'Help's on the way. I'm ex police. We're going to get you all out of here.'

Another woman turns to look at him, tears pouring down her cheeks. The mother then. Alongside her is a man, face white. The father.

'What should I do?' The man's voice is breaking. 'What should we do?'

'Stay with her. Talk to her. Help's coming.'

Another man steps forward, his face steadier. 'Marine. A parent. My wife and son are on their way out. What can I do?'

Another slim, tall woman in a black suit joins them, her face white with terror. 'We have a lot of students in anterooms out the back. We don't know what to do. Is it safe to bring them through? Two of my ushers have bolted. What should I do?'

'Right. Take me to them. They're opening more doors. The crush will reduce soon. How many shots were fired? Did it sound like an automatic weapon?'

'I don't know. I don't know. We didn't hear shots . . .' The woman's voice is shaking.

'OK. You – with me.' He points at the marine and the woman in the dark suit and leads them both through the choir stall to a narrow stone corridor with two large oak doors. There's a single usher standing just inside one door and he can hear crying.

Matthew steps into the first room. 'Right. There's been a shooting but we are going to keep you all safe. This is . . .' He tilts his head at the marine.

'Tom.'

'This is Tom. He's military and he's going to stay in here with you and bolt the door. You'll be safe in here until the police arrive. I'm going to give you a password. The password is ICE CREAM. OK, Tom?' The marine nods. 'You don't open this door until you get that password. You hear me. Now shut this door and bolt it inside.'

He moves along to the second anteroom and repeats the instruction to the woman in black who agrees to stay with the students. 'You're safest in here for now. The password is ICE CREAM. Don't open until the police give you that password. Yes?'

He retreats to the main part of the cathedral just as the first uniformed police officers appear at the far end.

Matthew dials Mel again. 'We've got scores of students in two locked anterooms inside. They're safe. Heavy doors. I've given them the password ICE CREAM. I'll pass it on to the first teams who've just arrived. Can you circulate it as well?'

'Good thinking. Will do. Any more shots? What kind of weapon, Matt. Automatic?'

'We don't know. But it's not safe to move the students just yet, Mel. There's still a terrible crush. But no more shots. No sign of the gunman. One victim. Girl. Looks in a bad way. But the shooter could still be around.'

'Really good work, Matt. Thank you. You OK?'

'No. We need that armed team. But I can see two more doors being opened. Good. And your guys are here at last. I'll hand over. But I can't stay. I've got Sally and Amelie in town.'

'OK. Hand over and go to your family, Matt.'

'Password – ICE CREAM. You get those students out fast as you can, yes? They're terrified and some of the parents won't move away until they see their kids.'

'Course. You stay safe, Matt. And *thank you.*'

Matthew moves forward to speak to the first uniformed team to reach the doctor tending to the injured girl. They are on their radios checking the ETA on the ambulance. He tells them about the students and the password and they nod, then frown. They all know the ambulance won't be allowed through until the all-clear is given on the gunman.

'I'm ex-job. Matthew Hill. DI Mel Sanders knows me and can vouch for me. I've done what I can but I can't stay. I have my own family in town. Do you need anything more from me?'

The officers shake their heads and Matthew glances around the cathedral again. 'Up there. That balcony is my best guess for the shooter position. No sign of anyone now. But who knows?'

And then he moves forward one last time to speak to the parents of the bleeding girl. 'The ambulance won't be long.' The doctor is continuing the CPR. 'She'll be in hospital soon.'

Matthew then retreats, using the door back out to the green by the laburnum. From there he jogs down a side alley and runs at a steady pace, using back streets to avoid the chaos on the high street. At first there is no phone signal. He hears more and more sirens as he nears the outskirts of the city, dialling Sally as he runs. At last. Three bars . . .

'I'm safe. I'm on my way to you. The police are there now.'

There is this terrible sound. Like an animal howling.

'Where are you, Sal?'

There's a pause. Sort of gulping on the end of the line.

'Asda car park. I did what you said.'

'Good. On my way.'

He hangs up and continues jogging, replaying all the scenes in his head. The girl on the ground in the pool of blood. The sound of the fences hitting the ground. Smash. Smash. The students, crying and terrified in those two anterooms.

Ice cream. Ice cream.

He steadies his pace until he finally turns a corner to see the supermarket across the road.

There are quite a lot of people milling about – white-faced – and he can hear a steady stream of questions.

What's going on? Is it safe? What do we do?

He sees the red of Sally's coat in the distance and continues towards her.

As he reaches them, Amelie's still crying. Sally too.

And then to his shock there is this blow to his left arm as Sally hits him really hard, tears pouring down her face.

He just stands there as she keeps hitting him.

'Why did you do that? Leave us. Why . . . did . . . you . . . do . . . that?' She punctuates each word with another blow.

He just lets her hit him over and over until finally she stands still and looks at him, the anger on her face changing. Next her shoulders are heaving with sobbing.

'I thought you were going to get yourself shot.'

Tears are still streaming down her face now and he gently puts his arms around her, kissing her cheek – 'It's OK, I'm safe; I'm here now, Sally' – before pulling back to lift Amelie, who is also crying, from the ground to hold her tight too.

CHAPTER 3

THE FATHER - *NOW*

He watches his wife, watching their daughter.

Through the window, beyond the hospital bed, he can see a nurse on the main ward talking to the uniformed officer who's guarding their cubicle.

The staff say Gemma may be able to hear so they're watching the news on the TV above the bed with subtitles instead of the sound. It's Thursday. Twenty-four hours since the horror of the cathedral, yet the scrolling words confirm nothing's changed. Still the police are saying there's no evidence to suggest terrorism. There's nothing, in fact, to confirm or suggest any motive or suspect at all. The appeal is repeated for photographs or video recorded on the many smartphones at the graduation ceremony.

He has to steel himself for a moment, remembering the screaming and the blood on the stone floor. Some news channels have been running appalling footage on a loop which brings it back so vividly time and time over, making his stomach churn and his wife cry. He tenses, worrying that the images may appear again right now. Gemma on the floor. That pool of blood. His baby girl's blood . . .

He grabs the remote from the bedside table and turns off the TV.

His wife spins her head, her eyes full of questions. He takes in the exhaustion and the fear on her face. Also an ache that he recognises – that longing for better news. Any news, actually.

'There's nothing new, love. And in any case, DI Sanders is due soon. If there's anything new, she'll tell us . . .'

'Shhh. She's listening. I know she's listening.' Rachel turns back to Gemma to smooth her hair and kiss her forehead with a gentleness that is almost unbearable to witness.

'We're here, darling girl. Daddy and me – we're right here. And we'll be here when you wake up. Just rest for now. You're not to worry about anything. You just sleep.'

He clenches his right fist and feels the nails dig into the palm. He finds that he likes this discomfort and so digs the nails a little deeper.

He tries to keep his eyes from moving to the terrible little hill within the bedding. There's a frame beneath the blanket over her left leg, or rather where her left leg used to be.

How will they tell her? Still he digs his nails deep, deep into his flesh. When she comes round – *if* she comes round – how the bloody hell will they tell her?

Last night his wife stayed at the hospital and he dashed home to pick up some things. Clothes. Books. Toiletries. Gemma's favourite perfume. He looked at the flatness of Gemma's double bed at home – no hill; no nasty frame beneath the duvet – and in the end he swept everything from the top of Gemma's dressing table, breaking a mirror and a little china dog that she loves. In the early hours he tried to superglue the dog back together, but it looks a mess. Like his daughter's body.

He hasn't told his wife yet. About the dog. About Canada . . .

Instead he brought Gemma's grey rabbit to the hospital with some perfume that his wife has sprayed around the room. She seems to think their daughter will smell it from her coma and somehow be comforted. He thinks this unlikely but has not said so; not out loud.

He stares at the rabbit – a grey rabbit that has been a favourite since Gemma was last in hospital as a tiny girl. Asthma attack. At the time he thought it was the scariest thing he would ever endure as a parent. Four nights in the high-dependency unit. It was bad. But he had no idea back then just how bad 'bad' could be . . .

He watches his wife pull her hair up into a high ponytail. For all the exhaustion and the greyness of her skin and the black circles beneath her eyes, her back is straight. She's extraordinary. His rock. His everything. He remembers her pacing while Gemma had the surgery – up and down the corridor outside the operating theatre. Up and down. Up and down. And the doctor coming out with updates. The two body blows.

They were unable to save the leg. *But the baby is OK.*

Baby? What baby?

He was actually sick. Retching over and over in the nearest gents.

Kneeling over the toilet bowl, he was looking down at his own knees, wondering what they did with his daughter's leg. Do they burn it – an amputated limb? Some kind of incinerator? That was what made him vomit. To think of a part of his beautiful little girl. Separate. Gone. Her flesh and blood. His flesh and blood.

Now, back on the ward, in this small and claustrophobic cubicle, he tries very hard not to think of any of these details, but there it is again. The little blanket hill in the bed. His beautiful girl. All chopped up.

'She's here.' His wife signals with her head the arrival of DI Melanie Sanders who's talking to the uniformed officer outside their little box.

'We just need to get a drink, my darling.' Rachel again kisses Gemma's forehead. 'We'll be back very soon.' Next, she raises her finger to her lips so that he'll say nothing more until they're outside.

Waiting for them beyond their daughter's room, DI Sanders looks pale, which he takes to mean bad news. Or rather no news.

'How's she today?' she asks.

'The same.' Rachel is careful to close the door to the cubicle before taking a seat alongside the police inspector. 'They say the coma is the body's way of taking a break. It will give time for the swelling on the brain to go down. It's probably a good thing actually. The coma.' His wife tucks her hair behind her ear and he wonders if Rachel realises that she has told DI Sanders this already. More than once. 'We don't know how long it will be.'

The doctors explained last night that Gemma's blow to the head when she hit the stone floor was every bit as serious as her leg injury from the gunshot. She has severe swelling on her brain. Her pupils are responsive but there's no way of knowing what the long term holds. It's a waiting game. The medical staff are all very careful not to make any promises.

'It's important that you know we are doing everything that we can to piece together what happened. I have a good team. A strong team.' DI Sanders is also repeating herself.

'So there's no more news? No leads yet?' He wishes that he sounded less critical but it's hard to hide his frustration. A whole twenty-four hours. He'd expected progress and wants so badly for this to be explained, for this to have nothing to do with Canada . . .

'Nothing concrete yet. We're still working on Gemma's phone and laptop; also going through all the footage that people have shared. I'm waiting on the forensics report on the cathedral. Who knows what we'll find. Sometimes it can be the smallest thing that unlocks something.' DI Sanders pauses and then takes in a long breath before turning to him.

'I asked last night if either of you noticed any change in Gemma. Anything troubling her. I was wondering if you'd had time to think about that? I mean – if you had any suspicions about the pregnancy? If there had been any discussion or hints or any kind of upset over it?'

'What are you implying?' Yesterday DI Sanders' questions were brief and practical. Gemma was only just out of surgery. They were distressed and the interview was short. Today he senses a change in the officer's tone and there's something in her gaze he doesn't like.

'I just mean that it must be a shock. The pregnancy. If you knew nothing at all about it.'

'It is a surprise.' He's careful to speak slowly. 'But nothing compared to the shock of seeing my daughter gunned down at her graduation ceremony. With respect, I don't see the pregnancy as the key issue here. And how we feel about it is hardly the priority, Inspector.'

'No. No. Of course. I understand. But if it was something you knew nothing about, it may in some way be connected. At issue. It must have been stressful for Gemma too. I have to ask these questions, I'm very sorry.'

She doesn't look sorry. She looks borderline cynical now. He wonders what she's thinking, this detective inspector. Does she imagine some row? Some meltdown or confrontation with the father of his daughter's child.

'We didn't know she was pregnant, Inspector. We told you that last night. There was no discussion with Gemma. No conflict over it. We knew *nothing*.'

She holds his gaze a little longer and then turns to his wife.

'I appreciate this is a difficult line of inquiry for you both. But we have to consider who may be the father of the child, in case it's relevant to what's happened. I understand she'd recently split from her boyfriend. Alexander?'

'Yes. It came as a surprise to us – the split. They'd seemed quite happy.' Rachel clears her throat with the fake little cough he knows so well. She does it when she says something embarrassing and is aware that people are staring at her. He wants to tell the inspector to leave his wife alone. That she is going through quite enough, thank you very much.

'And they parted two or three months back, I understand. From speaking to some of Gemma's friends?'

'Yes. About that. She didn't tell us immediately. We did have plans in place for a joint dinner to mark the graduation. The two families. We obviously cancelled all that.' Rachel clears her throat again.

'Have you spoken to Alexander?' He's the one now staring and DI Sanders narrows her eyes before she replies.

'Yes, we have. Only briefly so far. He's in shock too. Understandably. We've been careful so far over what we've shared with him but my reading of our initial interview is that he doesn't know she's pregnant.'

'Right. But this won't be made public? The pregnancy, I mean – it's not really anyone's business, is it?' Ed is suddenly afraid of what will happen when the papers get hold of this. He imagines it splashed across the front page. All over the telly.

'We'll be very careful but sometimes these things do get out.'

'Well, I should warn you that no one will hear it from us. And I'll be very angry indeed if this . . . *gets out*.' He holds the inspector's gaze again and watches her nod.

'It's just we find it difficult. All the journalists.' His wife has lowered her voice as she speaks. 'Are they still outside the hospital? They keep messaging us on social media.'

'Yes, I'm sorry. The media interest is always difficult. I do sympathise. Have you thought again about the family-liaison officer?'

'No, no. We don't want anyone here. Not yet. Maybe when we're home.' Rachel's tone is adamant; she can't bear the thought of anyone else hanging around the hospital. Bad enough needing a police guard.

'OK. Well, as I say, we'll be careful but we do need to ask questions – about your daughter's relationships. This is an attempted-murder inquiry. I promise we'll be sensitive but I want to be straight with you too: I can't give an absolute guarantee that at some point, our line of questioning won't lead to this information being shared by the people we have to question.'

His wife's crying now and he reaches out to put his arms around her shoulders as she feels in her pocket for a tissue.

'And nothing more's come to mind since we spoke yesterday?' DI Sanders is watching him closely again. She's a strange woman. Intense. It feels as if she has some kind of laser vision. Some instinct that is both promising in terms of the investigation. And personally dangerous.

He thinks of Canada. He thinks of the phone calls he made secretly late last night and wonders if the inspector will have his phone records examined. Damn. How the hell will he explain himself?

'No. Nothing.'

CHAPTER 4

THE DAUGHTER – *NOW*

She sleeps most of the time and is grateful for the calm. But even in sleep, she hears the sea whispering and knows that it's waiting for her.

Each time she wakes, she is somehow not in the real world at all but instead beside the ocean. There's only the colour blue – the soft blue of the sky and the deeper, brighter blue of the sea. She can feel the breeze on her face and the salt in the spray with the echo of each rolling wave – yes, whispering.

Sshhhh.

Always she is right at the water's edge so that she can feel the lapping of the waves. Sometimes she's up to her ankles in the water and sometimes up to her knees but she's always dressed and so never ventures out to swim.

The first time all this happened, she thought she was *truly* awake. Now she knows this is not the case. It's happened over and over, as if on a loop. Just a different and special kind of dreaming from which the only escape is more sleep.

She opens her eyes right now and there it is, same scene as always. Blue sky. Blue sea . . . whispering.

Today she just stands in the water and lets it lap around her legs. Oddly, one leg is warm and the other is very cold. She looks down but can see only seaweed, floating on the surface. Next she waits for the objects to float by. Every time in every dream, there are strange objects that float by – like clues in some game she doesn't yet understand.

Mostly they are things from her home and from her life – as if they are shipwrecked with her here by this beach. A bottle of perfume. The brush from her dressing table. Today there is the mortar board from the ceremony in the cathedral. She watches it, bobbing up and down in the current, just out of reach. She remembers now that she was worried this would happen – that it would fall from her head. She straightens her back and remembers walking very upright with everyone clapping. And then she saw her mother's puzzled expression. Yes. She looked down at her dress. Is that when the mortar board fell off?

She watches the board move closer and stretches out her hand. She wonders if she's supposed to collect these objects? Is that it? Some kind of test? Trying to find the pieces of some puzzle. If she collects all the objects in these dreams, maybe she can go home? Is that it?

But her feet are buried too deep in the sand and she cannot move them. She tries harder, stretching out further, but it's no good. The mortar board floats past and she feels that she is going to cry.

Next the direction of the waves seems to change and the mortar board's floating even further away. She tries to call out but still she's mute; her voice gone. She moves her lips but there's no sound beyond the whispering of the waves.

Shhh. She's listening. I know she's listening . . .

What was that? She turns her head. She was so very sure she heard a voice. A voice she knows . . .

She keeps very still and listens but there's silence now. It is too late. The mortar board drifts further and further away and she's so very tired again.

She closes her eyes and is somehow moving through the water and the clouds and the blue of the sky all at the same time. And now the strangest thing. She can smell her favourite perfume – all around her.

And as she drifts or flies or floats, she suddenly feels this wetness on her forehead.

Like the spray from the sea. But no; it isn't spray.

She holds her body very, very still.

We're here, darling girl . . .

It feels like a kiss – this touch to her forehead.

Yes.

She's crying again.

This feels just like a kiss.

CHAPTER 5

THE PRIVATE INVESTIGATOR

Matthew checks his diary on his phone. Blank. Good. He moves from his desk through the door that connects to the adjoining flat and turns on the coffee machine. He sighs as he watches the light flashing red, knowing it will be a while before it signals the correct temperature.

Once upon a time he was more patient; he would tell anyone who would listen that good coffee was always worth waiting for. Now? As a parent and the owner of a growing business, his life's unrecognisable. A see-saw of different worries. He either has too much work or not enough. When business is hectic, he worries about balancing it with family life. When work's slow, he worries about paying the bills. The upshot is he worries more and sleeps less.

And he's not so good at waiting . . .

He glances around the small kitchen and thinks back to the time he lived in this flat right alongside his office. That different version of Matthew before he met Sally. Before the gift and the puzzle that is their lovely Amelie.

He slumps on to the stool at the breakfast bar, willing the light on the machine to hurry up. At last there's a little buzz as the colour blinks from red to green. He presses the button for a double espresso as his phone rings – the display confirming DI Melanie Sanders. *Again.*

'Hello Mel? How's it going?' He's surprised to hear from her so soon. It's Friday – two days since the horror of the cathedral – and she's already phoned several times, on each occasion sounding more and more stretched. It's unlike her.

'Listen. I know I shouldn't ask but do you have time to meet at our café, Matt?' Her tone's uncertain and her voice is quieter than usual. He can't read it.

'Yeah – sure. Not much on here today actually. An hour?'

'Perfect. Thank you.'

'You OK, Mel?' He's surprised she even has time to meet him.

There's a pause. 'No. Not really. The politics on this one are off the scale, Matt. We've got the media crawling all over us. I'm wondering whether I'm up to this.'

'Don't be ridiculous. Of course, you're up to this.'

'Everyone wants a decision on whether the final graduation ceremony should go ahead next week. I mean, we've ruled out terrorism, but it's an odd case. So public. I'm not sure I can make the call yet. We'll have the CSI team on site a while.' She's talking too fast. 'Don't they realise I have to put the inquiry above everything else? Above the politics. Above the economic worries—'

'Right. Take a deep breath, Mel. Save it for the café. One step at a time. We'll talk it all through.' He pauses. 'Order carrot cake. A huge slice. You need sugar.'

At last she laughs. 'Thank you, Matt. I appreciate this.'

'No problem. See you in an hour.'

He hangs up and sips at the coffee before quickly dialling home. Sal texted earlier to say their daughter was playing up again.

'Hi there, honey. How's Amelie?'

'Complete nightmare.' Sal's whispering. 'She *still* won't go to nursery. I've tried absolutely everything.'

'Tummy-ache routine again?' Matthew's frowning. They let Amelie stay off an extra day after all the drama but he'd expected it to blow over by now. Day three.

'No. Hang on, Matt. I need to move . . .' There's the click of a door at Sally's end. 'Sorry. I don't want her listening in. She says she's worried the bad man will come to the nursery with his gun.' Sally pauses again. 'She says she feels safer at home.'

'Jeez.' Matthew stands and checks his watch. He should go home but is now torn. He needs to leave straight away for the café if he's not to hold Mel up. Or rather let her down. 'Right. Well, we need to talk this through some more this evening; maybe I underestimated.' He rakes his fingers through his hair, taking in a long, slow breath. 'I'd hoped she'd just forget it at her age. Maybe we should take advice. Get someone professional to talk to her.'

'Like a psychiatrist? Oh goodness. You really think so? You don't think we just need to give it some time?'

'I honestly don't know. Look. Do you want me to come home now?'

'Are you busy?'

'Sort of. But—'

'No, then. It won't change today. I've written off nursery for today.'

'OK, so let's try reassuring her together again when I get home later and see how the weekend goes. But let's take some advice too. What about the school? Maybe we could talk to her teacher?' Amelie's nursery is attached to the primary school she'll be attending soon. It's a brilliant place. Long waiting list.

'This is my fault, isn't it?' Sal sounds close to tears now. 'For saying those things in front of her. For mentioning the gun, for saying I thought you were going to be shot . . .'

'Sal, you have to stop that, love. This is no one's fault but the bastard who shot that poor girl in the cathedral. Amelie will get past this with our help. We'll make her feel safe again, Sal. Kids are resilient. We just need to give her a bit of time.'

He waits, sipping again at the coffee. The truth? He's feeling now that this is *his* fault for charging off in the opposite direction; for heading to the cathedral into danger instead of protecting his family.

Sally lets out a long sigh. 'You're right, Matt. OK. I'll try to distract her today and play it down. We'll talk to her again later. Yes?'

'Course. Together. Look – I've just got a meeting and then I'll be home early. Promise. Love you.'

'You too.'

In the car, he finds the faux-jolly banter of a music quiz irritating. He keeps thinking of Amelie bursting into tears when he caught up with them in the car park after the cathedral. He flicks from radio station to radio station. Some are running updates on a hurricane that has hit an island he's never heard of. Meltona. Everyone stranded. He searches for a local news bulletin and at last there's an update on the shooting. It repeats that police are still trawling through the huge array of photos and video footage of the graduation ceremony. There's a sound clip in which you can hear someone in the background shouting, 'She's been shot. Oh no. She's been shot.' Then screaming. He snaps off the radio, his heart rate increasing again.

He's picturing once more the small oak door by the laburnum tree. The faces of all the terrified students in that anteroom, unsure whether to make a run for it.

Ice cream. Ice cream. You wait for the password . . .

By the time he reaches the café, he feels inexplicably tired even though it's barely 11.30 a.m. Mel's already seated in their favourite alcove.

'Hi Matt. I've ordered coffee and carrot cake for both of us.'

'Good. You look as if you need both.' He takes in the dark circles beneath her eyes. 'So the pressure's really on then?'

'Understatement.' She checks her watch. 'The suits upstairs and the press office want updates every five bloody minutes.'

'And you so love politics.' He's trying to make her smile but it doesn't work so he changes gear. 'OK. So do you have a big enough team?'

'Well there we do have a surprise. They're throwing resources at it like you wouldn't believe. Most unusual. I'm told I'm to do whatever needs to be done, mostly because of the national media crawling all over us. Universities up and down the country are watching like hawks. Everyone wants to know what to do. If this is a one-off. Or some weird new MO.'

'And what are counterterrorism saying?'

'All clear. No terror link and no intel so they're backing right off. First twenty-four hours, there was talk of cancelling every graduation across the country until there was a proper steer. PM in the loop. Now it's all suddenly changed. I was briefed first thing. They've found absolutely nothing. There's been some big meeting and the new focus is to reassure the public this is *not* terrorism. My job to make everyone feel safe.'

Matthew at last understands Mel's demeanour. 'So all back on your shoulders?'

She just stares at him by way of response as the waitress arrives. They both lean back as the server places down their coffees, apologising as froth spills into one of the saucers.

'Don't worry.' Matthew grabs a paper napkin from a stainless-steel carousel in the centre of the table to mop up the spill; the

34

waitress smiles, saying the cake will be just a couple of minutes. He watches the woman return to the counter.

'So my immediate problem, quite apart from finding the bastard, is calling what to do about this final graduation.' Mel stirs the cocoa into the coffee. 'The university wants to know what to announce. They've cancelled the two ceremonies which were supposed to be this week, but we expect to release the cathedral from forensics early next week so they want to know if they should go ahead with next Friday's ceremony which is the last of the year. My call apparently.'

'You mean the chancellor doesn't want it on her shoulders.'

'Something like that. Quite apart from public confidence, there's a lot of money at stake. Hotel bookings and so on. Maidstead tourism bosses are panicking. *Everyone's* looking to us to buoy confidence and wrap this up. You know how rare shootings are outside of drug crime. Let alone at a major event . . .'

'OK. So where are you on the forensics?'

'Your guess was right. The gun was fired up in that balcony. A handgun with a silencer's the best assumption from all the video footage we've reviewed. Just one bullet into the girl's leg. We've recovered the bullet but it's not giving a lot away.'

'And the sweep of the balcony?'

'Unhelpful. Lots of people went up there to take pictures before the ceremony. A million footprints and fingerprints and no matches to anyone on our systems yet.'

'What about the exit path for the shooter? Anything on the footage?'

'No. There's an easy exit from the balcony. A staircase to the lower corridor with a small side door straight outside. It's tucked away – a bit like the door you used to get in on the other side. Usually locked. Sometimes left open on the quiet for staff which was the case during the ceremony. No CCTV nearby.'

'OK. Not good.' He lets out a long, slow breath. 'So – motive. What are you thinking? Is this personal – to Gemma or the university or the cathedral – or just some lone lunatic?'

'I honestly have no idea.' Mel frowns as if weighing something up. She goes to say something but then changes her mind, sipping at her drink.

'Come on, Mel. You called me so spit it out. You know you can trust me. And like it or not, I'm sort of involved . . .'

'The victim's pregnant, Matt. Parents didn't know. I think her friends may be hiding something. She'd recently broken up with her boyfriend. He's on my list obviously. Been questioned but nothing on him so far. Word is he fled early on and we're still checking that against the footage.'

'Right. Jeez. So do we know for sure who the father is?'

She shakes her head as the waitress places down their cakes and they again wait for her to retreat out of earshot.

'Not yet. But we both know the pregnancy's going to come out, Matt. Next round of questioning, it's bound to leak. Her parents are dreading it.'

'Yeah. Tough on them – but we can't help that.' He watches her scoop some of the topping from the carrot cake on to her fork and suck it, the pleasure of the sweetness lighting up her eyes for just a moment.

'Anything from her phone and laptop yet? And what about a diary or blog? She studied English, didn't she? A writer. Could be a diary?'

'Apparently not. We've checked her flat and her mother said she didn't keep one. Her phone's locked so we don't have full access yet. First scan of laptop hasn't found anything yet. We've put in the request for social-media access but you know how slow that is. My team's going through the phone-company records, checking all the numbers. Popular girl. It's a long list.'

'And this is all assuming she was a deliberate target. What about the university or the cathedral? Anyone sacked recently? Anyone with a grudge? Any known weirdos hang out at the cathedral? Local gun clubs? Any religious protests?'

'Are you sure you won't just come back on my bloody team, Matt? It would make my life *so* much easier.'

He half laughs. Then he feels his expression change and watches Mel's change too. A lifetime ago they trained together. Worked together. When he left the police force over a difficult case – a child's death – Mel said he was making a big mistake and she was probably right. But he won't go back. Too late to turn back now . . .

'So weird that you were in the city, Matt.'

There's a long pause.

'What is it?'

'Sal's not very happy with me. For diving in.'

'Right. Sorry. I didn't think . . .' She looks away across the café and then back at him. 'Selfishly I was just bloody glad you got there ahead of my team—'

He raises an eyebrow.

'Seriously. You were amazing, Matt.'

'I deserted my family, Mel. Not sure Sally would call that amazing.' Matthew finishes his cake and pushes the plate away. 'Also – Amelie heard too much.'

'Oh no. I'm sorry. I had no idea.'

He watches Mel take this in properly and her eyes soften. He and Mel have liaised unofficially on several cases. The last time – a stalker inquiry – Mel was heavily pregnant. He was booked privately to help the victim. Mel was the official investigating officer. She took maternity leave afterwards but her son George is still tiny. Only just walking.

Matthew wonders how on earth Mel manages. Her husband Tom is a wildlife campaigner, working with a charity. A decent bloke. Matthew likes him.

'Does Tom worry? About the job? Do you talk stuff through with him?'

'The truth?' She wrinkles her nose. 'I play everything down, especially any risks. I think he'd make me quit if he knew.' She dusts her fingers on the napkin. 'Right – so my immediate worry is Gemma's messages.'

'Messages?' Matthew notes the gear change. Also how very pale Mel looks. Not herself at all.

'Gemma's phone records show several Facebook notifications on the morning of the shooting. One of her friends told me she'd had some really odd direct messages and was stressed about them.'

'What kind of messages?' Matthew wishes he had the courage to ask if she's really OK. Is she struggling too? Work and home? Dare he ask? Should he ask?

'That's the problem. We don't know yet. Like I say, we're not into her phone yet. We've got the paperwork in to Facebook but Lord knows how long that will take. Gemma's friend doesn't know any details. Also.' Again she pauses to finish the last of her coffee. 'There's something a bit odd about the dad.'

'Something – like what?'

'Oh, you know me. Gut feeling. I don't know exactly—' And now her phone interrupts them. 'Sorry, Matt. Got to take this.' She holds up her hand to register the impasse as she answers, her expression darkening. 'Right.' She stands up. 'So is anyone hurt?' She glances to the ceiling as she listens some more to her caller. 'Understood. I'll be right there. Try to calm things down. Reassure the staff. And for goodness' sake, keep him away from the family.' Mel ends the call, plunging the phone into her jacket pocket.

'Sorry, Matt. Crisis at the hospital. I've got to go.'

CHAPTER 6

THE MOTHER

I'm putting moisturiser on Gemma's face when it all kicks off.

As I rub my hands together, waiting for the slight stickiness to be absorbed, there's suddenly some kind of commotion outside the cubicle and across the ward. At first there's just distant remonstrating. I'm utterly stilled rather than panicked, holding my breath. *We have a guard . . .*

I can't make out the words and don't know if this is benign – some other family rumpus, some staff or visitor dispute . . . or to do with *us*? I look at Ed and he holds my stare. The police guard beyond our cubicle window stands. There's a beat of silence but next comes full-on shouting, maybe at the entrance to the unit or just outside in the corridor.

I demand to see her. You can't stop me. The bitch has been lying to me. Cheating on me.

Now comes true terror. I stand and Ed stands too. We exchange a look of pure and mirrored dread, my stomach cramping and my mind racing. The voice sounds young. Male. But the angle of the window into our cubicle means we can't see who it is.

The police guard glances at us through the glass, signalling with his hand for us to stay put before striding out of sight. I feel a new and terrible wave not just of fear but complete disorientation. *What to do?* Ed moves to close the door to our little cubicle, holding the handle in place – pushing it upwards to try to stop anyone getting in.

I can hear one of the nurses arguing with the intruder and then an older male voice, presumably our police guard. 'You need to put that down right now. You can't go through. We've told you that. Let's keep this calm. Let's move this downstairs and talk this through calmly . . .'

He's immediately interrupted by a loud thud and a woman screaming. I can feel my heart racing wildly and let out this low groan.

Next, we hear more shouting, unintelligible, and the sound of apparent scuffling followed by loud clanging as if something metal's been knocked over. A chair? No. The noise suggests something much bigger. Maybe some kind of trolley as there is a cacophony of different metal notes and the sound of breaking glass. I imagine various instruments strewn across the floor. One note continues – a horrible low whirring as if a metal bowl is circling on the floor. Round and round. Round and round.

I've moved to the side of Gemma's bed. Ed has stretched his right hand across to the bedside table, his left hand still tight around the door handle. He grabs my iPad and holds it up high as the only available weapon. I'm now standing between the window and Gemma's bed, stretching out my arms to widen my shield and trying not to think of the cathedral and how useless an iPad will be if the man is armed.

Don't let it be a gun. Don't let it be a gun again.

There's another little impasse – this strange and chilling moment of quiet – then a male voice calling out in pain. I'm holding my breath when a nurse suddenly appears on the other side of our cubicle window. She has her hand up to signal for us to keep still. She glances across the room then back to us to mouth, 'It's OK.'

Next, we hear the voice of our police guard giving instructions, apparently to a hospital security guard. He says there's police backup on the way and the young man is to be held until backup arrives. We wait. One minute. Two minutes.

At last there's a knock on our door. 'It's your police guard here. You can open up now. It's all clear.'

Ed slowly opens the door to find the guard still on his radio. 'Thank you. Yes. He's cuffed. The situation's contained.' He's leaning his chin down as he speaks into the radio while also checking his watch. 'I have assistance from hospital security but I need that backup fast. And we need to update DI Sanders. Will you do that for me?' A pause. 'Good. And keep me posted.'

He then takes his finger off the radio and turns to us. 'I'm so sorry. I just want to let you know that you're absolutely safe. The young man making the scene claims he's your daughter's boyfriend. Alexander.' He lowers his voice. 'He's making various accusations. Demanding to see Gemma. We've got him handcuffed in a side office. He'll be taken to the police station for questioning. But I just wanted you to know what's happening. I'll be staying here with you, once backup arrives to take him to the station.'

I can't believe it. *Alex?* All that rage.

'Was he armed?' My voice is so high that I hardly recognise it. Alex. The boy who came on holiday with us. The boy who always seemed so kind around Gemma. Devoted.

'No, no. Not armed. Well – not exactly. He grabbed a water jug. Threatened one of the nurses who wouldn't let him through. No formal weapon. Just very overwrought. DI Sanders will be here soon, I'm sure. She'll talk to you once we know what he's saying.'

'Was anyone hurt?' Ed's voice is steadier than mine.

'No. He knocked over a trolley at the nurses' station. There's broken glass, which needs clearing up, but no one hurt. Are you both OK? The nurses are talking to all the patients in the other cubicles. I'm very sorry you've been put through this.'

Ed reaches out to touch my arm and lets out a long sigh. 'Thank you, Officer. We're fine. Just a bit shaken. So what's he's saying? Why did he come here? He's her ex, you know. Not her boyfriend now. He sent us a card, asking to see Gemma, but we didn't reply. I mean – she broke it off with him. We were respecting her decision.' Ed turns to me and then back to the guard. 'So do you think it was *him*? At the cathedral, I mean?'

'Best we don't jump to any conclusions. I suggest you wait to speak to DI Sanders after he's been interviewed properly. Do you still have the card? She'll want to see that.'

I nod. There have been so many cards from people but I've kept them all. I move to my holdall in the corner to look for it, struggling to take this in. The venom in Alex's voice. *The bitch has been lying to me . . .* Unrecognisable. And what did he mean – *cheating on me*?

I can feel my lips trembling and put my hand up to my mouth, suddenly remembering Gemma. Horrified that she may have heard all this.

CHAPTER 7

THE DAUGHTER - *BEFORE*

Essay notes – romanticism module. Third year.

OK, so these are obviously *not* my notes on the romanticism module . . .

The truth? It's Thursday night, *late*. I'm sitting at my laptop, and it tells you everything that my hands are actually shaking and I'm hiding this in an 'essay prep' folder in my coursework files because I need to be as sure as I can that Alex won't somehow read this. Find this.

Paranoid? Going off the rails? Maybe a little bit of both. I don't know.

All I know is that I am doing this, writing this I mean, because last night we had the worst argument ever and I have no one to talk to about it. He was off-the-scale angry. Alex. My supposedly perfect boyfriend. Not physical, he didn't hit me or anything, but he did for the first time actually *scare* me. I honestly had no idea his temper could be that bad.

I've actually never seen anyone rage like that tbh. My parents don't really fight. I guess I'm lucky that way. They're more sulkers.

They don't even raise their voices; they just hole up in different parts of the house when they're upset. Until it blows over. So I'm not *used* to this. I don't know how to handle it, what to even think. And I have NO idea what to do . . .

I haven't written anything like this – like a diary, I mean – since I was a kid. I blog sometimes. I rage and rant about politics all over social media. Words are how I process things. This feels a bit child-ish, actually – the diary vibe – but I can't post this stuff anywhere and I just don't know how else to handle it. I keep picking up my phone and thinking I should call someone. Mum? No. Maddy . . . But I can't do it. I don't know what I'd say. And if I've made too much of everything and Alex and I are fine again, I won't want anyone to know it ever happened.

It's just my mind is all over the place. Alex is always saying I overreact. Over-think things. Maybe I do . . . Maybe that's the real problem here. Mum's been telling me for years to 'go away until you calm down' whenever I get wound up, so maybe I'm actually the one at fault? Maybe I do just overreact . . .

But this thing between me and Alex felt really serious and I feel we've sort of crossed a line, and I can't figure out who is on the right side of the line – who is the most in the wrong. Him. Or me.

So – deep breath. The story.

It all started because I decided I couldn't go on without at least testing my theory (paranoia?) about Alex hacking my Facebook profile. Even writing that sounds terrible, doesn't it? He says I'm paranoid and sometimes I worry he's right. He says I see things that aren't there. Anyway, whatever . . .

I couldn't help getting worried because some really, really odd things have been happening lately with my social-media accounts. So, a couple of times I've sent Maddy photos after a night out by DM – just for us. We're not on Insta or anything, we're more private like that. Just stupid and completely innocent stuff. Us doing vodka shots. Us pouting and making faces for selfies. Usual nonsense.

Alex has always – right from the start – been a bit weird about my girl nights. I used to think it was sweet that he worried about me getting home safely. He made me text him when I got back to the flat. So he would know I was safe. I liked it. I probably even encouraged it because it made me feel looked after. It was a bit like when Mum used to wait up at home – a part of me was irritated and another part was pleased she cared that much.

And then with Alex, the 'checking in' escalated. It started to be every time I did anything – even completely safe stuff. Not late at night. I tried to say there was no need to text if I wasn't waiting, or walking on my own in the dark or whatever, but he still pushed it. At first, I realised that it was partly my fault because I said that I'd liked it to begin with.

This last term though, it's got much, much worse – to the point where I've felt he was being borderline controlling. I also kept noticing him looking over my shoulder when I was on my phone or my computer, so I put a password lock on my laptop. Then, after I did that, I realised it wasn't normal to feel the *need* to do that and so I told him. He felt really bad. He said it was only because he loved me so much. I let it go but I did say it was important we trusted each other and that we should have our own lives as well as our couple life. He seemed a lot calmer for a bit and I thought things were OK. Sorted. I started arranging a few more girls' nights with Maddy, to sort of test that he was genuinely pulling back and giving me some space. And that's when the weird stuff with Facebook started happening.

He said something to me that made me think of one of the DMs I sent Maddy last week. Something about the colour of the vodka glasses and me wearing his favourite dress. I was really spooked. And annoyed. I asked him how he knew that stuff when he wasn't there and he just said he knew the bar, that's all. And we were always drinking vodka. And that it was a lucky guess I'd wear that dress.

I pretended to let it go. I suppose it was just possible that he was telling the truth.

But then I deliberately sent a photo to Maddy of us with a bunch of people from our course – including some fit guys – and sure enough Alex was in a foul mood the next time I saw him. Grilling me about who I'd been out with and who else was there from the course, name-dropping some of the people in the picture. He had to have seen the photo.

Which means he must have got into my Facebook account and read my DMs. Argh. Hacked the page? Or worked out the password (to be honest it wasn't that safe).

So yesterday I changed all my passwords (most of them were the same one, I'm hopeless at this stuff) and I told him I'd done this as I was worried someone had hacked my account and was looking at my direct messages.

Well. He went mental! I thought he'd be embarrassed and even a bit ashamed (as it's obvious it was him) but I never dreamt he would lose it like that . . . I tried to calm him down. A part of me felt guilty that I'd provoked him, like he's always saying. I mean, I did send the group shot deliberately. But it turned into this massive fight about trust and him loving me so much more than I love him; him wanting to keep me safe. The hairs were literally standing up on the back of my neck because it all felt so wrong. So weird.

Then he started crying – properly sobbing. And I didn't know what to feel. I tried to leave but he said we needed to talk it through some more and work it out. He was still crying and he sort of grabbed my arm, not to hurt me, I know that, but just to stop me leaving. Anyway. I had to wrench it away.

Oh. My. Word. The look in his eyes. It was scary.

So that's why I'm babbling here. Because he's supposed to be coming with me next weekend to visit Mum and Dad again. We've got an expensive fancy afternoon tea booked as an early celebration for my birthday. And I don't know what to do.

He's been bombarding me with texts today, apologising. Sending me pictures of us all loved up etc. He keeps saying that all couples argue, which I suppose is true (though I told him before that my parents aren't like that). And that getting past this will make us stronger . . .

I keep thinking about films and soaps, and rerunning TV dramas in my head. Is it normal to fight as badly as this? Can you get past stuff this bad? Do I expect too much? Is he right that I overthink everything?

And the thing is I am always boring everyone about how great he is. The *perfect* boyfriend. And yet suddenly I don't know what I think of him at all – and what does that say about me? About my judgement?

So do I cancel the visit home? Do I confide in Mum after all?

The problem is, she really hates any kind of argument. I don't exactly know why. Gran said some difficult stuff happened when she was a kid but I don't know the details. So if I tell her about this, she'll probably worry herself *sick*. She was the one in the early days telling me I was way too young to be thinking about a serious relationship. I was the one trying to convince *her* how fab and special Alex is and how 'serious' we are. Argh.

It's all unravelling so quickly that I haven't even told Maddy yet.

I don't even know what to think.

I just . . . don't . . . know.

CHAPTER 8

THE FATHER - *NOW*

Ed closes the front door behind him and hangs his waterproof jacket on one of the hooks on the wall. He throws his keys into the little wooden bowl on the narrow side table and listens to the familiar jangle as they settle.

Next, he stands perfectly still in the hallway, taking in the silence. Not so long ago, he would have rejoiced to come home to this. An empty house. The rare treat of the place to himself. He would have made a large pot of coffee and taken it into the conservatory with Radio 4 on his phone, piped through the speaker on the shelf. He would have luxuriated in doing precisely what he wanted with no jobs allocated by Rachel and no pleas from Gemma to help with her new CV, which in recent weeks she has been changing almost daily.

He's walked through this front door a million times and thrown his keys into that same carved wooden bowl a million times and yet it is as if he doesn't recognise the place. The bowl. The hall.

It's still Friday but late. His second trip home to pick up things they need. He stares at his coat, dripping water on to the parquet floor. He hadn't even noticed it was raining. He checks his hands.

Wet. Feels his hair. Wet too. He wonders how long this daze-like existence will continue. When he might start to feel human again.

The problem, since the cathedral, is working out how he's supposed to fit into the world around him. It's not so bad at the hospital. There his purpose is clear. There Ed Hartley is the parent of a very poorly child. In Gemma's small and oh-so-clinical cubicle, it's all bleeping machines and nurses with tests and updates and his job is to listen, to watch the numbers on the machines, to press the doctors for information and above all to stay strong. His job is also to care for his wife who's always been so much tougher on the outside than the inside. He runs errands for coffee and sandwiches and watches Rachel with all her hands-on care of their daughter, so tender and so patient that it's almost unbearable to him.

But back here in the house, collecting things for Rachel and checking the post, Ed has absolutely no idea how to *be*. The house is just the same but their life is completely dismantled. It's as if there are two worlds and he has no idea how to transport himself between one and the other.

He hears himself take in a long, slow breath and finds that he cannot bear the silence. *You need to do something.* The voice in his head sounds afraid. *You need to get a grip and you need to phone Canada again.* He glances at the landline and wonders if it's safer to use his mobile this time. Will the police really check their phone records? He has no idea.

All he wants is confirmation that everything in Canada's OK. He's already tried emailing her parents but the email bounced, the address no longer valid. His first frantic call to the unit – late that first night – was a complete waste of time. They couldn't help him and told him to phone back in the morning. He couldn't; he was back at the hospital.

He watches more drips fall from his coat, pooling into a tiny puddle on the floor. If Rachel were here, she would appear with a cloth, worried about a watermark on the wood. He thinks of her earlier, before the scene with Alex, brushing Gemma's hair – turning their daughter's head from side to side ever so carefully.

He realises that he should have said something to the police about Canada from the off but leaving it this long has somehow made it more and more impossible to find the right explanation.

At last Ed takes his mobile from his trouser pocket and moves into the kitchen. A plate with toast crumbs is still on the side from his last dash home for toiletries and clothes. Rachel wants to stay at the hospital full time, using the little room provided for the family of seriously ill patients for rest. But the bed's a single. They've tried taking turns but neither of them sleeps properly so Rachel says he should be the one to collect more things, check the post and grab some rest at home too.

He didn't want to leave, after what happened with Alex. But now? It's a window to try Canada again. He scrolls through the contacts in his phone and then remembers he didn't store the number. He googles the unit and dials, working out the time difference in his head. Five hours behind – the unit should be fully staffed.

A female voice answers. 'The Meridale Centre. Can I help you?'

'Hello. I'm ringing, please, to inquire about one of your patients. Laura Berkley. I just want to know how she's doing, please. Nothing urgent. A general call.'

'And you are?'

He pauses, his pulse quickening as he tries to decide whether to lie.

'It's just we can only share information with relatives. Are you a relative?'

'Sort of.'

'I'm sorry. I don't understand. Can I take your name?'

'Look, I simply want to know if Laura Berkley is there. And if she's OK. Surely you can at least tell me that?'

There's a longer pause and some noise at the end of the line as if the woman is checking with a colleague or maybe a computer screen.

'Excuse me. But are you a reporter?' Her tone's curt suddenly and Ed ends the call, aware of his pulse in his ear as he keeps the mobile pressed against it.

Why did she say that? Why did she think the media might be interested in Laura?

He's shaken and to steady himself he moves to sit on the high stool at the breakfast bar. *Are you a reporter?*

Ed has no idea what on earth to do next. He thinks of his beautiful daughter in that hospital bed with the nasty frame shielding the stump which was once her leg.

He thinks of the cathedral. The moment Gemma fell . . .

And then he thinks of that *other* cathedral, all those years ago. The clock. The first sight of *her*.

Is it possible it's simply a coincidence? *Two* cathedrals? Is he deluding himself as he clings on tight, tight, tight to the hope that this could just be a terrible and horrible coincidence?

CHAPTER 9

THE MOTHER

'That's probably enough for today, darling. It's late.' I put the bookmark in place and close the novel, smoothing its cover with my palm. Ed found the book in Gemma's room on his first trip home and I've been reading to her to try to restore a sense of calm after the horrible scene earlier.

I still feel shaken and find myself gripping the novel too tightly. I stare at my white knuckles and loosen my grasp, turning the book over to examine the strange cover.

It's an odd book about a group of girls who find themselves alone on an island with the option to send only one three-word text message each day to the outside world. No incoming messages are allowed and no other connection to the internet. The cover of the novel has an oasis of palm trees in a sea ominously coloured red. It's well written and certainly unusual but I'm a little surprised it's to Gemma's taste, to be frank, and am worried it's turning too dark. Borderline horror, which is clearly not the right choice just now for her or me. I consider telling Gemma this but don't want to sound preachy. I may just get Ed to look for a different book. I'll message him in the morning before he returns.

'I think I'll just sit and doze for a bit,' I tell her. 'The nurses are changing shift. You just rest. I'm right here if you need me.'

Each time I talk to her like this I still get this same flutter of disappointment when she doesn't move. I try to be patient and pragmatic but the truth is I simply cannot help searching her face, her hands, her whole body actually, hoping that she will find some small way to signal that she can hear me. A flutter of her eyelids or a tiny movement of her fingers perhaps. But I scan and scan and there's absolutely nothing.

Always this complete stillness.

At first in here, I held her hand almost constantly and told her that she could squeeze it ever so gently if she could hear me. I truly expected her to do this. It was a terrible shock to feel nothing. Just flesh on flesh. It was then I realised that in my head I had this absolute conviction that I was going to get my 'moment'. Any minute. Any hour. I had conjured this ridiculous movie version of our situation; only now I'm slowly starting to dread that here in the real world there's to be no Hollywood moment. I was simply creating too much pressure for both of us. Disappointment for me and, worse, possibly continual frustration for her. And so I stopped asking her to squeeze my hand. Now I just tell her that she's not to worry about anything; I say that I know in my heart that she can hear me but it doesn't matter if she can't confirm this to me just yet. I don't mind. She's not to feel any pressure.

Still, I find it hard to take my eyes off her in case I miss the first movement. The first sign.

There's a change suddenly through the glass on to the main ward – a dimming of the lights, signalling the night shift proper. The new nurses on duty have already been in to check on Gemma, logging all her readings on the little clipboard at the end of her bed. They know my routine.

I tell Ed that at night, I'll sleep in the little room they've provided for us on the floor below but this isn't true. I only nap in there in the day when he's here to watch her in my place. When I send him home to rest, I can't bear to leave our little cubicle in case something changes so I just sleep in this chair. The nurses don't seem to mind.

I find I do a lot of thinking in this late-evening phase – when the lights first dim. I feel too awake to try to settle or doze and instead tend to just stare at different objects, one after another with my mind wandering through the silence. Through the years. In these shadows and in this stillness, I think a lot about the last time we were in hospital with Gemma, when she was sick with asthma as a toddler. It was terribly frightening but in a very different way. I slept in a chair alongside her that time too but it was not the same at all on the children's wards. All the parents stayed over – some on camp beds set up in the playroom and others covered in blankets in tall-backed chairs. There was a kitchen where we could make hot drinks and I had long conversations with the other mothers in the early hours – each of us fighting different battles with different illnesses but all in the same horrible boat together, wearing the same dark circles under our eyes. A sad but comforting camaraderie in that kitchen.

Here, there's no camaraderie. Only this sense of shock that what's happened has separated my whole family from the rest of the world.

There are three of these single cubicles with windows looking out on to the wider ward, which has three additional open-plan beds. Patients seem to come and go and most have visitors only part of the day and evening. The majority seem to come in after road accidents and the like, spending a few hours here after surgery before transfer to the general wards.

Everyone knows that Gemma was shot. I see it in their eyes as they glance towards our cubicle. The shock. The pity. I watch them take in our police guard and then keep themselves to themselves.

Like I say, no camaraderie here and probably best that way. Safest.

I find that I'm staring now at the controller for the bed – a grey plastic brick with little arrows to move the mattress up and down. My eyes blur, so I blink and move my gaze up to the window where I can just see our police guard has taken a seat right alongside the door to our cubicle. Good. I like it when he sits where I can see him, especially after the commotion earlier.

I scratch my nose. Hospitals have such a distinct smell, don't they? When Gemma was born, I had to spend five days on the ward after an emergency Caesarean. Initially I couldn't bear it – that distinct mixture of antiseptics and polish and hospital food. Now? I am already used to it again. My new norm. I can't imagine being at home. The scent of home.

I stare at Gemma and wonder if she can smell as well as hear? For a moment, I consider asking her if she smelled the perfume I sprayed, but change my mind. I need to let her rest.

You know the thing that really upsets me now? Ed's not at all sure that Gemma can hear us; he's said as much several times. I don't challenge him because I don't want an argument, but I can't bear to think that he may be right. To imagine her in another place entirely out of reach. All quiet and lost. No. I reach out to smooth the corner of the blanket on her bed.

Gemma can hear me.

I am watching her breathe – in, out, in, out – when the police guard stands. I can make out that he's talking to someone and am anxious but then there's a knock at the door and I realise he would not allow this unless it was safe. I wonder if Ed's returned for some reason but when I move to open the door, it's DI Sanders. I feel my chin pull back towards my neck with the surprise of this. We were expecting to speak to her together tomorrow.

I'm frowning. Good news? Bad news?

'Please don't be alarmed, Mrs Hartley. I'm sorry to call in so late but I was just passing the hospital on my way home and thought I'd check on you. After the upset earlier. How are you doing?'

'Oh right. I see. Still very shaken but OK. I'm sorry – but I thought we were going to go over it all properly tomorrow. Has something happened?'

'No, no. Nothing's happened. But we've interviewed Alex now and I wanted to bring you up to date.'

I feel for my phone. 'Should I ring my husband? Ed's desperate to know what's going on. We both are—'

'No, no. Please don't disturb him. I'll come back again tomorrow and talk to you both together then.'

'Right. Sorry. Can we talk outside, please?' I move through the door to the pair of chairs placed just outside our cubicle. I take one. The inspector sits alongside. I lower my voice and hope that with everyone sleeping, we won't be overheard. The nurses are in their corner office.

'So – was it him? The shooting? Was it Alex?' Even as I ask the question, it sounds surreal. I picture Alex at our breakfast table, laughing on one of his weekend visits. I just can't see it. Alex with a gun? Alex hurting Gemma?

DI Sanders lets out a breath before speaking. 'We're still making inquiries. Alex is in custody. We've been unable to track his exact movements across all the photos and footage. It's early days. I'm not going to lie to you. At this stage, he *is* a suspect. But we have no evidence yet.'

'Don't you test his clothing or something? For residue. I've seen that on the television—'

'We're doing everything we can. Everything's in hand. But—' She looks down at her lap and back up at me. 'With everyone fleeing the scene, it's been more difficult for forensics. People have washed their clothing, for instance.'

'Right.' All sorts of thoughts are swirling around in my head. 'So the aggro earlier? What's he saying about that? I really thought something terrible was going to happen again.'

'We've charged him with breach of the peace and criminal damage. As I say, he'll stay in custody for now while we make more inquiries. You're safe here. He's calmed down and he's claiming to be very sorry for the scene here.'

'You're not expecting me to feel sorry for him?'

'No, no. Of course not. But we have no hard evidence at this stage to suggest he was in any way responsible for the shooting.'

'But he's a suspect?'

'Yes, he is.'

Once again I picture him in our house. In our life. And the images fire another thought. 'I've been meaning to ask you, by the way. Whether we can have Gemma's laptop and phone back? It's just she always took the most photographs in the family. And she keeps them on her laptop.' I think of the batch I most long to see. Gemma in that pink dress we chose together. She gave her phone to the assistant to take the picture – better camera than mine. And she has pictures of her birthday tea too. I so regret now letting Gemma take all the photographs. She's much better with the technology but never remembers to message them to me.

'I'm sorry but we normally hold on to all evidence until we have a trial. A mobile phone is often crucial.'

'But what about the laptop? She keeps the photos backed up there. More storage. It would mean a lot to me.'

DI Sanders looks at me intently and I see a softening in her expression. 'I'll see where we are with checking the laptop. But I can't make any promises. And we'll need to keep the phone.'

'Right. Thank you. And Alex: that's why you came here, is it? Just to talk about the scene earlier.' I still don't quite understand this visit.

'Not only that.' Again, she pauses, picking at imagined fluff from her trousers. 'Alex is suggesting that Gemma had started a secret relationship. With one of her professors. He says that's why they broke up.'

. . . she's been cheating on me . . .

All at once I'm holding my breath again. It's both shocking and offensive; it doesn't sound like Gemma at all and my first instinct is to defend her. And yet? I think of the change in Gemma in recent weeks. That distant tone on the phone. That disconnect which I could never understand. Her reluctance to explain her split from Alex.

The baby. Dear God. *The baby.*

'You knew nothing about that?'

'No. Nothing.' It's my turn to pause. 'Do you not think he's just saying that – making this up, I mean. To get back at her. To cover his tracks.'

DI Sanders rolls her lips together.

I continue. 'So why is Alex saying he came here? Why did he cause the scene and frighten us all? Because he's angry. Bitter? Surely that makes it more likely that he could have been involved in the shooting.'

DI Sanders ignores my question and presses on. 'Have you ever been aware of either Alex or your daughter involved with guns in any way? Shooting club? Clay-pigeon shooting? Anything like that?'

'No. No. Absolutely not.' I scrape the hair back from my forehead but then I turn away. 'Hang on. They did go on some country weekend once. Scotland. I think there was shooting but Gemma was upset about it. I don't think she took part.'

'And Alex?'

'I don't know. I don't remember.'

'Do you think you could check? Perhaps look back at the photographs and the dates for me. Find out the name of the place.'

'Yes. OK. If you like.' I take a tissue from my pocket and try my question again. 'So what is Alex saying about why he came to the hospital? Is it because we ignored his note? You got the note? I asked the guard to pass it on. Alex was asking to see Gemma.'

'Yes, I did. Thank you.'

'And we were right to ignore it, weren't we?' My mind is racing suddenly, wondering if we could have handled it another way. 'I mean – there's no *way* we could let him see Gemma. Not after she finished with him.'

'Yes. Completely understandable.' DI Sanders pauses. 'Look. Alexander says he came here because he wants to know if the baby is his. Or from Gemma's new relationship. He says it's his right and that's why he made the scene.'

'I see.' I don't, actually. I don't see or understand anything any more. The whole world no longer makes any sense to me. More scenes are swimming in front of me. I remember Gemma's phone call to me, explaining that they had suddenly split up and that we needed to cancel all the plans for the joint graduation dinner. The summer villa holiday together. When was that? I'm trying to do the sums.

I also remember that when I asked questions about Alex, she started to raise her voice, to get upset. *Shouting.* And with the echo of the shouting, other pictures start swirling around my brain. From much further back. Years back.

My father slumped at the bottom of the stairs and my *mother* shouting, shouting, shouting . . .

Opening my lunchbox at school and finding tea bags between the bread and everyone laughing. *Tea-bag sandwiches. Come here. Rachel's got tea-bag sandwiches . . .*

I feel very hot suddenly. Confused and terribly hot.

'Are you all right, Mrs Hartley?'

I can hear DI Sanders' voice but I feel this sort of daze.

I close my eyes and see my parents in the kitchen. I look down. Pink pyjamas with white embroidered hearts. Rabbit slippers. And then there's screaming. My mother is screaming . . .

'Here. Sip this, Mrs Hartley.'

I open my eyes to find DI Sanders handing me water. She must have fetched it from the corner of the ward. But I don't remember her moving.

'I'm sorry. I'm very tired.'

'It's understandable. Shall I leave? Talk again in the morning?'

'No, no. Go on.' I need to know what she knows. Why she really came here tonight.

'I'm sorry to ask but have they been more exact about the stage of Gemma's pregnancy?'

I don't want to say it but she keeps staring at me, raising her eyebrows and then tilting her head to the side. She has quite a nice face, actually. Ed doesn't like her, I can tell. But she has warm eyes, for all the difficult questions. I guess she's just doing her job.

'Fourteen weeks.'

'Right. Thank you. And she split up with Alex when?'

Again – I don't want to say it.

'I'm sorry but I have to ask. It's important.'

'About three months ago. I can check. We had to cancel a few things. I can look that up.'

'Thank you. That would be a help.'

I look away, my brain spinning once more as I do the sums again. I had assumed this baby *had* to be Alex's. It never occurred to me it wouldn't be. I supposed Gemma found out after they split and hadn't wanted to tell anyone. Not even me – her mother. But could it be true about this affair? Is *that* why she couldn't bring herself to confide in me?

'Did he give a name? Did Alex say which professor he claimed Gemma was seeing?'

'No. He said he heard rumours but didn't know who it was. You're right. He could be making this up but we'll be speaking to all of Gemma's tutors as part of the inquiry.'

I find myself trying to think back to conversations with Gemma about her work. She was always mentioning which modules she liked best. Postmodernism was a favourite. But I don't remember her mentioning the names of any staff. I feel bad for not knowing more. For not asking more questions.

I glance at the window into Gemma's cubicle and feel close to tears. How could I miss *all this*, Gemma?

I expect DI Sanders to stand and to leave but she doesn't.

'Is there something else? I'm sorry but like I said, I'm actually very tired now.'

Again, she's looking right into my eyes.

'I just wanted to ask a few questions about your husband, Mrs Hartley.' For a moment it is as if the air cools. Yes. The ward, which I normally find so stuffy, feels momentarily colder. 'Whether there's been any difficulties between you. In the marriage, I mean. Again – I'm sorry to pry but we have to ask these questions. And your husband has been quite difficult with our inquiry. With me. You must have noticed that.'

'Our daughter's been shot, Inspector. Of course, he's finding it *difficult*.'

'Yes. Quite. But I didn't mean that. I think you know what I mean.' That intense stare once more as if she can read my mind. 'I just wanted to say that if there's anything bothering you. Anything you might want to talk to me about privately, you can. Now. Or at any time.'

I wonder if I should just say it. Get it over with. On and off since we arrived here, I have wondered if I should mention her. The strange woman. I've been afraid of the consequence – what I did afterwards, I mean. And I can't really believe it has anything to do with any of this. But what if I'm wrong?

I look at the floor and get this vivid picture. I can see the scene so clearly – that first day I saw the odd woman, looking at me so strangely from the end of our drive. Right at the house.

It was a Thursday and it was raining. I was looking out of the kitchen window and she was just standing in the rain, staring at the house. No. Not just at the house. She was staring at the window, through the window . . . at *me*. I've been trying to push all this to the back of my mind because I'm ashamed of my own behaviour *afterwards*. And I haven't wanted to admit what I did to anyone; Ed will never forgive me if he finds out what I did.

'So is there anything else you want to tell me? Anything at all that might help the inquiry.'

I'm completely torn, fighting tears now.

'No.'

CHAPTER 10

THE PRIVATE INVESTIGATOR

Matthew has switched the office landline to answerphone but with the speaker activated. He listens to it ring – two, three, four rings . . .

Matthew Hill, private investigator. Please leave a message and I'll get right back to you.

He grimaces through the long beep. A puzzle that, away from a microphone, his voice echoing in his head sounds utterly unremarkable, yet on playback it's excruciating.

He clears his throat, wondering which version of his voice other people hear. At last the beep ends. A pause. And then the voice of a woman with an alarmingly breathy tone.

I need you, Matthew.

There's a longer pause after which the caller rambles about her love of good jewellery – *and why shouldn't a widow wear her good jewellery, Matthew? Am I supposed to be embarrassed by my wealth?* She talks of the problems of isolation since her husband's passing. *He was a very successful man, Matthew.* Another pause. *Potent . . .* Matthew hears himself gulp. At last the caller continues and it rapidly becomes clear that what she actually 'needs' is a bodyguard to accompany her on holiday while she wears her biggest diamonds. Two weeks. South of France. She mentions having booked a wonderful villa but in a rather remote area. She's prepared to pay a premium on his usual rate and will be happy for him to join her for restaurant reservations. *I know some wonderful places.* She leaves her details. Matthew finds that his eyes are still wide, uncomfortable now through lack of blinking.

There have been a number of similar approaches in recent months – all politely declined. He should laugh it off but in truth, it depresses him. Why don't people take his work more seriously?

Sal reckons it was the stalker case he worked on. His wise wife had always warned against anything too close to security work. He took on the stalker case strictly as a one-off as he felt very sorry for the woman involved. A journalist – Alice Henderson. It was a legitimate and intense inquiry – at times emotionally gruelling, also dangerous – and although it worked out in the end, he's promised Sally not to take on anything remotely resembling bodyguard duties ever again.

No Kevin Costner gigs, Matt. It sends the wrong signal. Promise? Promise.

Sadly, despite greater clarity on his website, potential clients – many of whom appear purely rich and lonely – are not yet taking the hint. Matthew fears he's losing credibility while Sally is losing patience.

These women clearly fancy you, Matthew. It was that picture in the paper. And that new TV series. People get the wrong idea . . .

Don't be ridiculous, Sally.

The 'local hero' newspaper coverage of the cathedral shooting hasn't helped. The local Sunday ran another big feature yesterday. And while high-profile cases are technically good for PR and hence business, Matthew's still quietly disappointed he's not being offered the kind of legitimate and complex investigative work he craves. Interesting cold cases. Shoulder to the wheel. Is that really so much to hope for?

Matthew pours a dash of hot milk from the jug on his tray into the remnants of his coffee and sips. *Better.* It's borderline obscene how quickly good coffee revives him. He's just about to google advice on options to help Amelie – whether in fact they should turn to a professional counsellor – when the entry buzzer signals someone at the door downstairs.

Matthew frowns and checks his watch. Mondays are normally quiet. There's nothing in the diary and 'walk-in' clients are rare now that his website urges a phone call or email as first contact. He moves across the office to the intercom, praying it's not someone breathy who wants him to go on holiday . . .

'Hello. Matthew Hill. Can I help you?'

'I'm so sorry to turn up here without an appointment, Mr Hill. It's Ed Hartley. Gemma Hartley's father. Can I come up? I really need to speak to you, please.'

Matthew's puzzled. His office is nearly an hour from Gemma's hospital. He presses the buzzer and issues his regular warning about the steepness of the flight of stairs.

He holds the door ajar and waves his arm to signal for Ed Hartley to take a seat over to his right.

Matthew sits in his own chair behind the desk but, seeing the ashen nature of Ed Hartley's face, gets straight back up.

'You look quite shaken, Mr Hartley. Must be such a difficult time for you. Can I get you a coffee? Or a glass of water?'

'Both please. Very kind.'

'No problem. To be perfectly honest, I'm surprised to see you. I imagined you'd be at the hospital.'

'I'm on my way back there right now actually. Haven't had time for breakfast. My wife's staying at the hospital full time still. I've just been nipping home to fetch bits and bobs.'

'Oh right. I see.' Matthew doesn't see at all but parks his surprise and moves straight through to the adjoining kitchen to make yet more coffee.

'I used to live in this flat next to the office.' He raises his voice so that Mr Hartley can hear him through the door connecting the two spaces. 'We sometimes think about letting it but I rather like having the kitchen space. And strictly between us, I've been known to take a little nap in the flat after a long night.'

Ed Hartley lets out a small, nervous laugh but his mouth remains tight and Matthew watches as he taps his hand against his lips. Tap, tap, tap. His visitor runs his fingers through his hair, crosses his legs and then jerks his right foot up and down repeatedly.

By the time Matthew emerges with a cafetière and hot milk in a jug – he decided against the noise and delay of his espresso machine – Ed's face is even paler.

'Are you sure you're alright, Mr Hartley?'

'Well no, I'm not actually.' He takes the mug and nods as Matthew offers to pour in some hot milk but shakes his head to sugar.

'How's Gemma doing? Any change?'

Mr Hartley just shakes his head again. Matthew takes in a long breath.

'OK. So why are you here? What can I do for you?'

Gemma's father starts a strange rocking in response to the question, his eyes darting around the room as if trying to find the answer among the furnishings.

Matthew waits.

Mr Hartley sips at his drink and then stares at his feet. 'This is probably going to sound a little odd. Irregular even. But I was wondering if you might help me find someone, Mr Hill. It's to put my mind at ease. Purely to put my mind at ease.'

'I'm sorry. I'm not following you. Find who?'

He does not reply.

'I'm very sorry, Mr Hartley, but you are going to have to spell this out for me. Is this something to do with Gemma? With the inquiry? Because if it is, I need to be clear that this is perhaps something you – we – should be discussing with the police. With

66

DI Sanders. This is a live and complex investigation as you know. There's no way I could be taking on—'

'No, no. I can't talk to DI Sanders. And this isn't connected to Gemma. At least – I'm ninety-nine per cent certain it's not connected. I just need the reassurance, you see. That's all this is. To set my mind absolutely at rest.'

Matthew glances at his mobile on his desk. Mel Sanders will definitely need to be updated on this, but he will need to tread carefully.

'How about you just tell me what this is. This one per cent of worry. Who are you worried about? Who's missing?'

'My wife, Mr Hill.'

'She's disappeared from the hospital?' There's a punch to Matthew's stomach. He's picturing the police guard. Has something gone wrong again at the hospital?

'No. No, no. Not Rachel. I mean my *ex*-wife. My first wife.'

'I'm sorry. I didn't realise you'd been married before.' Matthew's frowning again. He doesn't recall Melanie mentioning this when they've gone over the case.

'No one knows.' Ed looks up to take in Matthew's expression.

'I think you'd better tell me everything, don't you?'

Ed resumes rocking, his agitated expression heightening. 'She's called Laura. My first wife. And she became unwell. It was all very difficult. It was why we parted.'

'Unwell?'

'It's complicated. I really don't like to talk about it; not to anyone. But the thing is . . .' Another pause. 'The thing is it's probably just a coincidence . . . Not connected in any way at all. But it's been preying on my mind, you see.'

'What has?'

'We met in a cathedral. Me and Laura. We met in a cathedral, Mr Hill . . .'

CHAPTER 11

THE FATHER - *BEFORE*

Ed Hartley has come to spend a lot of his time wondering about fate. The weather. Timing. He will muse most of all about the rain that Thursday in Wells; had it been dry, he would never have met Laura.

Fact is, his first marriage only happened because of a deluge. He was in Wells to give a presentation, pitching for new clients for his agency, but it was all cancelled at the last minute because the rain was so severe it caused a landslip and disrupted all the trains. And the only reason he went into the coffee shop was to shelter from the relentless downpour. And if he hadn't gone to the coffee shop, he would never have gone to the cathedral.

He was twenty-five – just a few years out of uni. He'd been in a marketing job for a mid-size agency for just eighteen months and was still enjoying the novelty of travelling for pitches and meetings. A hotel on expenses. But with his presentation suddenly cancelled, he was at a loose end. He was bored with his hotel which had over-enthusiastic air conditioning so he'd wandered into town, optimistically hoping the rain would ease. It didn't. And so, on his second cup of coffee, he found himself tuning into the conversation of two women at the adjoining table. They were hurrying their drinks and checking their watches, apparently anxious to make it to the cathedral '*in time for the clock thingy.*'

What clock thingy?

Ed couldn't help himself. He turned to stare at the women as they gathered up their things and for a beat considered asking out loud. But that would mean owning up to earwigging so he turned back to his coffee instead, pretending to consider adding a sachet of sugar.

One of the women was now telling the other to hurry. *Come on. Noon is the best time for the clock. We need to get a shift on.*

That decided it. Ed liked clocks, especially unusual ones. But what could be so special about a clock in a cathedral?

He reached into his jacket pocket for the tourist pamphlet, picked up from hotel reception, just as his two neighbours made for the door.

Wells Cathedral had half a page – and yes; the clock had a special mention. It dated back to around 1390. Right. *Decided.* He stood, slurped the last of his coffee and headed for the door himself.

It was too windy for his umbrella so by the time he reached the cathedral, he was pretty much wet through. It was not the largest of cathedrals, but he loved the mellow colour of the stone. The arches. At the information desk, he was told there were no official tickets that day. A woman in a bright pink blouse signalled the voluntary-contribution box. He dropped in some pound coins, asked about the clock and was told to hurry. *There's a guide at midday to explain it all.*

It was easy to see where to head. A small group of visitors were craning their necks to view something high up. A guide had a small torch that he was shining up on to the wall, sweeping his other arm as he continued his spiel.

Ed moved forward to perch on a little stone shelf that others were also using as a seat. Somehow, he lost his grip on his redundant umbrella and it slid with a clatter to the floor. All eyes turned. A woman with long strawberry-blonde hair smiled at him as the guide paused to check on the noise before moving the torch back to the clock high up in front of them.

The story was impressive. The oldest clock face in the world, apparently.

'But what you will enjoy, ladies and gentlemen, is the unusual action with the chime.' The guide checked his watch. 'Just a few more seconds and you'll see what I mean.'

Ed stared up at the clock and wondered what to expect. Some kind of unusual bell? Music? He was surprised to find the anticipation so enjoyable. An unexpected boost to this dismal, wet day.

At last the chimes began and little doors at the top of the clock opened to reveal the twist. Not cuckoos, not birds of any kind but knights on horseback . . . *jousting*.

He smiled and turned to see everyone in the little crowd smiling with him. Two sets of knights were on some kind of circuit travelling in opposite directions, so it really did look like a mini joust. Very clever.

Given the time, the display lasted through the whole twelve chimes and Ed at last understood the noon recommendation. When the chimes finished, everyone clapped. The tour guide then turned off his torch and, to Ed's slight embarrassment, encouraged them all to join in a little prayer together.

It was not that Ed was an atheist, more that he was entirely indifferent about religion. But he paused politely as a short prayer and blessing was announced. And it was during this little 'moment' that the woman with the strawberry-blonde hair caught his eye again, apparently stifling a laugh.

As everyone then slowly dispersed, Ed was surprised to see the woman move towards him.

'I'm so sorry. That was very rude of me. Disrespectful. I didn't mean to cause offence. Are you religious? Please forgive me if you're religious. I can't help it when I get nervous; I really didn't mean to—'

'It's fine. Not offended at all. I'm not religious myself.' He had lowered his voice to a whisper. 'But jolly good clock. I just came in to shelter from the rain, to be honest.'

'Me too.'

'So, have you had a look around the rest of the cathedral?' He realised, even as the words escaped his mouth, that this sounded like an invitation. Was that his intention?

'No. You?'

She had rather strange eyes. Not quite green and not quite brown. His own mother had green eyes, and he was wondering what percentage of the population did too. Not many, he suspected, as it felt unusual; he would look it up. Wasn't it an Irish thing to have green eyes? But she didn't sound Irish. A soft accent that he hadn't yet placed. He was staring now. The eyes looked greener. Odd. Was it a change in the light? She didn't look away.

'Please say no if I'm intruding, but if you fancy some company looking round?' She was smiling, still holding his gaze.

'Oh yes. Lovely. Though I'm no expert. Cathedrals, I mean.' He signalled with his hand for her to take the lead and they set off towards the far end of the cathedral.

Ed pretended to read labels as they moved from one area to another but was in truth stealing glances to take in his new companion. She was wearing a deep-red coat with a battered black leather satchel. It was worn across her body on a long, wide strap that dug into her shoulder, making quite an indentation in the fabric of the coat. Evidently heavy. He found himself wondering what was in the satchel. None of his business, but after a while it burned like the curiosity over the women chatting alongside him in the café.

'I hope you don't mind me asking, but your bag. It looks quite heavy.'

'It's all right.' She leant forward conspiratorially. 'It's not a bomb.'

'Well that's a relief.' He didn't get the tone quite right and she kept her expression entirely neutral which for a moment alarmed him. He could feel his face reddening.

'I'm teasing. Music manuscripts. Lots.'

'Right. OK. And you're carrying them because?'

'Because I teach music and I'm technically on my way to work. I'm freelance but I teach at the Elderbury School now. Piano and violin. I've only been there a few weeks so I'm still playing tourist.'

Now he was really interested. Ed had not a musical bone in his body and both admired and envied those who did. He had tried guitar lessons; his teacher had made an admirable effort, but Ed just couldn't make sense of the music on the page. Odd because he was good at numbers and so had imagined it would be similar. But he just couldn't get the hang of it. Three terms and he finally threw in the towel.

Once again, he realised that he was staring at his new companion.

'Lunch. I was going to get myself an early lunch,' he said. 'I don't suppose you fancy joining me? I'm afraid I don't know anywhere but we could busk it.'

'The Hedgehog Café.' She was smiling. 'Don't worry. They don't serve hedgehogs. That's probably illegal. There's a story behind the name of the café but I've forgotten it. One of my pupils recommended it. Cool place. Great soup.'

'Soup it is then.'

She then linked her arm through his, with the satchel on the other side of her body.

'I'll see if I can hail us a canoe.' He winked and she laughed and he felt a little bubble in his stomach. It was the perfect surprise on this wet day and he felt light and excited and happy.

He will come to look back on that moment often, with his head in his hands and the heaviest of hearts. Thinking, yes, about fate. Destiny. The fluke of timing. For he could not know that this would be the woman he would marry.

He could not know that within two years he would be living an entirely different life with her in Canada.

He could not know that one day, he would wake up to visit the bathroom and she would be screaming and screaming and screaming.

And everything would suddenly swirl and spiral into a dark, dark place like the rainwater rushing for the drains as they hurried to the Hedgehog Café that very first day.

CHAPTER 12

THE DAUGHTER – *BEFORE*

Alice's Adventures in Wonderland – *the quest for identity?*

I haven't even re-read it for the essay yet. The book, I mean. I have no idea if it's a quest for identity or not. I'll have to make a big pot of coffee and pull an all-nighter. There's no way I can ask 'S' for special favours. Not after . . .

Crazy – I've only just realised the irony. Tea parties. Mad Hatters. It's how my whole life feels right now. Down a stupid rabbit hole.

It's as if I've gone mad myself. What I get now, way too late, is that I should have trusted my first instinct. I should have cancelled the birthday celebration; I should have told Mum the truth. Most important of all, I should have told Alex straight up that we needed a break. Instead? Typical disastrous me; I was too *confused*. I went for the easiest and most cowardly option which was to do nothing. To go with the flow.

It's a Mum thing really. 'Why don't we all just go with the flow? Lighten up.' I used to think it was so good – that my mum hates arguments so much, that she works so hard to avoid them. It was only when I hit my teens and had friends round that I realised, through them, that it was a bit weird. Unusual.

She sort of goes into this zone, my mother, any time anyone in the family gets upset. She says things like, 'I absolutely will not let this build into something silly. No. No. I'm not listening to you. I'm walking away. You can talk to me when you've calmed down.'

She would go into the kitchen and bake something. Later she'd present the cakes or flapjacks or whatever and I'd think – *here we go*. And of course, I'd feel a *bit* better; cake always makes you feel better. But as I got older, I sort of wished I'd been able to stand my ground sometimes, because I think what I'm realising now is that I don't have the courage to tell my mum any stuff that will upset her.

I remember I did push it once when I was doing my A levels. I got really mad at her – some argument over how much revision I was doing – and when she was walking away – *you need to calm down, Gemma* – I started shouting. I wanted her to listen. I wanted her to thrash it out with me for once. She retreated as she always does – to the kitchen. I shouted down the stairs at her. I said she was a coward. That I hated her stupid cakes. And then I went down and found her sitting on the kitchen floor with her back to the cupboards, sobbing.

She claimed she'd tripped and that was why she was crying but I didn't believe her. She wouldn't say what it was. She wouldn't even look at me and her whole body was like, trembling. I felt so, so guilty. It freaked me out. So from that day, whenever Mum gave me her 'look', I just backed down. Piped down.

That's why I didn't tell her about Alex scaring me. It would have upset her so badly. And I just didn't want any of that.

You see, Mum had booked two treats for my twenty-first – a trip to Paris, just her and me in a month's time, and the family weekend thing with Alex, including champagne afternoon tea at this posh hotel. She'd gone to so much trouble, I didn't want to prick her balloon. I didn't want to *upset* her.

Alex had been so sorry after his meltdown – so calm and apologetic and considerate – that I started to think I *had* overreacted. I decided to go along with the visit home, just because it was simpler. For Mum. For me. For everyone. And do you know what? He was great. Perfect company. The textbook boyfriend.

On the train home, he fetched my favourite snacks from the buffet. He backed off; let me read my book without interrupting. He caught my gaze now and again and gave me his little wink and smile and it felt just like it did right at the beginning. As if the argument and all the stuff with social media had never happened.

He brought a lovely gift for my mum without even telling me. She collects ceramic jugs and he'd found a small, very unusual one in a gallery. You should have seen her face. *Well, goodness me, how very thoughtful of you, Alex.*

And the afternoon tea was fab. Dad ordered a tea he'd never tried – silver leaf, which made super pale tea. We thought it would have no flavour but it was divine. There was champagne too and the food was incredible. I had to take so many photos. Little spiced crab things. These amazing little treats on edible soil. And the cakes! More like works of art. We were absolute pigs, all of us. The waiter brought us a box for the leftovers, but we were embarrassed that there was hardly anything to go in it.

I am writing all the detail because I want to hang on to it. The memory of it. I honestly can't believe that was just three weeks ago and so much has changed.

I feel so ashamed and confused, and disappointed with myself. I want to go back to that tea. I want to be sitting there again with the crab things and the beautiful cakes and I want to take my mum home and quietly and secretly tell her the truth about me and Alex.

My doubts. My worries. I want to go back and do that, without making her sit on the floor and cry . . .

Maybe if I'd done that, found a way to talk to Mum, I wouldn't have so stupidly confided in 'S' instead . . . (Not saying his name!)

Oh my word. What's the matter with me? I'm supposed to be *intelligent*. I'm supposed to be heading for a first . . . so why am I such a complete and utter disaster?

OK. So this is what happened. We had the lovely weekend, we caught the train home, and everything was fine. And then the second we got back to my room at the flat, Alex's face changed right in front of me. No kidding – it was like Jekyll and Hyde. He started asking me why I felt it was OK to openly flirt with a waiter in front of him.

What waiter?

The one at the tea, he said. *The waiter at the hotel. And don't pretend to be innocent. You were practically eyeballing his crotch . . .*

What? Shocked doesn't even come close. I had absolutely no idea what he was talking about. Sure, the waiter was friendly. He made a fuss because it was my birthday. He made it nice for all of us. But there was no flirting. No way.

At first I was too surprised to know what to do. Then I told Alex to leave but he wouldn't. He walked right up close to me, banging on about the waiter. I remembered that time he grabbed my arm and I felt nervous. I didn't feel completely safe so I went through to the kitchen and told him I would stay there and scream for help if he didn't leave. I had my phone in my hand and I almost rang my mother. I wish I had. But in the end after about half an hour, when I threatened to knock on my flatmates' doors, he finally left.

I didn't sleep. I decided it was *definitely over* with Alex. I realised I should have finished it before the weekend away. I knew that I needed to stop worrying about pride, to make a clean break, and tell my parents. Face up to my mistake and my embarrassment too.

I had a meeting with 'S' – one of my English tutors – scheduled for ten thirty the next morning. I had this strange feeling in my stomach about it and I nearly cancelled. I realise now, yet again, that I should have listened to my instinct but I didn't. Instead, I had a couple of strong coffees to try to wake myself up. But the problem was my brain was still really, really foggy. I had hoped to blag my way through the session. And here's the thing. I always look forward to my sessions with him usually.

Everyone likes 'S'. He's a bit older, maybe forties? But the coolest and smartest of the professors.

OK. Honest truth? Most of the undergrads have a bit of a crush. We joke about it. But I absolutely swear that I never in a million years imagined . . .

Anyway.

You can probably guess where this is going.

I don't even know how it started. How it happened. What the hell I was thinking.

I was just sitting there in this sort of daze, and then he was looking at me in this weird way.

You don't seem yourself, Gemma. You look pale. Is anything wrong? Is there anything I can help you with?

It's the worst thing, isn't it, for someone to ask if you are OK when you are not OK. It's the last thing you need. And I'm just not used to it because that's not how things roll in my family. Asking. Prodding. Talking about feelings . . .

I should have said I was fine, or pretended I was ill. I should have gone back to the flat. Or to Maddy's – if she wasn't so loved up with her new guy.

But I didn't. I started crying. *Of course.* And everything after that is just this big and embarrassing and totally humiliating blur.

This was three weeks ago. And I have stupidly made things so much worse. I seriously can't quite believe what I've done. Worst of all, I can't even confide in anyone about Alex now, because of what I've done.

So, I'm staring at the title of this essay I haven't even started, and I realise that I am *her*. For real. I am Alice down the rabbit hole, and I don't see any way back for me now.

CHAPTER 13

THE PRIVATE INVESTIGATOR

Matthew has never seen Mel this agitated. At first, she won't even look at him.

'Give me one good reason why I shouldn't drive straight to the hospital and arrest him for obstructing our inquiry.' Mel Sanders is stirring her coffee vigorously as she speaks, the froth spilling on to the saucer and the teaspoon clink, clinking against the china.

'His daughter's in a coma, Mel. She's lost a leg. He's a father. He's in agony.' Matthew pauses. 'Also – the tabloids will have a complete field day if you arrest him. Quite apart from the fact this is very much a long shot. I mean sure, it needs checking out. And yes – he should have told you about the first marriage; I made that crystal clear to him. But at this point, we've no idea if this first wife really is a suspect. Ed Hartley doesn't think so. He's just nervous about the cathedral coincidence—'

'But what if she *is* a suspect? What if he's called it all wrong? We've lost days, Matt. It's unforgiveable for him to withhold this from us.'

There's a pause. At last Mel looks up from her drink and Matthew's trying to read his former colleague's expression. He knows she's just blowing off steam. If she really planned to arrest Ed Hartley, she would have done so already. But she does still look very tired.

'You sure you're OK, Mel?'

'Just a bit tired. George has decided now's a good time to become allergic to sleep.'

'Oh dear.' Matthew remembers the 'no sleep' phase all too well. Small child. Big case. Not an easy combination. Suddenly he understands why Mel's not quite herself.

'I'll be fine. Just really need to get somewhere with this case.'

Matthew checks his watch. Gemma's father has agreed to meet Mel at the police station around noon to answer questions about his first wife. It took all of Matthew's negotiating skills to achieve even this. To be frank, he's no idea himself what to make of this new twist; Ed Hartley shared only the bare bones of his story before dashing off in a huff to the hospital.

'Look. You have the first wife's full details now, Mel. We know there was some kind of mental-health crisis and Ed Hartley gave us the name of her clinic. So is there any word from Canada?'

Matthew has tried the clinic himself but drawn a blank – patient confidentiality. He's praying Mel's had more luck.

'She discharged herself. A good while back.'

'You're *kidding* me?' Now he understands her mood.

'I wish. Also – the paperwork's missing. The clinic's had some bad media coverage lately over standards and security. Patients being released without proper supervision and follow-up. An undercover reporter did some secret filming, posing as a nurse. It's been something of a scandal over there.'

'Oh no, that's not good. So do you know where the ex-wife is now?'

'We're liaising with the Canadians but you know how slowly those wheels grind, especially as I don't yet have the full picture – proper grounds, I mean. They're doing me a favour at this stage, checking the family address he gave you. But it seems out of date.'

Matthew twists his mouth to the side and narrows his eyes. 'So why didn't you arrest him, really? If you're that cross. That worried. Why did you want to meet me instead?'

Melanie Sanders takes a deep breath and leans back in her seat. 'OK. Cards on the table; I have something to ask you, Matt.'

He's full-on curious now, widening his eyes to signal that she should continue.

'As I said before I have the rare treat of a proper budget. They want this sorted so I have carte blanche to run this inquiry the way I want.'

'Grief. The suits upstairs must *really* be worried.'

'They are, Matt. We've got universities and tourist boards all over the country in meltdown. They know it's not terrorism but some are worrying about copycats. They're worrying about absolutely everything, to be perfectly honest with you. There's loads of chatter online among students and parents, none of it good. And now I need to worry if someone in Canada is involved. So I need to work fast. And I need help.'

'So?'

'So I want to *hire* you, Matt. Officially. As a civilian expert. Profiler. Whatever you want to be called. I know I'm always joking about this but I'm deadly serious this time. I need you.'

Matthew pulls his chin back into his neck. 'Can you even *do* that?'

'On this one, I can do what the hell I like so long as I get the job done. Please say yes, Matt.' A pause. 'I really need you.'

Matthew feels a wave of something travel right through his body and cannot make out whether it is adrenaline, excitement or blind panic. Ever since he left the force, he's wondered if there would be a road back one day but has always pushed the thought away. Setting up the business and working as a freelancer have created financial pressures that have demanded an entirely different mindset.

He looks at Mel and realises that deep down he's hoped for this moment. But what about Sally? With Amelie playing up she'll be wary, especially after the danger he put himself in at the cathedral.

'This is a surprise, Mel. I honestly don't know what to say.' Fact is they've cooperated together informally on several cases and Mel's forever joking about getting him 'back on the force', but never officially. Never openly.

'There will be proper paperwork. A contract. Invoices and all that jazz. I can get HR to sort it all out, if that's what you're worried about.'

It isn't that he's worried about. It's Sally he's worried about. Also Amelie's nightmares and her reluctance to go to nursery. Will working with Mel make this all worse for his family? Or better?

'I need to think about it. And talk to Sal. You know how upset she was after the cathedral.'

'Right. Yes. Of course.' She's staring at him. Her pale face is strained which he now realises is pure exhaustion. 'Look, Matt. I'm going to the university next to speak to the chancellor. We've liaised by phone but she wants face to face to make a decision fast about the final graduation ceremony this Friday. The press want to know what's happening. I'm not going to lie to you, I'm feeling the pressure and I'm worried about making the wrong call. I can't win. If we cancel, we're admitting we can't keep people safe. If we go ahead and anything happens . . .' She takes in a deep breath. 'Will you come with me? Sit in on this meeting and the interview with Ed Hartley afterwards. Tell me what you think?'

'And how will you explain me tagging along?'

'I'll think of something. Please say yes, Matt. Sit in with me today, see how you feel, and give me your decision about a more formal arrangement tomorrow. How does that sound?'

'But don't you need approval for this, Mel? I thought the National Crime Agency supplied their own experts?'

'We're short on numbers, as well you know. It's pretty hand to mouth out there; they're hiring retired detectives all over the country.'

'But I'm not retired.'

'Ex-job. Same thing. This will be up to me, Matt. Please say you'll at least consider it? I'm up against the clock here.'

'OK. I'll do today. See how we go.' He downs the rest of his coffee, trying once again to put a label on the feeling in his stomach.

Is it excitement? Or is it a warning? A signal that putting himself in the firing line one more time might just be pushing his luck too far.

CHAPTER 14

THE MOTHER

I glance across Gemma's bed at Ed. He's pretending to read his book but hasn't turned a page in ages. He arrived late this morning and looks tired. Snappy too.

Look – things just took longer than I thought, Rachel. It's not easy you know, juggling everything.

I don't rise to it. Does Ed really think Gemma wants to hear conflict? But it feels awkward sitting in silence today, both of us pretending to read. I know from his expression that there's something very wrong.

Beyond the obvious, I mean.

For myself, I keep daydreaming; thinking about that little moment with DI Sanders and how I wanted to tell her about the odd woman who turned up not once, not twice, but three times this past month. I can't honestly believe that some strange woman is going to have anything to do with all of this but I still feel guilty for not mentioning it. The problem is my mind goes round and round in circles. If I tell the police about the woman, I will have to tell them what I did *afterwards* about it and I don't want Ed to find out.

I look across at my husband again. Make no mistake, Ed is a good man and a good father. I love him very much and I would say that we have a good marriage, but what is it really – a good marriage? Is it strong enough to survive what's happening to Gemma? Is it strong enough to survive what I did over that stupid woman?

Is it strong enough to survive the fact that I don't always tell the truth? Can't. Won't.

Certainly there's sometimes this odd space between Ed and me which I can't quite explain. When we first met, he said he'd been hurt badly in the past but he wouldn't talk about it. Boy – if anyone can understand not wanting to talk about something from the past, it's me. I didn't push him and he didn't push me. I just assumed it was classic commitment phobia. A guy making excuses. He lived in Canada for a bit and said a business venture had gone pear-shaped there; he didn't like to talk about it because it made him feel a failure. He wanted a clean slate. A fresh start.

I remember feeling this extraordinary bubble of hope because that was *exactly* what I wanted too. A clean slate. A fresh start . . .

It was as if we were made for each other. Anyway, I was wrong about the commitment phobia because he's the loveliest and most loyal of men. We did get married, we made a good life and, most of the time, we're very happy together.

But every now and again, when I ask the wrong question – especially about the past – he gets like this. Defensive, wearing an expression that is warning me off. No. It's worse than a warning. It's like it's not my Ed at all.

And I know it's completely hypocritical of me to push, given that I hate people doing that to me, but this is different. This is about Gemma.

'Is there something wrong, Ed? Something beyond this, I mean.' I glance at Gemma in the bed. 'Something we need to talk

86

about. Outside?' I signal to the door but he doesn't answer. Just looks at the floor.

OK. So here's the truth. After I caught that really odd woman staring at me through the kitchen window, I had this flutter of suspicion that maybe Ed was having an affair. That maybe he had had enough of me flouncing off to the kitchen whenever we had a little upset; that the woman was his mistress and was checking me out. I tried to tell myself not to be so stupid but the whole thing got worse. This suspicion grew and grew because I caught her watching me on two more occasions. The second time was at the hairdresser's about a week later. I had a head full of foil for my highlights so couldn't go out on to the street to confront her, but it was definitely the same woman and she was watching me specifically through the window again. And the third and final time, I was just out in town window-shopping. I fancied a new coat in the sales and was just strolling from shop to shop when I caught her reflection in one of the windows. She was standing behind me, just staring again.

This time I'd had enough so I called out to her. *Who are you? And why are you following me?* She stepped forward then and leaned towards me to say something really odd.

He's not who he says he is. I have to warn you. He's not who he says he is.

So here's the embarrassing confession. After that, I completely freaked out. There was no way I was having this out with Ed directly – he'd only lie – so instead I hired a private investigator to see if Ed was having an affair with her. The thing is, I started asking Ed where he'd been and what he'd been doing and if everything was alright with the marriage. If he would ever lie to me. He got quite defensive – and I read in a magazine that can be a sign of infidelity.

My suspicions just sort of spiralled and I found the PI online. I'm ashamed now because the private investigator charged quite a lot of money but found absolutely nothing. *You have a faithful husband, Mrs Hartley.*

'Our daughter has been shot and you want to start this all up again? Questioning me? Navel contemplating? Picking at the marriage?' He's whispering, still looking at the floor.

'No, Ed. I just feel a bit guilty that I find it hard . . .' I pause. 'Well, you know. That I find it so hard to talk about difficult stuff. But we need to be there for each other.'

'I *am* here for you.'

'Yes.' I pause and take in a deep, slow breath, feeling even more guilty. 'You are.'

I turn to look at our daughter, her skin pale and her eyes firmly closed. Can she hear this – even when we're whispering?

For just a second, I drift away again. I can hear my father's voice booming from the kitchen. I can hear plates and glasses smashing . . .

I am standing in the doorway, just a little girl, and I can see my mother's eyes glaring at me.

Go to your room, Rachel. Go now!

I told Ed and Gemma too that I had a happy childhood, that my parents' split was amicable . . .

I listen again to the smashing sounds from the kitchen all those years ago and I remember covering my ears and looking down at my rabbit slippers.

'We really mustn't squabble in front of Gemma. We should go outside.'

'Oh, Rachel. For heaven's sake. We can't go outside every time we need to talk. It's ridiculous. I'm sure she can't hear whispering.'

I keep quiet for a while, just looking at Gemma, watching her chest rise and fall ever so gently. I can feel this tightening in my stomach, pushing away all the pictures from the past . . .

'You know how much I love you both? Isn't that enough?' Ed's tone is really strange.

'I'm sorry, Ed. It's the strain and the lack of sleep.'

He reaches for my hand and squeezes it. 'The police want me to go and meet with them again, Rachel. I said I'd go to the station; I know it upsets you when they come here.'

I spin my head to look him in the eye. 'But what do they want? Do they have a lead? Is it to do with Alex? Shouldn't they be talking to both of us together?'

'I have no idea. They said they'd explain when I get there. Will you be all right this afternoon – here on your own, I mean? I can try to put them off, if you'd prefer?'

'No. No. Don't put them off. It might be a breakthrough. It might be news about Alex . . . Maybe something's come from his interviews. Or the phone footage.' I frown, only now realising that I have a headache starting. 'And would you ask again about the laptop? If we can have the laptop?' Once more I'm thinking of all the visits. All the photographs. All of us smiling. 'You don't really think Alex was the one who did this, do you?'

Ed doesn't answer and I look at the cabinet beside Gemma's bed where he's placed sandwiches from the deli. Crab for me and Brie and caramelised onion for him. I wonder if Gemma's kept all the photos of her birthday celebration. Afternoon tea with Alex. All those fancy sandwiches.

It feels a lifetime ago; Gemma and Alex broke up soon afterwards but she never explained why. Did he really do this to her?

I look back at Ed and realise I will have to tell the police about the odd woman. Just in case. But will DI Sanders tell Ed about the private investigator?

Ed holds my stare and I can't read his expression.

89

'Whatever happens with the police . . .' Ed's voice is slower. Very quiet. 'You know that I love you? You and Gemma? I love you both more than anything in the world.'

'Why did you say that? What do you mean – *whatever happens with the police?*'

'It doesn't matter.'

I turn to see that his eyes are distant and there's this new and dreadful feeling deep in the pit of my stomach.

'Why did you say that, Ed?'

He shakes his head and turns away from me. I stare at his profile, widening my eyes and willing him to explain, but there's only the bleeping of Gemma's machine breaking the silence. *Bleep, bleep.* I can feel the gap between Ed and me widening – stretching and stretching – *bleep, bleep.* I close my eyes and just don't know what to do.

I'm thinking again about that strange woman.

He's not who he says he is.

Was she just some loner? Some misfit.

Or did she really mean Ed after all?

CHAPTER 15

THE PRIVATE INVESTIGATOR

In the chancellor's office, Matt's head is still swimming with the news that Ed's first wife is AWOL. Also Mel's surprise approach.

They travelled in separate cars from the café and there's been no time yet to ring Sally. He's done a very quick check of the diary on his phone – two surveillance jobs booked for messy divorce cases. It's the kind of bread-and-butter work he despises but can't afford to refuse. He'll need to honour those bookings but can't deny that working on this case officially is a great deal more appealing than fielding calls from rich widows.

The chancellor's office isn't small but manages to feel claustrophobic. So much wood. Matthew glances around at the panelling, the two huge wooden desks (why two, he wonders?) and the floor-to-ceiling bookcase entirely filling one wall. He doesn't recognise the wood, which has quite a yellow tone. Yew, maybe? Whatever the timber, it makes him think of saunas. He feels hot suddenly, pulling at his shirt collar.

'We have a meeting of the senior management team later.' The chancellor's repeating herself. Ms Emily Brockenhurt, as neatly confirmed on a small, inevitably wooden name stand on her desk, is dressed immaculately in a turquoise suit with white blouse and pearls and the foil of huge red glasses. She looks very focused but also hot, suddenly sliding off her jacket and hooking it over the back of her chair.

Matthew takes the coffee cup handed to him as Ms Brockenhurt holds up a bowl with sugar. He shakes his head to the sugar and watches Mel out of the corner of his eye. She's playing her usual, clever game. Silent. Waiting.

'We need to make this decision about the final graduation ceremony. Whether to go ahead on Friday. I need to let everyone know by the morning. Parents want to know whether to claim refunds on hotels. It's getting tight.' The chancellor clears her throat. 'I'm sorry. Insensitive of me. I meant to ask first if there's any more news on the poor girl's condition. My staff have been in touch with the hospital, but not being family—'

'Stable. No change. *Gemma's* still in a coma.' Melanie's tone is steady, and Matthew likes that she emphasises Gemma's name. 'We're all under pressure, Chancellor. I do understand. Been a tough weekend.' Mel puts her own cup down on the edge of the desk.

'And are we any nearer finding who did this, DI Sanders – since we last spoke?'

'We're doing everything we can and I have good people.' Mel turns to Matthew.

'Right. Good. Of course. I've asked our head of communications Amanda to join us, by the way.' The chancellor starts sifting through papers in front of her. 'She's drawn up the report you wanted on all the extra security arrangements. Also the press statement we'd put out when – or rather if – we go ahead.' The chancellor looks at her watch. 'She'll be with us in just a few minutes. I just wanted to give us some time alone in case you have anything you wish to share with me privately. Do you have any leads?'

'As you know from the papers, we have someone in custody but no firm evidence yet. We have to assume that the person who shot Gemma Hartley could still be at large. There's no denying that cancelling Friday is the safest option.'

'And is that what you recommend, Inspector?'

Matthew watches Mel closely. He knows that senior officers want the public reassured. They don't want to signal that the force can't keep the peace; can't keep people safe.

'We don't want the public thinking we can't keep them safe. It's a balancing act.' Mel reaches for her coffee cup again.

'I'm going to be frank, Inspector. We already have foreign students cancelling their courses. The blow to income is considerable. Parents are ringing in constantly. I want people to be safe too. But I also want my university to *survive*. It would be a lift if we could end the summer with a happier memory.'

There's a knock at the door before Mel can answer.

'Ah, that will be our press officer.' The chancellor lowers her voice. 'I should mention, strictly between us, that she took it hard – what happened in the cathedral. Amanda. She's having counselling. Great asset to the university. Very capable. She's been working round the clock – all weekend.

'Come in.' The chancellor shuffles the papers in front of her into a neat pile.

A tall woman then enters the room, carrying a stack of reports, and Matthew recognises her as the woman who helped him with the students in the two holding rooms at the back of the cathedral directly after the shooting. She was very shaken, he remembers, but impressively capable, nonetheless. She didn't flee.

'You may remember Amanda from the cathedral, Matthew. She tells me you were marvellous.'

Matthew nods and Amanda's eyes look strained suddenly. He can understand why it would haunt her too. *Ice cream. Ice cream.*

He feels a little guilty for asking so much of her and Tom that day. Must have been difficult. The student panic in the locked rooms. The reason for the counselling?

'Amanda did very well,' he says. 'And Tom. There was a marine who stepped up too. I'd have struggled without your help. Both of you.'

'Thank you.' She pauses, then shakes his hand and Mel's too before passing each of them a document. 'Right. So here, we've summarised all the extra security suggestions.'

Matthew quickly glances through it. The list includes use of a specialist consultancy and a range of measures, including airport-style scanners in marquees outside the cathedral.

'We're assuming the police would also offer extra support?' The chancellor's looking directly at Melanie again. 'Amanda's drawn up a draft statement for the press.'

'*If* we go ahead,' Amanda says suddenly.

'Quite.' The chancellor's expression is difficult to read.

'We'll do a sweep of the cathedral and have uniformed officers for reassurance,' Mel says. 'Senior officers don't want an obvious armed presence. But we'll have backup on standby.'

Matthew glances at Amanda who's still looking tense. The chancellor seems to notice.

'Look, I like directness so you should know that we have divided opinions in the senior management team over what to do.' The chancellor clears her throat. 'Our head of student counselling has concerns. But we have terrific support in place. For the students and the staff too. The bottom line here is we have to get past this and, like it or not, we have to think of the bigger picture. The future of the university. So you're not advising *against* going ahead, Inspector?'

Mel narrows her eyes. 'It's a difficult call but – no, I'm not.'

'Good. Good. And are we likely to see anyone charged this week? Before the ceremony, I mean?'

'In an ideal world. But I can't say.' Mel takes in a long, slow breath. 'By the way, there is one line of inquiry that you might be able to help with.'

'Fire away.'

'There's a suggestion that Gemma may have been having an affair with one of her tutors. A member of staff.'

The chancellor looks shocked. She looks over at Amanda, then back at Melanie. 'And do you have *evidence* of this, Inspector?'

'No. But have there been rumours?'

'I've heard nothing. Amanda? Are you aware of this?'

The press officer shakes her head.

'Right. Well, we'll need to quash that. Probably just tittle-tattle.' The chancellor's fiddling with the pearls around her neck.

'Possibly. But we'll need a list of all Gemma's tutors for interviews. And if you do hear anything at all, you'll be sure to let us know?' Mel is staring at the chancellor now.

'Of course.'

'And that other list I asked for? Any staff sacked. Tribunals. Anyone who might hold a grudge.'

'It's in hand. Unfortunately, my head of people is in Meltona, would you believe.'

'Oh goodness. The *hurricane*?' Matthew widens his eyes. The chaos on Meltona island has been on the news for three days. So that's why the list's been slow to arrive.

'She's safe, thank God. They all got to higher ground. She managed to borrow some reporter's satellite phone to contact family but all comms are down again. She doesn't expect to be flown out for a few more days. But I've got other staff working on the list for you. By tomorrow, latest.'

'Thank you. Though I'd really like to speak to your HR lead on Meltona if that's at all possible. What's her name?'

'Molly Price.'

'Right. We'll try the comms our side but if she gets through again, would you ask her to ring me?'

'Sure.'

'And you mentioned student support. Can we run another check on whether Gemma was seeing anyone? A counsellor. Anything like that?'

'That would be confidential.' The chancellor is frowning.

'In an attempted murder inquiry, I'm afraid *nothing* is confidential.' Mel stands to signal the meeting's over. 'Right. Forensics are nearly finished on site. We'll release the cathedral back to the authorities by tomorrow. And I look forward to your board's decision.' She doesn't shake hands again, just heads to the door.

'Of course. We meet at six p.m. I'll email you straight afterwards.'

Matthew follows Mel but at the door she suddenly turns back. 'Oh, by the way, I heard some rumblings of redundancies. Could we have that list too?'

Matthew suddenly understands why Mel's so keen to speak to the HR lead.

The chancellor's also standing. 'All universities are up against it, financially. No secret there. We hope to use voluntary severance. There's no list yet, Inspector. No decision. No disputes. We have a happy ship.'

Mel pauses and then smiles before leaving the room. Matthew follows and they're careful to say nothing until safely out of the building. As Mel fires the central-locking key towards her car, she leans into the rear passenger door.

'So what do you make of them? Our chancellor and our head of communications?'

'Not sure. But they clearly disagree over the final ceremony.'

'And what do *you* think, Matt? Have I called it wrong? Should I have played safe and advised cancellation?'

'Like you said before, you can't win either way.'

Mel opens her driver's door. 'Which gives me precisely four days to crack this case . . . with your help.' She grins.

He tilts his head but is careful not to reply.

'What's your gut saying, Matt?'

He pauses to think but not for too long. That would defeat the object. 'My gut's saying it's to do with the baby. We obviously can't press for paternity tests while she's in a coma. Legal nightmare. But we do need to find out who the father is.'

'OK, Matt. I think I might agree with you. Meantime let's go see Gemma's dad. Find out why the hell he's been lying to us, eh?'

CHAPTER 16

Lemon

The cot is assembled now and I'm pleased with it.

The curtains are up too – lemon, of course – and I have found a matching duvet. Lemon with little white elephants.

There's still work to be done, so many boxes in the corner to be unpacked and sorted, but I feel it is all finally coming together and I like to come in here in the evening now and sit in the tall-backed chair. It feels so calm and special. Stops all the noise and the stress. All the questions in my head.

Why, oh why, are there always so many questions?

Sometimes, you know, I feel as if my head is actually going to explode with them. I told a doctor this years ago and he said that we could try a different prescription, but I got tired of the battles over the drugs. All the wretched side effects. It seems to me that drugs try to fix one thing but simply create another problem. And then you need a different drug to fix the new problem. But do the doctors listen? Do they sympathise? No, they don't.

I think I may look for a mobile next – to hang above the cot. When I was small my mother used to sing this lullaby . . . I know the tune but I can't for the life of me remember the words. I may look online.

YouTube perhaps? Imagine if I can find a mobile with little elephants to match the duvet.

That would be just perfect, wouldn't it?

That would blank out what happened. All the blackness and the noise in my head.

That would make things nice and calm again.

A lemon mobile with white elephants. Yes. I'll look online. Maybe they sell one to match.

That would be just perfect.

CHAPTER 17

THE PRIVATE INVESTIGATOR

'So what do you think? Be honest, Sal.' Matthew's in his car, mobile clamped to his right ear as he watches Mel, ready to pull away ahead of him.

He's holding his breath but she doesn't answer for a time and so he ploughs on. 'I won't say "yes" if you hate the idea. But I think this could be a good thing for us; for Amelie, I mean. We can tell her Daddy's going to help catch the bad person and she doesn't need to be afraid.'

More silence.

'Please say something, Sally.'

'This is someone with a *gun*, Matt.'

'I know, I know, love, but I also know what I'm doing. And I can help them solve the case faster if I'm on board officially.'

'But this isn't your problem, Matt. The whole thing really scares me.'

'I understand and I won't agree to anything until we've talked it through tonight. I just wanted you to know straight away about the approach. Look, I've got to go.' He lifts his hand as a signal to Mel that he'll follow her car. 'I love you, Sally.' He means it. He really does. He just wishes he could make her not worry.

'I love you too.'

Matthew's just about to fire the ignition when he spots Amanda, the PR, leaving through the main doors. A thought suddenly sweeps in and he quickly steps out of the car.

'Amanda. Sorry to hold you up but have you got a minute?'

She glances at her watch, frowning. 'I've got a meeting actually.'

'Don't worry. Won't take long. I just wanted to say thank you properly. How grateful I was for your support at the cathedral. You and Tom. Keeping the students safe until the full team arrived.'

'Oh that. Right.' She looks embarrassed. 'Well to be honest, it wasn't my finest hour. I was pretty petrified actually.'

'Me too.'

She smiles at last.

'Seriously. I was sorry to ask that of you. Put you and Tom on the spot. But most people at the cathedral just bolted. You didn't.' He won't mention that he knows she's having counselling. The chancellor clearly shouldn't have shared that.

'No. Well, we had the students to think of.' She looks away for a moment. 'They were terrified too.'

'And the other thing I wondered . . .' He waits for her to look back at him. '. . . is how you feel about this final ceremony. If it goes ahead, will you be involved? Did I pick up back there that you have concerns?' He pauses. 'Off the record.'

'Oh, come on.' She tilts her head. 'You and I both know that there's no such thing as *off the record*, Mr Hill.'

'Matthew, please.'

'I'm a press officer. I'm hardly going to speak out of turn, Matthew.'

'Of course.' He bites into his bottom lip then plunges on. 'But I'm going to be asking around. I'm going to find out anyway. So – is this senior management team very split?'

She takes in a long breath as if weighing something up. 'Look, it's no secret around campus that opinions are divided. Some badly want a morale boost to see us past this. Others think it safer and easier to just bump it all.'

'And you share the latter view?'

'I didn't say that.'

He looks at her intently. 'It's OK to be nervous, you know.'

She lets out a long sigh. 'Is it? Our chancellor's thankfully made of stronger stuff.' Her eyes look haunted for a moment and Matthew remembers her in her smart, black suit alongside the marine as he barked instructions at them.

'As I say, I asked a lot of you. And if I remember, they shepherded the chancellor out of a side door pretty quickly.'

Amanda glances around her again. 'Actually, there is something I should probably mention to you.'

Matthew's more curious now.

'Oh – nothing significant. Just something on my mind. It's just my sister Helen knows the family. Gemma's mother – they live in the same area. Helen asked me to fix good seats for them in the cathedral. We're really not supposed to do that; the demand for seats is a hot potato every year. Anyway, my sister went *on and on* about it so in the end I did. Wangled for the Hartleys to be right up the front. It's why they saw it all so clearly. I feel bad about that now.'

'Right. So you *know* the family?'

'No. Not me, not personally. But my sister's fond of the mother. Helen asked me to give some tips about the uni when Gemma first applied. And this last year she asked if I could help Gemma with work experience. I'm afraid I fobbed her off. We're always so busy. I feel terrible about that now.' She looks crestfallen.

'Well, you couldn't know.' He smiles. Everyone hated babysitting trainees when he was in the force. Then he remembers that Mel's waiting.

'Oh, and just one more thing. More personal. I read in the paper that the university is offering counselling to students and staff.' He's keen to be diplomatic even if the chancellor wasn't.

'Yes – that's right. We have a very good team.'

'It's just my daughter's having nightmares. She was there that day – on the high street with my wife and heard too much. I was wondering if you could recommend someone. A counsellor from your team? I'd be happy to pay privately.'

'What age is she?'

'Four.'

'Poor thing.' Amanda's eyes soften. 'Well, our team specialises in student and adult counselling, but I know they have contacts who work with children. There were a few younger siblings at the cathedral. I can have a word with our head of student counselling if you like.'

'Would you?' Matthew hands over his personal card. 'Email and mobile are on there. As I say I'm happy to pay privately but would love a recommendation. We need someone good.'

'No problem. Happy to help. And about the seating. Do you want me to come clean with the chancellor? It's just I'll be in a bit of hot water but I'd rather tell her myself if it's going to be an issue. I've been a bit worried your investigation might question why they were up the front. In the VIP section.'

Matthew realises it had never occurred to him to wonder. He looks down at the ground and then back at Amanda.

'No. I don't think it's important. Mum's the word.'

'Thank you.' She looks relieved.

'And try not to worry. If the ceremony *does* go ahead, DI Sanders will keep everyone safe. She's good. *Very* good.'

Amanda just nods and looks at her watch again. 'Sorry. But I really ought to be going. The meeting.'

◆ ◆ ◆

Twenty minutes later, as Matthew finally pulls up at the police station, Mel's waiting on the steps, scrolling through her phone.

'So what happened to you, Matt? On the phone to Sally?'

'You should be a detective.'

Mel laughs.

'Yeah. I spoke briefly to Sal but I also had a quick word with the PR Amanda. We were right. She's trying to be diplomatic – typical PR – but she clearly doesn't agree about the final ceremony going ahead. She's more shaken than the chancellor realises.'

'Interesting. And what about Sally? What does she think about my offer?'

'We're going to talk tonight. My guess is she'll want me in a bulletproof vest minimum.'

'Well, at least you're skinny enough to carry it off.' Mel's smiling as she leads them through the front office, using her security card to take them into an inner corridor. 'I look pregnant again in mine.'

Matthew's turn to laugh. It was a standing joke when they last liaised over a case. Mel was in the final stages of her pregnancy and was so large that everyone, Matthew included, was sure she was having twins. She wasn't. It's funny to see her tiny again – her son at home. Separate and growing up fast.

He follows her to the lift, thinking also of Amelie and hoping that Amanda may help source a good counsellor. He wonders how anyone would even approach this – with a child so young.

'You all right, Matt? You look distracted.' Mel's turned her head.

'I'm fine. Sorry, mind in overdrive. One thing. Did you ever wonder why the Hartleys were right up front for the ceremony?'

Mel frowns. 'No. Just assumed they got lucky. Why? Is something worrying you? Something relevant?'

'No. I just wondered if it was better or worse for them. To have seen it all so clearly.'

Mel considers this. 'Better to be nearer, I'd say. Given the crush you described. At least they got to Gemma pretty quickly.'

'Yes. That's what I think.' Matthew pauses. He'll tell Amanda this if she gets in touch about the counselling. That she shouldn't feel bad about the favour. Might ease his guilt over asking so much of her after the shooting.

'Come on, then. Let's do this.' He takes in a breath and next they're moving swiftly through the CID offices to the small suite of interview rooms where Ed Hartley's waiting for them.

Mel leaves Matthew momentarily, he assumes to explain to her team why she's leading on the chat with Ed Hartley and taking him through too. He waits outside the door of the office but can't quite make out what's being said – though he imagines the eye-rolling. It's not a formal interview but most inspectors would still bump this to a sergeant. Though Mel's never been one for protocol.

Next they're sweeping into the small, square room to find Gemma's father drinking coffee at the central table. He stands.

'I've been waiting ages.'

'Sorry. We were at the university. We got held up.'

'Do I need my solicitor?'

'Why would you need a solicitor, Mr Hartley? This is just a chat.'

'Right. That's what Matthew said. Just an informal chat.' He sits down as they take up their own seats opposite. 'So you won't be recording this or anything?'

'This is just a chat, like I said. You've agreed to meet me. You're not under arrest. So why don't you tell me about your first marriage. And why you're worried that your first wife might in some way be involved in Gemma's shooting?'

'I didn't say that. I just said that it was a coincidence that I met Laura, my first wife, in a cathedral. So that was sort of preying on my mind and I felt I should have told you. So have you checked things out? Is Laura OK? Is she with her parents or is she at the clinic?'

Matthew bites into his lip, wondering how Mel will play this.

'Your first wife is missing from the clinic, Mr Hartley.' Mel pauses as Ed Hartley's face pales. 'The clinic's under investigation for breaches of standards and security. Cost-cutting cock-ups according to the local media. Upshot is right now we have absolutely no idea where she is. Which is why I think you'd better tell me absolutely everything, don't you? About her condition. How you parted. When you last heard from her. And whether she has any reason whatsoever to wish you or your daughter harm.'

CHAPTER 18

THE FATHER - *BEFORE*

It came right out of the blue. Laura's illness. Like a trip on the pavement, your face suddenly smashed on to concrete.

And for Ed, it was the *speed* of the unravelling that shocked him most.

He and Laura had been married just six months. They'd recently moved to Canada where her parents lived and her father had given him a job, handling the marketing for his building company. It was going well. No, better than well; they were truly happy.

Thursday night – a month into his new job – they went to bed around eleven as usual. Friday morning, he got up early for a pee and suddenly it was as if someone flipped a switch on his life.

That trip on the pavement . . .

By the time he padded back to the doorway of their bedroom, Laura was bolt upright in bed – first just staring at him, her eyes wild, and then screaming in apparent terror.

He felt a spike of adrenaline. The rush of his own mirrored fear. *An intruder?* He spun his head this way and that, trying to work out where? Who? What the hell he was dealing with. He grabbed a candlestick from the top of a bookcase in the hallway and swung his head and his weapon. Left. Right. Left. Right.

But there was nothing. No shadow. No sound of footsteps. Nothing.

He checked the hall and the second bedroom. Again – nothing. By the time he was back in the doorway of their room, Laura had stopped screaming but was still staring directly at him, eyes bulging with alarm. It was as if she was looking at him but also through him, without proper recognition. His next thought was a night terror. He'd read about that. Maybe she was actually still asleep and wasn't seeing him at all. There was a feature in one of the Sundays once; it said that sometimes sleepwalkers moved around with their eyes wide open.

'It's all right, it's all right. I'm here. What's happened? What is it? What did you see? It's just a dream, Laura. I'm here. You're safe.' He was still in the doorway but now took a step into the room.

'No, no! You stay right there. Don't you dare move.'

So she could hear him; see him. He didn't understand, his head spinning.

Next she picked up the phone by the bed and was dialling. 'I'm calling the police.'

'The *police*?' He stepped back into the doorway. 'What's happened? I can't see anyone, Laura. There's no sign of anyone.'

'Who *are* you?' Still she was staring at him, unblinking. 'I told you not to move. I mean it. I'm trained. I can take you down.'

'What do you mean – who am I? Put the phone down. This isn't funny, Laura.' Not for one minute did he actually think this was a joke and he regretted saying that instantly but he didn't know what else to say. What else to do.

Christ. She was actually dialling . . .

'No, no. Don't ring the police. You're perfectly safe, I promise you. Just look at me, please. You're safe.'

She seemed to pause then as if changing her mind. Puzzled rather than terrified. His mind was still spinning while hers seemed in freefall.

She pressed the end button on the phone and just continued to stare at him. She tilted her head to the side as if trying to better compute what she was seeing. Next, and most ominously, she picked up a torch – kept alongside the bed in case of power cuts – and held it up as her own weapon.

Instinctively Ed lowered his hand holding the candlestick, but Laura did not copy; she kept the torch high in the air.

'What do you want?' Her eyes were still wide. Unnatural. 'I'm not afraid to use this. And I'm warning you – I'm trained. And I'm stronger than I look. I can take you down.'

This time he said nothing for a while. Very gently and slowly he put the candlestick back on the top of the bookcase. Maybe if he just waited she would calm down. Wake up properly? She watched him. He watched her. They both waited for maybe a minute.

'What have you done with my husband?'

'Look. I don't know what this is but you must have been dreaming, darling. It's me. It's Ed. Look at me. You're safe. It's *me*.'

'I'm going to ask you one more time. What have you done with my husband?'

He felt a strange pull in his stomach, his mind moving to a new place. He took in her wild eyes and her pale skin. Her trembling hand. Laura was clearly unwell. In some kind of psychotic state. What had brought it on, he had no notion. Night terror, sleepwalking or whatever. All he knew for sure was that he wasn't equipped to deal with this, not on his own. He needed to get her to snap out of whatever this was. But how to do that safely, without making it worse?

'OK. So how about we get someone to help. Someone to come and help?' What he was actually thinking was that he needed to buy some time. He was still assuming this would pass soon. That she would wake up properly very soon and this peculiar state would *pass*. 'Shall we ring the doctor, Laura?'

'Doctor? Why would I need a doctor? How dare you. You come into my home . . .'

'OK. So how about your mother. Why don't you phone your mother? Get your mother to come over here? Help us sort this out?' He was wondering in fact whether he could phone the doctor secretly once Laura's mother arrived. Laura's parents were just ten minutes away by car. If this passed, they could explain when her mother arrived and then see what the doctor advised. He was remembering now that his father once had a bladder infection that went untreated and caused him to hallucinate. He thought there were locusts on the carpet. Maybe this was something like that? Some kind of infection causing her to see things?

'You need to tell me what you've done with my husband.'

'I *am* your husband, Laura. Look at me.'

She raised the torch higher.

'OK, let's just ring your mother. Get her to come here. Alright?'

She glanced to the left and right as if thinking. 'No – the police. I think we need the police here.'

'Let's get your mother here first. And then if she thinks we need the police, fair enough. I promise you I'm not going to come into the room and I'm certainly not going to hurt you. You're not in danger. It's me. It's Ed.' He was looking at the heavy torch in her hand. What on earth was going on in her mind he had no idea, but he needed to calm this all down. Keep the police out of it. Could disorientation from a bad dream last this long? She'd never talked in her sleep. Walked in her sleep. But if it was some kind of infection, she would need antibiotics. He could phone the doctor discreetly once her mother was here.

Now at last she was dialling the phone again. She pressed it against her ear. 'Mum? Listen. I need you to come over urgently. Something really terrible has happened. A man's here in the house. He looks just like Ed but he *isn't* Ed. I don't know what he's done with Ed. He won't tell me.'

There was a pause and Ed could just make out the confusion and panic in her mother's raised voice on the other end of the line.

'I don't know, Mum. I don't know what's going on. Can you just get in the car and come over here right now otherwise I need to call the police?' Another pause. 'No, no. You can't speak to him. I can't let him in the room. It's too dangerous.'

And then she just hung up. She raised the torch again and continued to stare.

'She'll be here in ten minutes. You don't move, you hear me. You don't move a single muscle or I'll take you down.'

CHAPTER 19

THE DAUGHTER – *BEFORE*

Waiting for Godot – *did Samuel Beckett truly write for performance or did his work pose restrictions for actors and directors? Discuss.*

I don't understand it. I'm never late. I'm always careful. I've been on the Pill since I was seventeen and I've never had any problems or any serious scares. Why now? Why a scare now? As if I haven't got enough going on.

OK – so I need not to panic here. It could be stress. Ten days over could still be stress. I read about that. Stress can mess up your cycle big time.

And I have been stressed . . .

The truth is I haven't written anything about 'S' for a few weeks because it's literally been changing daily, let alone weekly. At first he was so lovely and so honourable. He backed right off. Left it entirely up to me. He said that he had really strong feelings for me but didn't want to put me in a difficult situation. I decided at first that it was best to write it off as a mistake. Just that one time. But the more I saw him and realised how he was struggling with his feelings, the more I kept thinking about him. About how different it felt with him, compared with 'A'. (I've only just realised what an idiot I've been writing HIS name out in full. I'm having to sweep through and change that . . . I mean, if 'A' does ever get into my computer, he'll do a search for his name, won't he? Fake essay titles won't be enough. *Why* didn't I think of that before . . .)

Anyway. Back to 'S'. I mean I do know it's a cliché. My tutor. And I was embarrassed and thrown at first by what happened. But it's so completely different being around someone older. It's so nice. The maturity, I mean. The proper *talking*.

And yes – I get that he's married. And it's complicated and technically very, very wrong but there's no way I would be seeing him if he wasn't, in effect, separated. The thing is – his marriage has been dead for a very long time. Years and years. He's tried to leave several times but she's apparently a little fragile and he's a really decent and kind bloke so he's trying to help her build her confidence and help her settle into a new job and a new life before they split up formally. So they're still living in the same home but more as a house share, not as a proper couple – sleeping apart, obviously – more as a front.

It was knowing this that decided things for me. I mean – it's not like starting something up with someone who's going to stay married, or is happily married. It's a question of timing when they separate. Not an 'if' but a 'when'.

So it was my decision to sleep with him again. He didn't push me. He's not like 'A'. He never loses his temper or gets wound up. He listens to me; he talks to me.

I think that's what I love the most of all. We talk things through. It's not like at home with Mum with her pottering off into the kitchen every time things get tricky. 'S' listens.

So – yes. We're a couple, albeit a secret one for now. And spending time with 'S', however briefly and however 'complicated', has made me realise just how immature and inappropriate 'A''s behaviour has always been. I've shared just a few details with 'S' and he was horrified. He says that in no way is that kind of behaviour acceptable, not ever, and I need to be careful. That 'A' is controlling and very, very bad news.

The only very tricky thing is I can't confide in any of my friends because the 'S' situation is so sensitive for now. Oh my word – why does everything have to be so damn complicated in my life?

I don't even know why I'm still writing this 'diary' in the fake essay folders and using initials . . . Surely 'A' can't remotely access my computer? Can he? Am I just being paranoid? No idea.

Anyway – for the record I got a first for my *Alice's Adventures in Wonderland* essay and that means I'm on target for a first overall. So proud. Mum will be thrilled. And 'S' promises me there's absolutely no way he would grant favours. I earned the mark on pure merit, which is exactly the way I want it. He says I have a really bright future, whatever I decide to do – teaching or going into media or communications.

So I just need this period to come, please. Enough of a scare. Next diary entry I will be sharing my relief.

I mean – I can't be pregnant.

I just can't.

CHAPTER 20

THE FATHER – *NOW*

Ed takes in the wide-eyed stares, the matching scepticism on both their faces – Matthew Hill and DI Sanders.

'You're seriously telling us that your first wife believes you're some kind of clone? That you're a replica who's replaced the real Ed Hartley?' DI Sanders' tone is unnaturally high. She glances at Matthew, eyebrows raised. This reaction, this precise look on their faces, is the very reason he never tells anyone . . .

'Look, I know how it sounds. Trust me, I was every bit as thrown and as sceptical as you are right now. But it's a genuine medical condition. Very rare but very real. Capgras Syndrome. Look it up.'

Ed watches the pair exchange another look of sheer astonishment.

'Google it.'

Matthew's taken his phone from his pocket. 'How are you spelling that?'

'Here. Look.' For speed, Ed taps it out on his own phone and holds up the screen to show them.

He waits while they put in searches on their own mobiles and watches closely as they both read, frowning as they skim between pages. He remembers his own disbelief when he first sat across the desk from the specialist who diagnosed Laura.

He jiggles his right foot up and down. He wants them on side but also wants them to hurry up; to get on with it. Surely they must see now that all he needs, urgently, is official help to check that Laura's OK. That she's with her parents somewhere. That she's in no way involved with what's happened to Gemma.

'Grief. I've never even heard of this.' DI Sanders is wide-eyed. 'So it's mostly women?'

'Apparently. Look – can you just phone Canada? The police in Canada.' Ed uncrosses his legs. 'I just want to know where Laura is, that's all. She's probably with her parents, don't you think? If she's been discharged. We just need their new address. They've obviously moved.'

DI Sanders now looks up at him directly. 'First, you need to talk us through exactly what happened. I need to understand what we're dealing with here before I speak again to the authorities in Canada.' She's checking her watch, probably working out the time difference.

Ed takes in a deep breath. It feels so alien, talking about this. Saying it out loud. He's spent so many years burying this deep, deep inside himself, it's almost as if he's made it not real. As if Laura is right and he isn't Ed Hartley; that this is the back story of a different person.

Who are you? What have you done with my husband?

It feels suddenly very hot in the room. Ed pulls at his shirt collar, wishing he was in a T-shirt. He looks up at the window in the corner of the room and, for a moment, it's like time travel. He's right back in his kitchen in Canada. He's slumped at the kitchen

116

table with his head in his hands – listening to the shouting from upstairs as Laura's mother tries to calm her daughter down.

Go and look for yourself, Mummy. It's not Ed. I don't know what he's done with Ed. He won't tell me . . . We have to find Ed. We have to find the real Ed.

He remembers a shadow cast on the wall from a plant on the windowsill. Laura loved house plants. Green fingers. Why is he remembering that?

'We had to call in a doctor, then a specialist. Laura moved in with her parents but she got worse. Became more and more difficult to manage. At first we all assumed it was something temporary. A psychotic episode that would pass. But every time we trialled her seeing me, every time I walked into the same room, she became hysterical. She couldn't understand why other people couldn't see what she was seeing. She insisted I wasn't me. It took quite a long time to get the proper diagnosis. It was all horrible. At one point she had to be sectioned. They had to sedate her and take her away in an ambulance. It broke her mother's heart.'

'And this was how long ago?'

'More than twenty years ago. I was twenty-seven. We were newly married. Just six months.'

He watches Matthew rake his fingers through his hair.

'Trust me, it was like being in a movie. Totally unreal. I couldn't talk to people because it sounded so bizarre. And I didn't want Laura to be labelled, because I thought she would recover. I didn't want it to blight her future. Her chance of getting work, teaching music and so on. I honestly thought she would get well.'

'And she didn't?'

'No. It all got much worse.'

Ed lets out a long sigh. He's wondering how much detail he should go into. Laura's dramas – smashing up her parents' house because she didn't recognise it. He remembers Laura's mother crying down the phone when they had to call an ambulance to have Laura sedated and taken to a special unit. By this stage, she was uncontrollable – furious that no one would believe her. Accusing them of 'being in on it all'.

'So, you understand now why I just want to know that Laura's with her parents. That she's OK. Accounted for in Canada, I mean.'

'When did you last have contact with her? What's her condition now? And has she threatened you ever, Mr Hartley? Do you think she's a danger to you? To your family.' DI Sanders has her pen poised to make notes. 'You realise you should have told us all of this from the very beginning.'

'Laura is ill, not violent. I thought she was still under supervision at the clinic. There's no way I believed she could be involved. I still don't.' Ed feels his body slump. He closes his eyes.

'And Rachel, your second wife, knows nothing of this?'

He feels close to tears now. It's unbearable to imagine Rachel's reaction. He knows that it looks terrible, not to have come clean.

'I should have told Rachel. I do know that.' He doesn't want to share just how bad things got when he returned to England. No job. Nowhere to live. He lied to friends; said that the marriage just broke up over an affair. There were antidepressants. Sleeping tablets. He didn't think he would ever be happy again.

For months and months, he lived like a hermit, refusing friends' attempts to get him to go out. And then finally they talked him into a dinner party. And there she was. This extraordinary woman in this beautiful red velvet dress. Rachel. It was like a light going back on in his life.

'I was a coward. I was selfish. I should have told Rachel, but I wanted a clean slate. I didn't want a pity party.'

'So Laura. She wasn't cured? She still has this syndrome?'

'There *is* no cure. She's been in and out of the clinic ever since. Her parents are wealthy. They pay for private treatment. She has

118

spells when she's a little better. And spells when she's really bad. They think she may have schizophrenia too but I was never convinced of that.'

'And you've kept in contact with her parents?'

'I did at first. For a good few years. But then they said it was better to cut ties. For Laura. And for me too.'

'Another question I have to ask.' DI Sanders is sitting up straight. 'Has Laura ever owned or used a gun, Mr Hartley?'

He knew this was coming. He shuts his eyes again. They're going to misunderstand. However he explains it, they're going to completely misunderstand.

'Well?' DI Sanders is again looking at her watch.

'Laura isn't a violent person. She's unwell. She became unwell.'

'That's not what I asked.'

'Look – OK. She was in the army for three years. The Canadian army.'

He feels the punch of their shock.

'The *army*? Are you seriously telling me she's got military training?' DI Sanders puts both hands on her head. 'Oh, dear Lord, I don't believe this.' She turns to Matthew and then back to Ed. 'You have an ex-wife with a serious mental-health condition who's used to handling guns and you don't tell us until today.' DI Sanders pushes her chair back from the table, stands and puts her phone to her ear.

'I'm sorry but it's not what you think. She was never a soldier. Not really—'

Mel puts her hand up to silence Ed as she waits for the phone to connect, walking to the door.

Ed stares instead at Matthew Hill, who remains seated.

'Laura signed up after university but she was a *musician*, Matthew. It was for the music. She was never a proper soldier. She only joined up for the *music* . . .'

CHAPTER 21

THE MOTHER

'I've no idea what's holding your dad up.' I put down the brush on Gemma's hospital locker and stare at it. 'I don't expect he'll be long. I've asked him to bring in a new book for me to read to you.'

I sit very still, fighting the urge to watch her eyelids for the tiniest flicker, and it's as if my body is absorbing the silence. The stillness. Sometimes it makes me want to cry, this vacuum that seems to seep into my bones, my very blood, and so, to challenge it, I reach forward to pick the brush up again, stroking the engraved pattern on the silver. Enjoying the feeling of the dips and the bumps on my fingers. My flesh.

It's not a very practical brush, truth be told, but it's so very beautiful. So special. It's a child's brush – real silver with especially soft, natural bristles – a gift from my mother to Gemma when she was small. Of course, Gemma stopped using it many years back, needing modern brushes, designed to retain heat – to tease and to tame. But she kept this brush with its matching mirror on her dressing table 'for show' and so I got Ed to fetch it from home. For my sake really.

When Gemma was little, she absolutely hated having her hair washed. Oh my word, the battle over the tangles afterwards. I used lakes of conditioner to try to ease things but there was still grumbling and moaning every single time. *Ow. Ow. You're hurting me. You're really, really hurting me.*

And so I would use a comb for the tangles first, holding the hair in sections and trying my very best to 'shock absorb' the pulling, and when that battle was finally over – *no more comb. Have we finished with the comb, Mummy* – I'd switch to 'Granny's brush' as a signal that the tangles were gone. Then I'd brush through her hair, stroke after gentle stroke, until Gemma was calm again. She would close her eyes and I would watch her shoulders relax and I would brush and brush and brush.

Of course, her hair has no tangles now that she can't move. Never moves. So I use 'Granny's brush', hoping she can feel the softness of it; that it might somehow soothe her. Calm her. Trigger a memory that might will her to come home. To come *back* . . .

I run my fingers across the soft bristles, again enjoying the sensation on my flesh. I think of my mother, sitting by the Christmas tree, when Gemma opened this present, rushing between us all to make us check our reflections in the matching mirror. Me. Ed. Granny.

She was really good at presents, my mum. Even when we had so little money after Dad left and she had to work two jobs to keep us afloat, she'd come up with treasures for me on my birthday. Something home-made – an outfit for a favourite doll – or a trail of riddles she'd made up herself, leading to a special box of chocolates.

Amazing how she found the time and the patience after everything she went through.

I look back across the hospital cubicle at Gemma, motionless in the bed. Her laptop's on the bedside cabinet. They sent it over this morning. A favour. Nothing relevant in it, the police say. I've looked at some of the photo files but have found it much harder than I expected. I can't find the photo of her in that pink dress and so the laptop's just sitting there alongside her. As if it's waiting for Gemma to emerge from a nap and start tap, tapping away.

I stare at her closed eyes and think again of my mother; of all the stories I've told Gemma about my own childhood. About her grandfather. Her gran. Did I do the right thing? I think so; what good would it do to hurt people you love with a past you can't change?

And it wasn't *all* invented. The stories from my early childhood were real. Precious. My father making me a rocking crib for a favourite doll. Reading me stories at bedtime. Building a hutch for my first rabbit. All those things really did happen, Gemma . . .

I let out a sigh and check my watch. *Where is he? Why so long with the police?* I picture DI Sanders and get a tightening in my stomach. I realise that I really must speak to her about that odd woman who bothered me a while back, just to exclude her. Damn it. Maybe I should just come clean with Ed first about the stupid private investigator I hired. Why I worried that he was having an affair. Maybe it will be better to face his disappointment in me than all this worry and this guilt.

If I can just persuade him *not* to make a scene. Not here. Not with all this going on . . .

And now suddenly I sense something happening outside the cubicle. I can just see the elbow of the police guard, sitting beyond the window on to the main ward. Ever since the awful scene with Alex, we keep the blinds at a careful angle – the slats closed enough to keep some privacy but with enough tilt to let me see what's going on out in the main ward.

The guard normally sits just to the left of our window on to the ward. They normally change shifts at lunchtime. I know most of them by sight but not by name. This is the tall guy. Friendly. I can see that his arm's moving; he's standing up. I can hear him talking to someone . . .

'This shouldn't have been brought up here. No gifts. Strictly no packages. We said no packages.' His tone's clipped, cross, and I can just make out that he's taking his radio from his pocket. A shiver runs through my body. I remember what happened with Alex. I stand up too, wishing Ed was here.

Where is he? Why's Ed taking so long?

'Right. Put it down. On the floor.' The police guard's raised his voice. 'Put it down now, please. Can everyone listen up? I need you all to stay calm, but I need everyone to keep back from this package while I call for some help.'

CHAPTER 22

THE PRIVATE INVESTIGATOR

Matthew's listening to Mel on the phone to her contact in Canada. She's pacing as if wearing a hole in the floor will somehow absorb her anger at Ed Hartley for keeping so much from them.

She's listing what she needs. *The parents' address. Is Laura with them? If not, urgent checks on her passport. Has she travelled? Is there any way she could have flown to the UK?* Every now and then, Mel pauses to listen and Matthew is praying she's getting cooperation. Liaison with foreign forces can be slow and frustrating, not through lack of will but lack of resources. Everyone always so stretched with their own caseload.

He feels his phone vibrate in his pocket just as Mel tells her contact that she'll have to ring back; has another call coming through from her team.

Matthew checks his own screen. It's Sally. He wonders for a second whether to message that he'll call her straight back, but he sees only now that he's missed a couple of texts from her while dealing with Ed Hartley.

He puts the phone up to his ear, still watching Mel who's taking her new call.

'It's horrible. Horrible, Matthew. You need to come home now. Right away. I don't know what to do.' Sal's voice is near hysterical. 'I thought it was from you. I thought it was a surprise. I would never have let her open it if I didn't think it was from you . . . What have I done?'

'Sally. Sally. You need to slow down. What's happened?'

'A parcel turned up. I thought it was a surprise from you. A gift. There was a card which *looked* as if it was from you so I let her open it. Oh, Matthew. I let her open it.'

'So what is it, Sally? What's in the parcel?' His heart's thumping in his chest and he raises his hand in a 'stop' sign to signal to Mel that there's a crisis. But instead of ending her call, Mel pumps the signal straight back at him. An emergency of her own?

'I'll get bomb squad, just in case,' Mel is saying. She moves her free hand from the 'stop' sign to the top of her head – her posture of disbelief.

Matthew's heart is now pounding. 'Sally. Hold one second. I'm getting some advice this end. It may be important.'

He listens again to Mel's side of her conversation. 'Right. So is it possible to evacuate the ward?' She pauses, closing her eyes. 'Do what you can until I speak to the hospital board. Ring you straight back.'

Matthew feels a new punch to his gut.

Bomb squad.

'Right. I'm back. So what's in the parcel, Sally? You need to describe it to me. Any wire? Anything like a battery? And where is it now?'

'It's a doll, Matthew. But it has blood coming out of it.' She's crying now. 'It's *disgusting.*'

'Jeez. Did Amelie see? Where's Amelie?'

'In the playroom. She saw it. Yes. I told her it was a Halloween joke. A mistake . . . It's all I could think of on the spot. But she's really upset, Matthew.'

'Right. So where's the doll and the box?'

'Here. In the kitchen.'

'OK. Did you hear me before? Can you see any wires? Anything like a battery in the box?'

'No, I don't think so. Nothing like that. Just the doll.'

'Right. You need to get out of the house, Sally. Leave the doll and the box there in the kitchen. Don't touch it again. Clean your hands, and take Amelie out to the summer house.'

Matthew's mind is in overdrive as he listens to the water running. They're lucky that their cottage has a long garden. The summer house a good stretch from the building. Safe distance. It's good there are no obvious wires. All the same . . .

'Are the neighbours in? Your mum. Is she home?' Sally's mother lives just two doors along in the little row of thatched cottages.

'No, she's out shopping. We're the only ones home.'

'Good. Good. Tell Amelie it's a game. Take some toys to the summer house and wait for me there. Leave the doll and the box. *Don't* touch it. OK? Go now. Right away.'

'You're scaring me, Matthew.'

'I'm sorry, darling, but just do as I say. OK? It's just a precaution. Playing safe. I'm on this. It's going to be OK. I'm on my way to you. It's going to be all right.'

There's a pause. It sounds like Sally's crying. Matthew badly needs to speak to Mel but can't bear to ring off.

'Is your phone well charged, Sal?'

He waits while she checks the screen.

'Sixty per cent.'

'Right. Stay on the line. Get Amelie and let me talk to her as you move outside. OK?'

'OK.'

Matthew can hear Sally calling Amelie through, but she's moved the phone away from her face. He can't make everything

126

out. There's quite a pause and then at last he can hear his daughter's voice in his ear.

'Daddy. I got a doll but it's broken. It's not nice. I don't like it.'

'Yeah. Mummy told me. Don't worry about that, princess. There's been a mistake. It was the wrong doll sent to the wrong house. Isn't that silly? We'll get you a better doll. It's a nice day so I'm going to finish work early and meet you in the summer house for a game.'

'What game? I want to watch television.'

'I'm going to let you choose the game but you need to be a good girl for Mummy, honey. Can you do that for Daddy? Be a good girl and wait in the summer house for me.'

'All right. Mummy says we need to hurry. Will you be long, Daddy?'

'No. I won't be long, darling. Put Mummy back on.'

There's a crackling noise and for a horrible moment Matthew fears his daughter has dropped the phone.

'Sorry. Sorry. It's me.' Sally's voice again. 'We're in the garden. Nearly there. How long will you be?'

'Half an hour tops. I'll get some people to come out. Check out the doll and the package. You need to ring off. Save your battery. You may hear sirens but that's just to make sure no one goes near the house. This is going to be OK, Sally.' He takes a deep breath. 'I love you. I'm going to make this OK.'

'OK.'

She rings off but he keeps the phone pressed to his ear. He wants to add that he's going to work with Mel and he's not going to rest – no bloody stone unturned – until he's found the bastard who's frightened his family . . .

How dare they. How *dare* they . . .

'What's happened, Matt?' Mel has stepped forward, looking right into his face. 'I overheard bits. You got a parcel too? At home?'

'Yep. Some kind of doll. With blood. Nasty—'

'But not a bomb? No explosives. Wires?'

'Nothing obvious.'

'Right. We play safe. There's a package on Gemma Hartley's ward too. Unopened. They're sending in a sniffer dog first. They're moving patients but it's too difficult to move Gemma. Too near the package. Too dangerous.'

'And what about her mother?'

'She's refusing to leave. She's staying with Gemma.'

Matthew puts his hand to his mouth. 'I have to go, Mel. I have to get home.'

'Of course. I'll get a team to your house too. Get going. I'll ring you en route. I'm on this. It's going to be all right, Matt.'

CHAPTER 23

Lemon

I'm tired of reading the platitudes in the paper. Telling everyone they're safe. That it's all OK. All in hand. Blah blah blah.

It's a disgrace – lying to everyone. Tricking everyone.

Well, they can't trick me . . .

I see. I know.

I found a cot mobile online. Delivered yesterday. It doesn't have the tune I wanted but it's the right colours – lemon and white – so I'm pleased. Things are looking nice and organised in here now.

I've set the mobile above the cot – high enough to be safe but low enough to be enjoyed. It soothes me to wind it up and sit in here a while to listen. As I say, it's not the tune I would have chosen but it's some kind of lullaby. Gentle. Sweet.

I'm not feeling great, actually, so I need to work hard to stay calm. I've had to limit my supply of everything. My drugs, I mean. Pace myself. So some of the time, I feel wired and then it's like jumping from a window and I'm incredibly tired. But no matter. It's to be expected. They've never really worked – the drugs. I know that now but I'm worried how it will feel without them completely so I need to make sure I don't run out.

So it's good to have this room to focus on.

I've put a calendar on the wall and it's not too long to wait. I can be patient. I can do this.

I just need to try to stop dwelling on the past and to think of the future when it will all have been worth it.

It's just such a shame that no one would listen to me before. Trust me? If people had listened to me, all this need never have happened.

CHAPTER 24

THE DAUGHTER – *BEFORE*

Is Tess in Tess of the d'Urbervilles *portrayed as being responsible for her own demise?*

I don't believe it. I am sitting on my bed, staring at the test stick with tears rolling down my face and I still don't believe.

Two blue lines. Pregnant. How? HOW?

I've been crying for so long that my face actually feels numb. But crying doesn't help. I need to do something. Anything. To write. To type. To figure out what the hell I am going to do next.

I honestly just don't understand how this could have happened. I've been on the Pill for years without a single scare.

I mean I know I get a tummy upset occasionally – irritable bowel syndrome, actually – but I never thought this would happen. *Could* happen. I've been googling the morning-after pill but that just makes me cry even more. Is it too late for that? Legal? Ethical? I haven't a clue about my dates, not really. I don't know what's legal and what's not. Can anyone get the morning-after pill if it isn't actually technically the morning after? Do I go to my doctor? Do I go to a clinic? Can someone at the uni help me? Will it def be anonymous? I feel that I should know this stuff but I don't and I've no one I can confide in. Maddy is out because I can't face telling her about the father. It's way too dangerous for him. Mum would never cope – it would literally kill her and I just can't talk to her about this kind of thing. And in any case, everyone will think it's 'A's. Which it can't be by my calculations . . . if the blurred dates in my head are right, that is.

And oh my God, do I tell him? The father. How do I do that? I suppose he has a right to know. A right to have a say, but it's early days for us. And he's married. And what if he thinks I did this on purpose, which of course I absolutely didn't.

OK. So I think what I'm going to do is this. I'm going to buy another test (why, oh why, did I only get one?). If that comes back positive too, I'm going to check my calendar and phone some helplines to work out where I am on my dates – also my options before I contact *him*.

Maybe he'll surprise me? I mean, I don't want to have a baby now. I want to get my career going. It would be completely bonkers to have a baby now. But I don't actually know if I can face the alternatives. Would I regret it? Ever forgive myself?

I don't know. I don't know.

I'm supposed to be at Pilates tonight but I can't face it. Can't face anything.

What an idiot, Gemma. What a complete and horrible nightmare.

It just feels surreal. I've had friends who've had scares and they've always turned out OK but I'd never really appreciated how it would feel. And I just don't know how I got here. Feels like Alice grew up into the worst possible disaster down that stupid, stinking rabbit hole.

CHAPTER 25

THE PRIVATE INVESTIGATOR

'Right. Talk me through what we've got so far.' Mel is staring through the glass screen to the interior of the forensic lab. The two dolls, the identical boxes and the various sample pots and bags are carefully laid out on a table within the sealed area. Hannah, the senior forensic scientist, is still in her protective clothing. She's doing them a big favour by agreeing to this preliminary briefing.

It's Tuesday, just twenty-four hours since the drama. The confusion. Matthew glances between Hannah and Mel, all the while thinking of Amelie and Sally in that summer house. The panic and the awful wait while the team sent in a sniffer dog to check the box in the kitchen. No sign of explosives. The careful removal. The phone call from Mel confirming that the hospital delivery was also cleared – no explosives.

Relief. Relief. Relief . . .

'It's early days.' Hannah sighs. 'I know I owe you one, Mel, but don't build your hopes up.' Her voice, relayed by speaker to the area outside the lab, is slightly distorted by the microphone inside her cubicle. Tinny. Mel and Matthew can't go inside without gowning up and they don't have time.

'I know, and I appreciate this. But do we have anything helpful yet? Anything at all?' Mel's fidgeting and Matthew shares a small, encouraging smile with her. She's under even greater pressure. The press have been told the final graduation is going ahead. Everyone assumed safe. And now *this* . . .

'Right. So the dolls are called Tiny Tears. Famous brand. Global success. First launched in the fifties and sixties. This modern version is by a new manufacturer – readily available. Not very expensive.'

'I didn't know they still made these.' Mel looks puzzled. 'My mum had one. Think it's still in the loft.'

'Well, you should get it out. Originals are collectable now.' Hannah adjusts her protective lab coat and goggles.

'OK. So the blood coming out of the eyes. How the hell?' Matthew's not interested in the value of the bloody dolls.

'Tiny Tears was designed to cry real tears and wet her nappy. Basically, you feed her water from a bottle and that's pumped back out of the eyes . . . and other parts.' Mel clears her throat. 'Our sender, as a malicious twist, decided to pump these two full of blood. Well – not real blood.'

'It's definitely not real?' Looked like real blood to Matthew. Thick. Dark. Nasty. Sally was convinced it was blood when she first saw the doll.

'It's good quality but definitely fake blood – the kind you can get from any joke shop. Popular at Halloween. We've run tests to try to identify the brand.'

Matthew stares at the blood on the dolls' faces, which is staining their lemon Babygros. He's remembering Sally's quick thinking when Amelie first saw the red leaking from the eyes when they set the box upright. *It's a Halloween doll. Sent by mistake . . .*

'OK. So we all agree our sender has a warped mind. But what about prints? What have we got?' Mel narrows her eyes as if dreading the response.

'Sorry. Nothing. All we've got so far are a few carpet fibres from the box. Regular wool mix. Not unusual. Very popular colour. Not very helpful I'm afraid.'

'And nothing else?' Mel looks crestfallen.

'Sorry, Melanie. I'll run the tests again. Update you when I do the full report.'

'Thanks. Appreciate that.'

'But good it wasn't explosives.' Hannah has lifted her voice but Mel has already turned away, and Matthew follows her out of the viewing area and through a door to the narrow corridor beyond.

'Right. So we'll get the team checking distribution of these dolls. We've got the hospital CCTV. It was a motorcycle courier, wearing a bloody helmet. He – or she, hard to tell – persuaded a hospital volunteer to take the gift up to the ward.'

'Still don't get how that was allowed.'

'Let's not go there. The volunteer was wearing a tabard labelled "Can I help?" Meant well. Had read about Gemma in the papers and thought it was nice for someone to send her something. She thought she was sparing hospital staff some time. So what about your delivery? Has Sally remembered anything else?'

'No. Just that she heard a motorbike too, then the doorbell. Bike had gone by the time she answered. She found the box on the doorstep and when she saw the message, she thought it was a gift from me to cheer Amelie up.'

'Yeah. That printed card – "For Daddy's girl". What do we make of that, Matt? Are we wrong? Is this from a guy, not a woman?'

'Not sure. Could be deliberate, to throw us off.'

'Suppose. Whatever – it makes me think you're right. This is about the baby, Matt. Gemma's baby.' Mel checks her watch. 'Right. I've got to speak to the suits upstairs. Meet you in the canteen for a sandwich later?'

Matthew pulls a face. He's delighted to have persuaded Sally last night to let him take up Mel's offer to work officially on the case. Now that it's personal. Now that they need to get this sorted, for Amelie's sake as much as anyone's. But he's not enjoying the prickly response from some of Mel's team. A few don't seem to understand why he's been brought in.

'Think I'll grab lunch off site if you don't mind. I'm trying to persuade Amanda, the uni PR, to meet me. I'm hoping she can recommend a counsellor for Amelie. And obviously it's more urgent now.'

'OK. Good. And once you've sorted help for Amelie, see what you can get from this Amanda about the professor affair rumours.'

'Still nothing from the formal interviews?'

'No. We've now seen all seven men who've taught Gemma. Nothing so far. But we need to find out who the father of that baby is . . . somehow. And *urgently*.'

'I'll try my best. Might hang around the campus a bit. See what I can dig up.'

'Good. OK. Excellent. How's Amelie doing?'

'Not good. Wet the bed last night, which she hasn't done for months.'

'Poor poppet.'

And then Mel's phone goes. She checks the screen, mouths 'Canada' before answering. Matthew watches her face concentrate and then darken. 'Right. Thanks for tipping me off. And you'll send all this through officially?' Another pause. 'OK. Thank you. I'll look out for the email. Appreciate the call.'

Matthew raises his eyebrows as Mel puts her phone back in her pocket.

'Laura – Ed's first wife – took a flight to the UK several weeks back.'

'You're kidding me.'

'I wish.'

CHAPTER 26

THE FATHER - *BEFORE*

When he was thirteen years old, Ed Hartley was called to the head teacher's study. An urgent message had been sent to the tennis courts where he'd just finished thrashing his arch-rival Ben McClaren. Ed was as confused as he was nervous. He knew it was some kind of serious to get a summons like this; he'd never been called to the head teacher before.

Ed was more people pleaser than troublemaker. A good pupil. Unless he'd been set up, he couldn't imagine what this was about. Unless there was a problem with the fees? His parents were always telling him how expensive his boarding school was. How tight they were finding it; how very lucky he was.

Ed had grown more used to boarding school in recent years. At first, he had terrible homesickness and had to fight hard not to let the other boys see him upset. He'd long since managed to get past all that but he still carried this slight undercurrent of unease in his stomach. Always a tiny bit on edge. It was, he decided later, an awareness of being exposed. Vulnerable. The realisation that he had to depend entirely on himself and not on his family day to day. There was just one weekly call home and he always told his mother and father he was *absolutely fine* as this was clearly what was expected of him.

This particular day as he walked to the head teacher's study, he turned over the possible problem with the fees and wondered if he would mind if he had to leave the school. He realised, bouncing his tennis racket against his knee as he walked, that he would actually be a bit disappointed. But not too much. Certainly not devastated. Maybe even relieved? And so he knocked on the head teacher's door with a strange mix of curiosity and hope.

His mood only switched to true alarm when he was called inside to find his Aunt Cathy, his mother's sister, sitting across the desk from the head teacher, dabbing her eyes. He hadn't seen his aunt in years. The sisters weren't close – some falling out, though he never knew the details. So what the hell was she doing here?

'Please sit down, Edmund.' The head teacher looked nervous rather than cross and Ed began to worry even more.

The news, when it was came, was both terrible. And also some dreadful mistake.

The head teacher was mumbling about an accident. *How very sorry. Everything was instant. They wouldn't have known a thing – your parents.* How terribly, terribly sorry they all were . . .

All Ed could think was how awful for there to have been this muddle. How terrible it would be when they found the right boy, the other Ed Hartley in some other school far, far away, whose parents really had been killed when a lorry knocked their car across the central reservation, right through a barrier so that it rolled down a steep bank.

Three somersaults of the car and then a burst of flames. The head teacher didn't tell him that. He read that later in the papers, when it turned out it wasn't a mistake. He was the Ed Hartley, waking from his dreams to see the car burst into flames in front of his eyes.

And now, here he was in Canada, all alone and once again awaiting news.

He was sitting in another smart office, again feeling small and strangely detached, wondering when someone was going to announce there had been a terrible mistake and it was another Ed Hartley this was all happening to.

After that first awful night when she couldn't recognise him, Laura moved back in with her parents, and for a time Ed was convinced her illness would be a temporary thing – that some strange infection would be discovered that would explain the delirium. The delusions. A week on antibiotics and everything would be OK. Surely?

And now, many weeks on, they still had no diagnosis – here in this fancy private hospital. With the fancy private specialist.

'So you haven't even tried antibiotics?' Ed repeated – irritated now by his fancy, bright orange chair which exactly matched the 'accent splash' in the blue and orange curtains.

Laura was one for 'accents'. A lime cushion here. A citrus throw there . . .

'There's no infection,' the consultant repeated. 'We've run every possible test.'

Ed glanced once more around the room. He wished they were back in the UK with the nice, reliable NHS. He liked the NHS. He knew where he was with the NHS with its tired look and its practical furniture. OK, it was horribly underfunded and it didn't have coordinated decor with fancy accents, but his experience across the few dramas of his lifetime – appendicitis and a broken leg – had been good. The staff brilliant.

He was still struggling to understand the Canadian health-care system. When he agreed to move to Toronto with Laura, the deal was they'd give it a year. He understood why she wanted to be near her parents, and having no real family left himself (Aunt Cathy lost interest and contact once he passed eighteen) it made absolute sense. Laura's family were welcoming and kind. Also doing well commercially. The job offer from her father was difficult to resist.

But right from the off, Ed had worried about the unfamiliar health care. He had wrongly assumed that Canada had an insurance-based system like America; that everything would be horribly expensive. One night he had a row with Laura in England. *What if I have a road accident? We could be bankrupt . . .*

She had smoothed his forehead and smiled, just as she did when he woke from the dreams in the middle of the night with the car bouncing down the embankment. She explained that Canada's health care was free, just like the NHS – funded through taxes. You had to pay for prescriptions and top-up services but that was nearly always covered by employment insurance.

So there is insurance?

Not like America, Ed. It's fine. It will be fine.

And now it wasn't fine because Laura's condition ventured into the terribly tricky territory of mental-health services and they were sadly as complex, funding wise, in Canada as anywhere else in the world.

This private care and specialist appointment was being paid for by Laura's father to speed things up. But Ed was conscious that private bills could very quickly become very large indeed, unless Laura could be properly diagnosed. And swiftly treated and cured.

She'd been referred by her own doctor who'd almost sounded excited when he said he had never come across anything quite like it. It was *distressing but also a fascinating case.*

Ed glanced again at the blue-and-orange curtains. *Fascinating* was not a word he would use.

There had been so many appointments already. He'd been asked a million times if Laura had suffered a head injury. *Any unusual behaviour before this episode?*

Over and over he told them the truth. *No.* He was as baffled as they were. Laura had been fine. And then suddenly she hadn't recognised him. It was just like his childhood. Playing tennis one minute. Orphan the next.

At first when Laura moved back in with her parents, she was calm and for the most part behaving normally in every aspect of life, unless and until anyone referred to Ed. Her parents had managed to convince her that she should stop thinking about him. That the episode that had so upset her would pass. She just needed to rest and very soon would see that Ed really was Ed and all would be well.

But this strategy collapsed whenever they tried to reintroduce Ed. They arranged low-key visits from Ed, pretending he had just 'popped by'. But however casual the approach, the episodes never stayed low key; they always ended in a meltdown. She would start screaming at her parents, demanding to know why they were not searching for her real husband. Why the imposter Ed was not in police custody.

This consultant – Mr Price – had himself arranged to observe one of these 'meetings' in the more-controlled environment of the hospital. They used a visitors' room painted green for its calming effect and dotted with huge pot plants in terracotta planters. Ed had strangely felt quite hopeful as he was led into the room to see Laura and her mother. Maybe a change of environment would help?

'This is Ed. Your husband Ed,' her mother had encouraged. 'See. I can see that this is the real Ed. It's all fine now.'

But Laura had stared at him, wide-eyed, and then stood up. 'This isn't Ed. This is *him*. This is the man who's taken Ed. Can't you see that, Mother? Look at him. Please look at him properly.'

The consultant, watching via a camera on the wall, had sent in a nurse to ask Ed to leave as Laura was becoming distressed. They had tried this kind of 'test' one more time with the specialist observing but Laura was even more upset the second time, thrashing her arms about until she had to be given a sedative.

It was decided that she should be given yet more general tests along with complete rest – a couple of weeks of 'watch and wait', living with her parents. The idea was that Ed should stay away and they would wait for the results of all the other tests and psychiatric assessments to try to introduce him for a third meeting to see if Laura's behaviour around him changed.

But things spiralled further. Although Laura had no problem recognising both her parents, she suddenly became suspicious of the family home. She'd lived there from birth. A beautiful sprawling five-bedroom home with a huge attic room which had been Laura's playroom once. When they were together in England, Laura had shared pictures and stories of the house. The attic had the most wonderful doll's house. Every birthday her parents gave her more miniature furniture to dress it. Laura loved the doll's house and she loved the family home.

But in their new nightmare, Laura woke up one day to announce to her parents that she wanted to be taken 'home'.

Her parents thought she meant back to her marital home – the flat with Ed across Toronto. But she didn't. She seemed no longer to recognise her parents' house. Her beloved childhood home.

'Why have you brought me here?' she asked. 'It's not your house.'

In despair, her father decided to try an experiment. One of the doctors had already mentioned the rare condition Capgras Syndrome which was on the long list of possible conditions that could be afflicting Laura. But it was so rare as to be considered highly unlikely. Nevertheless Laura's father, and Ed too, had done a lot of research. Laura's father David had found one suggested theory that driving the patient back to the 'right place' or the 'right person' sometimes worked by tricking the brain to reset. So he drove Laura a few miles in circles, telling her that they were going home.

Sure enough, when they returned to their same house, she seemed at first to recognise it. But this only lasted about half an hour. When she moved into the kitchen to make a cup of coffee, she again suddenly protested that it was not the 'right house'.

Why am I here? I need to go home.

David was now at a loss and tried desperately to reassure his daughter. He tried to show her familiar things. *Look – here's your favourite mug, Laura. Look at it.*

But Laura picked up the mug and threw it at him. She then began to smash other things in the kitchen, crying uncontrollably.

Eventually, she barricaded herself in her bedroom, clearly terrified. The family doctor had to be called out with a sedative and when things did not improve, the decision was taken that Laura would need 'hospital care'. As she wouldn't agree to this, she would need, in effect, to be temporarily sectioned for her own safety. The process in Canada involved a 'certificate of involuntary hospital admission'. But it all amounted to the same thing.

His beautiful wife Laura had been sectioned. The woman he had met, watching an extraordinary clock in Wells Cathedral, was the subject of the Mental Health Act.

That's how they ended up in this private hospital. With the smart orange chairs. And the fancy specialist.

'So what's the diagnosis?' Ed was struggling to sit still, Laura's parents sitting together holding hands to his left. He glanced across to see that Laura's mother was fighting tears.

'It's been *weeks*,' Ed added. 'You must surely have some idea by now. Some treatment plan.'

The specialist looked down at his notes. 'Our priority at the moment is to ensure Laura is kept calm. And safe.'

'Yes. But you can't keep her sedated forever and she can't live in the hospital. And she's my wife, for heaven's sake. *My wife.*' Ed felt his voice crack as if facing up to the true horror of his situation for the first time.

'These things can be very complex. And they can take time.'

'What things? What is it precisely that you think this is? Could it be this Capgras Syndrome you mentioned previously? Is that what you really think?'

The specialist took in a deep breath. 'It's a possibility but I'm not an expert. I've been in touch with a colleague in Ontario who's worked with Capgras Syndrome. He's written a paper on it. I've asked him to see Laura when he's next here.'

'And when's that?'

'Next month.'

'Next month.' Ed stood up and marched to the window. He looked out at the garden – at some kind of pink-flowered bush alongside an oak bench in a walled courtyard. He stared for a moment at the blooms. He didn't recognise the plant. He found himself longing for the pink camellias outside his flat back in London. Campion in the hedgerows on childhood holidays in Cornwall. The familiar. Familiar flowers. Their familiar flat back in England. All the familiar places where they had been so happy.

'Maybe I should take Laura back to England. See what the doctors there can do.'

'Don't be ridiculous, Ed.' It was Laura's mother. 'She can't even be in the same room as you.'

And then suddenly it was too much. The alien pink blooms slowly blurring before his eyes, though it was a while before he realised why.

Suddenly he could feel a tennis racket in his hand. An ache deep, deep in his stomach. An awareness that the life he had known was over.

And just like that boy in the head teacher's study, he could once more feel silent tears dripping from his chin on to his shirt.

CHAPTER 27

THE MOTHER

'I still don't believe it.' I feel giddy. 'You've been married before and you *didn't tell me*?'

We're in the nurses' small office at the entrance to the ward. I hate that we've had to leave Gemma with a nurse in the cubicle. I feel real physical distress to be out in this other world, away from our girl. What if we miss something? What if this is the very time that Gemma opens her eyes?

I feel light-headed, my arms tingling. 'I'm sorry. I feel faint again.'

'Sit on the floor. I'll fetch a nurse.'

'No. I don't *want* a nurse.'

'Well – put your head forward. I'll get some tea with sugar.'

'I want you to go.'

'Don't be ridiculous, Rachel. We need to talk. And I can't leave you like this.'

He doesn't move and so I lower myself to the floor and put my head forward. Ed just watches and we wait a few moments in silence. I'm thinking of my mother sitting on the floor of the kitchen crying all those years ago. I still feel giddy but I don't think

I'm going to faint after all. I just need to wait a while and I need Ed not to be here.

'I'm fine. I'm going to be fine. Just go. Please.'

At last Ed leaves the room and I'm relieved to be alone, words spinning around my head. *Laura. Canada.* Some ridiculous syndrome I've never heard of. That he probably made up to try to make his lies look better. I can hardly believe it. Ed married before. I find that I'm not only disorientated but jealous. What was she like – this first wife? This first choice? I have my eyes closed and am trying to work out what to do next when I hear the door again and Ed reappears, holding out a cup of tea.

'Sip it. Please, Rachel. It's got extra sugar.'

I don't want the tea and I don't want him back in the room either, but I also don't want to speak so I just reach out for the cup. Resigned. It's too hot but he tells me again to try sipping it. I do as I'm told. Tiny sips. It's horribly sweet, the punch of it hitting the back of my throat, and I'm sorry to find it's almost instantly waking me back up, sucking me back into this room. This new nightmare. I keep sipping, not because I want this new awareness but because it's buying time. He's quiet at last. Watching. And I'm trying to work out what to say to make him go; to leave so that I can return to Gemma and pretend this isn't happening.

By the time I've drunk maybe a third of the tea, he's repeating the bizarre story. The muddle of words, filling the room again. *Laura. Canada. Psychotic episode. Capgras . . .*

I try to shrink in on myself but the sugar's preventing the retreat. A mistake. I reach out to put the remains of the tea on the nearest desk.

'I should have told you. I wish that I had, Rachel. I'm so very sorry but I was so thrown when we met. So confused. And ashamed too. And I couldn't believe it when you didn't push me about my past. When you didn't ask questions.'

I look up at him. This new Ed. This liar Ed. And there's this part of me that always knew something like this was lurking. Waiting. And he's right, actually. I didn't ask because I didn't want to know. It was like a pact. I didn't ask questions; he didn't ask questions. Why did he have to spoil it? Why did the secret have to be *this big*?

'I can't do this, Ed. You need to go.'

'No, Rachel. I'm sorry that this is hurting you so much. I never wanted this. To hurt you – or Gemma. But I can't let you shut me down this time. We *have* to talk about this. The police say Laura's *here*. In the UK. She flew here a few weeks ago. I'm sure they'll sort it all out. That it's some kind of terrible misunderstanding. But until they do—'

And now I feel my eyes widening. My mind opening. My thoughts are expanding like a bird stretching its wings and in this new expanse of air and pictures and puzzles, there's the sudden realisation that Ed is not just confessing something bizarre about the past. Something *over*. Historic.

'Oh my God, so is she dangerous? Violent? Is that what you're really saying? This Laura. This first wife I knew nothing about. Are you seriously telling me that she may be involved in all of *this*?' I glance to the door on to the ward and am thinking about Gemma in her coma with the frame over her horrible stump, the confusion and the shock all at once changing to a new emotion. Real anger.

I glare at Ed and am shocked to find I want to hit him. I feel this terrible bubbling up inside as if all the years of pressing things down, all the pictures and the confusion from the past, from my childhood, are suddenly in the room with us. All the shouting and the secrets and the lies and the pretending. All suddenly too much.

'Are you saying that your first wife may have shot our daughter?' I pull myself up, using one hand on the desk, to sit back on the chair by the wall, unsure if I'm steady enough yet to stand.

'No, I'm not saying that. I don't believe that for one minute. She wasn't violent, Rachel, she was unwell. I would have said something right at the beginning if I ever thought that.'

'So why are you speaking up now? Why are the police suddenly in a panic about all this *now*?'

My eyes dart wildly around the room as I start to think of DI Sanders, remembering why I need to talk to her too.

I put my hands to my face as the awful reality dawns. *Click.* The two pieces in the puzzle suddenly slotting perfectly together. The woman *watching* me. The weird woman at the end of the drive and then outside the hairdresser's.

He's not who he says he is. I have to warn you . . .

Not Ed's mistress. Never Ed's *mistress.*

'I need to see a picture of her, Ed.'

He looks stunned at this request. 'Why?' He rakes his fingers through his hair. 'No. Rachel. You're upset. I won't let you torture yourself.'

'Your phone.' I stare at his pocket. 'Do you have a picture of her on your phone?'

'No, of course not. This is my past, Rachel. Decades ago. A lifetime ago.'

I glance right then left before shutting my eyes, trying to call up the image of the woman outside the hairdresser's. It takes a moment but suddenly I can see her more clearly. Open my eyes.

'Does she have striking hair, Ed?'

'I'm sorry?'

'Laura. Your Laura. Does she have strawberry-blonde hair?'

CHAPTER 28
THE PRIVATE INVESTIGATOR

As he pulls into the drive, Matthew can see Sally at the kitchen window, looking out for him. He raises his hand. She shares a small, nervous smile and then retreats, turning away towards the playroom.

Matthew finds that he's nervous too, wondering what the counsellor will be like and what exactly will be expected of him. He takes his phone from his pocket and scans the contacts. He starts to write a text but changes his mind. Too difficult to get the tone right. Dials instead.

'Amanda? Oh good. I just wanted to say thank you for helping us out. She's here at the house now. Lucy, the counsellor. I'm *so* grateful. Really.'

'Oh good. I'm glad she was able to come out so quickly. It sounded urgent.'

'Yes. I'm sorry I couldn't give you the details. Something happened. Sort of classified.' He can't share details about the dolls. They need to keep it quiet. Something for the interview room down the line – to hopefully trip up a suspect. 'But my wife and I are incredibly grateful.'

'Don't mention it.'

A part of him would like to ask her what to expect but he still feels awkward, knowing that she's having counselling herself.

'Also.' He changes his tone – more upbeat – as he gets out of the car, not wanting to keep Sally and Amelie waiting. 'Will you be at the update with the chancellor and DI Sanders later?'

'Yes. Why? Anything to add? We've still got the media crawling all over us. Expect you do too.'

'And some. No. Nothing to add. I'll be out of action, obviously, for this session. But DI Sanders will bring you up to speed. Just wanted to add that if you need anything from us – a return favour, do please ask.'

'No need. Happy to help.'

'Right. I must go. DI Sanders will update me after the meeting.'

'OK. Bye.'

'Bye.'

He fires the central locking and hurries inside to find Sally and Amelie seated around the small table in the playroom alongside a woman with a shock of dark, curly hair, held back by a bright turquoise band. She's wearing long, dangly earrings with white and turquoise beads and Matthew feels strangely reassured by how much she looks the part.

'Hello. I'm Matthew.' He shakes her hand.

'Lucy.'

'Look. We've got a worry jar, Daddy.' Amelie picks up a large empty plastic jar to show him and he's both surprised and pleased to see the energy back in her eyes. Amelie's clearly open to this; up for this. She's a frightened little girl just now, but above all still a curious girl.

'What's a worry jar?' He finds that he is ironically worried about the worry jar, still wary of his part here. But he smiles at his daughter and at Lucy and Sally in turn to signal he's up for this too.

He takes a seat and tells himself that he will try very hard to bury his default setting that 'therapy' of any kind is all mumbo jumbo. That talking never solved anything. He will try not to remember that when he left the force – when he woke night after night, sweating and calling out from his nightmares for the child he believed he had killed – he refused help. Refused therapy. Left the force instead.

He smooths the fabric of his trousers over his knees. This is not about him. This is for Amelie so he must park the prejudice and do whatever it takes to help his little girl.

'Well, *everyone* has worries,' Lucy says as she hands out paper. 'And everyone gets afraid sometimes. It's normal. Adults and children have worries. So sometimes we need to talk about them and maybe draw a picture. Or write some words. And then we put the worry in the jar and put the lid on. And we think of something happier to help us not to think about the worry.'

'I can write my name!' Amelie says, looking proud.

'That's very clever! And I bet you can draw pictures. Do you like drawing, Amelie?' Lucy is moving the pot of crayons and pencils closer to Amelie.

'OK, Mummy and Daddy. You need to write or draw a worry too.'

Lucy is widening her eyes and Matthew feels a pull in his stomach. He finds that he is unsure how he is supposed to behave here. Should he have spoken separately to Lucy first? Is he supposed to be honest? Or brave for Amelie?

'We need to be honest so we can work out how to deal with our worries,' Lucy says as if reading his mind. 'So that we know what to do when we have difficult feelings. When we have worries. And when we're afraid.'

'Do you get worried?' Amelie says suddenly, looking very earnestly at Lucy.

'Of course.' Lucy adjusts her hairband. 'But not too much. Because I know the tricks now.'

'Tricks?' Amelie looks very interested now, her eyes wide and hopeful, and Matthew feels his heart leap. He thinks of her crying when he ran to them in the supermarket car park after the cathedral. He thinks of her creeping into their bed in the night. *I've had an accident, Mummy . . .*

'Yes – the tricks are how to make myself feel better. That's what I'm going to show you.' Lucy winks and takes a piece of paper herself. 'So my worry is what people will *think* of me.' She starts to draw a stick person with a big stomach and in the belly she takes different-coloured pencils and draws lots of wiggles. 'I get funny feelings in my tummy – like wiggly worms – because I worry if people will like me.'

Amelie laughs and Matthew finds himself smiling and realises that he likes Lucy already.

'So what are you all worried about at the moment? Mummy and Daddy – write it down. And Amelie, you draw a picture of your worry.'

Matthew stares at his blank page and frowns. Sally starts to write immediately and Matthew wonders what the hell she's writing. Amelie draws a picture with crayons. She draws Sally with her blonde hair, using a bright yellow crayon. He is drawn very tall with big, baggy trousers and his curly hair a sea of squiggles. Next Amelie draws herself in a pink dress. Very small in the middle with stick arms and huge hands, reaching out to each parent.

She then pauses and all the adults watch as Amelie takes a red crayon and draws ugly lines across the whole family. Huge, fat red lines.

'That's the blood,' she announces as she presses harder on the paper, her face turning paler as she watches the family disappear behind all the red lines.

'That's my worry.'

CHAPTER 29
THE FATHER - *NOW*

Back at the house, Ed feels utterly overwhelmed. He picks up the new post from the doormat and adds it to the huge pile already unchecked on the side table. Lord knows what could be lurking in there. Unpaid bills. Final demands. Speeding tickets. But who . . . bloody . . . cares.

Until this moment, all the normal tiers of responsibility in his life – work, pay the mortgage, insure the car – have been kicked into the long grass, completely overshadowed by one thought only. Getting Gemma well.

Technically he's been freed up to concentrate on this one thing; he's been given compassionate leave by his agency and has no immediate financial worries. They have savings and Ed hasn't been thinking about work or the future or anything beyond Gemma and those blessed machines, ticking away in her cubicle.

But on the drive home and now here in the hall, staring at his face in the mirror by the coat hooks, there is this new and terrible pressure, crushing down upon him. The horror of an entirely new future, even if Gemma does come back to them. Has he blown it?

Will he lose it all anyway? His family? This home where they've been happy.

He stands very still for a moment and then turns from the mirror. He can picture Gemma running through the hall in a fairy outfit – her wings so wide that they brush against the staircase as she passes. *Look, Daddy. My wings are flapping. I'm flying.*

He turns his head, back towards the door and imagines packing boxes and a furniture van outside. The horror of another divorce. Another failure.

Rachel won't say why she wants a photo of Laura. She says she'll tell him when he gets back to the hospital. So how did she know about the strawberry-blonde hair? What the *hell* is going on?

The police asked for a picture of Laura too but he genuinely doesn't keep one on his phone and in any case their last contact was so long ago, he has no idea what Laura looks like now. Short hair? Long hair? Grey hair? So DI Sanders is chasing an up-to-date, official photo from the clinic in Canada and also from the passport office.

He told Rachel all this too; he told her that he only has a few very old photos in the loft but she still wants to see them. Says it's important. Ominously she says they may need to speak to DI Sanders again together but he doesn't understand why and, typical Rachel, she won't say. If they had a different kind of relationship he would press her but that's not how they roll, and how can he cause even more distress after what he's put her through?

He takes a deep breath and opens the under-stairs cupboard for the folding ladder. He drags it upstairs, click-clicking against each carpeted step. Normally he lifts the ladder high enough to prevent dragging but today he can't be bothered. On the landing, he looks at the narrow loft opening and sighs. For years they've been debating a loft upgrade with proper flooring, a larger access and a fold-down ladder but the project's always been bumped. How he wishes now that they'd gone ahead.

It's a ridiculous hatch and he has to twist himself awkwardly to get inside. He's forgotten the torch so takes his phone from his back pocket for its light. He knows exactly where the photos are. He tucked them in an old school book at the bottom of a cardboard box of boyhood treasures. A set of marbles. A prize conker. A favourite Lego kit. He put a stack of musty old comics and superhero annuals in the top of the box to discourage Rachel from rummaging. She hates comics. Hates anything musty.

Years back, long before he and Rachel moved in together, he sat in his old flat in his old life, wondering what he should do with the mementos of his life with Laura. Throw them all away to echo the pretence it had never happened? He decided to keep just three photographs of their wedding. It was a small affair, hosted at Laura's family home in Canada under a beautiful awning, decorated with flowers in the garden. Laura wore a sprig of white flowers in her hair instead of a veil.

He keeps very still thinking about it. It genuinely feels like it all happened to a different person. He closes his eyes and it's a while before he can bring himself to creep from rafter to rafter to reach the box, carefully placed in a corner near the water tank.

The photos, taken out of their frames, are now tucked into a fat copy of the works of Shakespeare – a prize given to him in the sixth form, just before he left boarding school. The head teacher had let him stay on after his parents' death, awarding a scholarship of some sort to discount the fees. He forgets the name of the 'award' but always suspected it was a kindness rather than something he earned. Decent of the school really.

Ed turns the pages to find the photos right in the middle. It's a shock. They both look so *young*. Is that what Rachel wants to see? How young he was? What Laura was like? He frowns, again wondering how on earth Rachel guessed the hair colour.

He takes a picture of the photos with his phone but there's no signal, not even one bar. He's promised to forward one to Rachel straight away and will need to go back downstairs so the phone can link to the Wi-Fi. The phone signal in their village is poor at the best of times but the Wi-Fi's good.

He's careful as he twists himself back on to the ladder, climbing down and pulling the hatch back into place. He moves into his study to send the picture, adding a simple message. *I'm sorry. I never meant to hurt you. Why did you need this, Rachel? Please tell me.*

He walks down the stairs, a pull in his stomach as he sits for a moment to stare at the phone, surprised at the ping of an immediate response.

A text from Rachel. *I'm calling the police. Come straight back to hospital. Will explain.*

He tries to ring her, desperate for an explanation, but her phone switches through to the answer service. No surprise and he can't think what to say by way of message, so he hangs up. Rachel struggles with tough stuff face to face, never mind on the phone. He sighs, reflecting that up until now this has suited him. All those times he's watched her descend these stairs to retreat into the kitchen to bake when things got tricky with Gemma in her early teens. *Just leave your mum be. Let it go, Gemma.*

He needs to hurry back to the hospital. Make her explain. Make it right and make her forgive him.

He stands, puts his phone back in his pocket and then frowns again as his mind seems to acknowledge something out of place. At first he can't figure out what it is. He glances around and then notices there's now a new letter on the doormat in a buff envelope. But he put everything on the side table, didn't he?

He assumes a circular of some kind but when he picks it up, he's surprised to find it's addressed to him. There's a stamp but oddly no postmark. The address is written out on a large white label, the writing childlike. Lower-case letters. He doesn't understand. There's no post at this hour. Much too late. He looks up at the frosted windowpane in the upper part of the door, wondering if this was somehow hand delivered, but there's no shadow. No sign of anyone outside.

He tears open the letter and feels a rush of adrenaline at the contents.

There's a single postcard tucked inside. No message.

Just a postcard of Wells Cathedral.

CHAPTER 30

THE DAUGHTER – *BEFORE*

Explore the relationship between fiction and meta-physics and/or ethics in any work by D. H. Lawrence.

Today has been just awful. The worst.

When I woke up and set off, I really was clinging to the hope there's an explanation; that 'S' has been telling me the truth and there's a reason he's not been in touch.

Over the last couple of days, after the second (and third) pregnancy test came back positive, I tried again and again to arrange to meet him, but he just didn't answer my texts. We keep messages to a minimum, obviously, and always delete them straight away, but he's normally pretty quick to reply so this really threw me.

These days we meet off campus – a small, low-key hotel somewhere. It's become too risky to meet up in his office as most students don't see their tutors very often – if at all – so 'S' has been worried someone would notice me coming and going. I've finished the module he was teaching so technically I have no call to see him, except in that 'tutor' capacity, and he says it would arouse suspicion to use that card too frequently.

He normally texts the name of a hotel, different each time, and I meet him in the room. Not in the bar, in case we get unlucky and anyone sees us. To be perfectly honest, I've hated this because it feels sort of dirty and seedy and underhand. And yeah – I get that an affair with a married man is, in theory, dirty and seedy and underhand but I've always told myself it's not like that with us because his marriage is over anyway.

In the end, I realised there must be something wrong with his phone. I couldn't find him around campus, not at all, and so I did something really risky. I'd already checked out where he lived online. Nosy. Jealous? Curious. Call it whatever you like, I couldn't resist seeing what his house was like. I found him on the electoral register and I used Google Earth to look at the place. Big red-brick affair with bay windows. Lovely actually. I got this horrible pang of proper, full-on jealousy when I first saw it. I suppose I've put the fact he's married in a box that I try not to think about. Looking at the house made it real, but then I remembered how he described his marriage – as like a prison, a place he just couldn't yet escape – and so I realised it was important not to over-think it all. I haven't forgotten that's what 'A' said I always do.

Over-think things.

I tried to put the house out of my mind but when 'S' didn't answer my texts, I couldn't help myself. I started to look on Google Earth more and more. I started to fantasise. To imagine us in a red-brick house with our baby. I started to tell myself that, yes, 'S' would be a little shocked when he found out about the pregnancy, but ultimately he would be supportive. Surely. He's a nice guy. One of the good guys. He cares about me. That's what I expected deep down; that we would work out a way to be together and for me to get my career going after settling the baby into our new lives.

When he still didn't answer my texts, I began to panic because I need to know how he feels about the baby before I make any decisions. I can't talk to Maddy or Mum or anyone still because 'S' will lose his job and Mum just won't be able to cope and so in the end I couldn't help myself. I didn't see any other choice. 'S' still wasn't on campus so I decided to make a trip.

I took the bus and used Google Maps on my phone to find his street. He's never given me his home address but, as I say, I found him on the electoral register. I don't know what I expected exactly – either to feel or to actually *do*. I certainly wasn't planning to walk up to his door or anything stupid like that. I just needed to be near him and maybe I hoped that he would catch sight of me at least and that would trigger him to contact me.

What a mistake. It was all so *horrible*.

I turned up mid-afternoon and I hid behind a bus stop on the other side of the street. I spotted his car in the drive and I could see right into the driveway with a clear view of the porch. A part of me was a bit worried that he might see me and be really cross but I didn't approach the house or anything stupid. I was hoping that if he did see me, he would just get in touch and we could sort everything out. That I would be able to explain it was the only way I could let him know that I needed to speak to him. Urgently.

And then the front door opened. *She* came out of the house ahead of him and it was such a shock. She was so much younger than I expected. And so pretty. She was carrying a picnic basket which at first partly blocked my view of her. Her long hair was in a ponytail and she was wearing sunglasses. The thing is she just looked so glamorous, so confident and so at ease. I had this picture in my head of her being some kind of mess – that's the way 'S' describes her – so it didn't fit. 'S' followed straight behind her, closing the porch door, and then came the next and even bigger shock. She put the picnic basket into the boot of his car and when she turned, I could see her properly. Her stomach. The bump. Not huge – maybe five or six months. I don't really know but it was like a physical blow. And then before they moved to get into the car, 'S' took her into his arms really tenderly. He pushed her sunglasses up on to the top of her head and kissed her on the mouth. Not just a peck. Not just a duty kiss but a really tender and *proper* kiss. Like the kisses he gives me.

I was dumbfounded. Anchored to the spot behind the bus stop. I was so shaken, I very nearly stepped out to make sure that he would see me and know that I had seen this.

They embraced for quite a while. He put his hand on her bump and she stroked his back – the very bottom of his spine – and tucked one of her thumbs into the back of his jean belt while he brushed the hair back from his forehead and kissed her again. And I just couldn't believe it. That I had let myself be so completely tricked. Such an idiot. That this was not a man who was living separately from his mess of a wife. This was not a man who was trying to leave his wife at all. This was a man who was having a baby with his wife.

As they separated and he took his place in the driver's seat and she moved round to the passenger seat, I leaned back against the bus stop and felt more shaken and more alone than I can ever remember.

As I keep saying, I haven't told anyone about the pregnancy because I just can't confide in anyone about 'S'. And now I have no one to talk to at all. No one to tell how truly *stupid* I've been.

Only now, much too late, do I realise what a cliché this is. I've been taken in by a player. A snake. And I feel too stupid to begin to know what to do next.

Since I got back to the flat, I've paced and cried and paced and cried. I've picked up my phone and thought about calling home; telling Mum that I need her to come and pick me up. But I just don't have the courage to dial. I can't do that to her.

So all I've done in the practical sense is get back in touch with the clinic to make a new appointment to go over my options. How many weeks I have left to make a decision about what on earth to do.

I'm just hoping and praying that I can get my degree finished and get through graduation before I have to make the call. Break both my parents' hearts.

And now, sitting here, I'm shocked at how angry I feel. Like I could hit something. Like I want justice. Revenge?

A part of me wants to find out the number and phone 'S''s wife. To let her know exactly what her husband's really like.

But guess what's happened to top it all? A new DM on Facebook.

He's not who he says he is . . .

That's the message. From a new 'friend' I don't even remember accepting.

It's made a shiver go right through me. I suppose it could be 'A' hacking me again but it's as if someone has read my thoughts.

Because that's *precisely* the message I would like to send to 'S''s wife.

CHAPTER 31

THE MOTHER

I reach for Gemma's laptop and rest it on the end of her bed in front of me, waiting for it to fire up. I've found the pictures from her birthday tea and click on the file. Gemma looks so happy. So pretty. There are photos of me and Ed too and it makes my stomach lurch to think of us back then. With no idea of what was to come.

I've looked through some of her other files – curiosity – but it's mostly coursework as far as I can see. A lot of essays. She was always telling me how much time she spent on them; pushing for that first.

I scroll through some headings. *Alice's Adventures in Wonderland* and another about someone I haven't even heard of. I just read the essay title and click away. I love books but wouldn't have a clue where to start; I feel out of my depth. I look again at some of the photographs – random shots with friends. Fancy-dress parties.

I let out a sigh and put the laptop back on the cabinet next to Gemma's bed. Extraordinary how the whole process of storing memories has changed in just a generation.

My mother's always loved taking and storing photographs. She began back in the day when you had to take your camera film to a chemist and wait for the photographs and the negatives. I remember telling a friend of Gemma's about 'negatives' and she didn't even know what I was talking about. I couldn't find any so had to show them online. Images of the long, dark strips with punched holes along the edges.

Mum also has stacks of photo albums on a shelf in that understairs cupboard; likes to get them out and re-tell the stories we've already heard a million times over. Me learning to ride a bike. Me learning the recorder. Me with my pigtails in the school nativity.

I think of my mother at home now. Flu or just a virus; we can't tell. Recovering well but still unable to visit Gemma. Messaging each day. I try so hard to keep upbeat when we talk but I know she watches the news and I worry how she will cope when she first sees Gemma. Like this.

And then I think again of when I was little. My mother looking after me when I was unwell. Her voice. *I've brought you some soup.* All those photo albums. Sometimes, you know, I wonder if childhood memories are all real or if we conjure some of them from the photographs and anecdotes shared by our parents. When I listen to the story and look at a picture in my mother's albums, I feel sure that I remember the incident. Smells come back to me – the floor polish in school. That soup on the stove at home. But with other photos, I suspect it's my mother's version I remember from her constant cycle of storytelling. I see images but fear I'm conjuring them to fit my mother's nostalgia.

All I can say for sure is this: my father didn't always drink.

I have some clear and real memories of outings in the car when I was little when my parents didn't argue. And when I wasn't afraid. Or anxious. Or confused.

I remember that we went to the New Forest once to see the ponies. We stayed in a small hotel for a long weekend treat and went on outings every day. Walks and picnics. I enjoyed the ponies but was a little bit scared as they had quite big mouths. I watched one chewing the grass and I could see huge teeth.

Why don't you offer the pony a Polo mint, Rachel? My father's voice.

No way. And I remember thinking the pony would 'have my hand off'.

I also remember my parents laughing and I'm sure that picture is real. I can't be certain of my age – six, maybe seven, I reckon. But I don't think my dad was drinking then.

My mum was a nurse. A really good one. She specialised in premature babies and worked part-time when I was in primary school while my father worked in a car factory. It was a very ordinary and solid sort of start, I guess. We owned our own little semi with a small garage and a small garden. My father worked hard and spent the weekends in the garden. And if you'd asked the little girl on that trip to the New Forest if she was happy, she would have said yes. But she would like a sister, please. Not a pony.

And then things started to change. Raised voices. More and more arguments. I don't know what triggered the change but I would see my dad staying up late with a glass of Scotch. He liked crystal glasses and expensive Scotch. It upset my mum.

Why don't you come to bed, love?

This went on for a while and then my dad lost his job. I learned much later that this was because of the drinking. I can only guess that towards the end of his time at the factory, he was what you would now call a functioning alcoholic. I didn't see him drunk back then. I saw him with a beer often. I saw him with those glasses of Scotch. But I don't remember as a small child seeing him drunk. Or difficult. Or belligerent.

That all came *after* he lost his job.

I've never properly talked it through with my mum. I don't know why. I don't want to cause her more pain or make her feel

165

guilty. It wasn't her fault. And there's not much point now, so I've put all this together myself. I may have some of it wrong but I do remember the creeping awareness of a dangerous change. It was like playing Jenga when someone has much too early removed the wrong blocks and made the tower prematurely unstable. You know it's all going to come down but you just have to keep playing. Moving ever so carefully.

Bottom line – my father couldn't get another job and so his drinking got much worse.

He no longer had to try to look sober to hang on to a job, so he didn't bother. My mother switched to full-time work, taking on the night shifts for better pay. She also signed up with an agency for extra weekend shifts and so was hardly home. She explained all this to me, sitting on my bed before she left for work, whispering that the 'difficult time' was temporary and she hoped with all her heart that she could be home more very soon. That things would improve when Dad got a new job.

He, meantime, became very argumentative and very bitter. He started to rant at the news on the telly. Rant at the news in the newspapers. Rant at anything and everything; and I started to see him drunk. A lot. They started to argue in the kitchen in the early evening when she was getting ready for work. I would be up on my bed, eyes wide and my hands over my ears, no idea what I was supposed to do.

And that's when the battle and the humiliation over my packed lunches began.

Mum didn't have time to make my lunch and Dad insisted it was his job. She was obviously wary and said that she would find time but it became like a red rag to a bull. An issue of pride. *Don't you trust me? Are you saying I can't make a packed lunch for my daughter? Is that what you're saying?*

Hot lunches were expensive and Mum made me a cooked meal before she left for her night shift so a dangerous new routine was agreed. Dad was supposed to make my lunchbox before he went to bed. I think I was around eight so maybe I should have been more independent and stepped up to make them myself. But I didn't.

My lunchbox became like this fuse. This ticking bomb.

The trouble started with small things. I would get to school and find that Dad had put something odd in. A lime instead of an apple. A can of sardines. People would laugh and I pretended it was a joke. That he did it deliberately to make me laugh.

I started to check my packed lunch in the playground. If there was anything too weird, I'd chuck the whole contents in a bin. But I got caught and the teacher got the wrong end of the stick; started to worry I had some kind of eating disorder.

I then tried making my own sandwiches but Dad got really loud. *Has your mother been talking to you? Move out the way. I . . . make . . . your lunch.*

I see now that it was never about the wretched sandwiches or the lunch, but something else entirely . . .

And then we had the huge meltdown over the tea-bag sandwiches. The final straw. The day I got it all wrong; blew it. And Dad took it out on Mum and everything in my world went all the wrong colours. Angry colours. That's it. I remember sitting up in my pink room with its pink bedspread and seeing only angry colours flashing around the walls as I heard the noises from the kitchen. Things smashing. Glass and pots and all manner of things.

I went down, in my rabbit slippers, and stood in the doorway. I was going to tell them that I would do my own lunch. I was sorry to cause this horrible argument . . .

But my mother was crouched by the bin, all ready for work in her nurse's uniform. She was holding up her hands to try to protect herself but I could see blood on the side of her face. And this terrible rage on my father's face.

Go to your room, Rachel. Go to your room now . . .

I don't let myself even look at this picture in my head very often. What's the point? It happened. It's over. I got it wrong. I told my mum about the tea-bag sandwiches, you see. I caused the horrible argument and I made the bad thing happen. I am only thinking of it all now because I am having precisely the same feeling. Of dread. Of fear. Of confusion. The booming in my head and the palpitations in my chest. I suppose it's the reason I just don't feel that I can bear this . . . or handle this.

Looking at the photograph that Ed has sent me, I know that we're all in very, very big trouble. It's her. Sure – she's very much younger but Laura is so distinctly tall and has such striking hair. That pre-Raphaelite Titian hair. How could it not be her?

The woman who was watching me on the drive. The woman who was stalking me outside the hairdresser's and the woman who told me, so weirdly – *he's not who he says he is* – was Laura. No mistake.

She's here. I don't know why. And I don't know what she's capable of.

All I know is that I need to wait for DI Sanders and my husband to get here. I'm going to have to come clean about the PI. And I feel all over again like that girl in the rabbit slippers who's hearing her whole world crashing around downstairs. With flashes of dark and horrible colours blocking all the sunlight from the room.

CHAPTER 32

THE PRIVATE INVESTIGATOR

Matthew Hill's dribbling honey on his toast when his mobile goes. He's feeling good. More relaxed today. Amelie's counselling is going better than they dared hope. Sally's just back from dropping her at nursery – just the morning session for now to see how it goes. Baby steps.

It's a week since the shooting, he's not due at work until late morning and is hungry. His mobile's on the work surface alongside the coffee machine and so he moves across the kitchen.

'Leave it. Have your breakfast.' Sally tilts her head to the side as she tosses her car keys on to the worktop. 'Surely Mel can wait five minutes for you to have your breakfast.'

'How do you know it's Mel?' He glances at the screen.

It's Mel.

'Sorry. Gotta take this.' He grins. Sally rolls her eyes as he clamps the mobile to his ear, marching through the French doors to their patio, toast in hand.

'Matt, so sorry. But I need you earlier than we said. I've messed up.'

'What do you mean – messed up?' Honey's running down the side of the toast on to the middle finger of his right hand. The phone in his left. 'Excuse the noise.' He bites into the toast to stop the honey trickling further. 'Eating toast here.'

'I had to let Alex go.'

'But I don't understand. Why?' He's now chewing as fast as he can. Though Laura's their front runner now, Alex remains a suspect too.

'He got himself a good lawyer. Some new phone footage from the cathedral proved he was right at the other end, near the main door, when Gemma was shot. He was with some friends. No gun. All verified.'

'So he got bail?'

'Yes. First thing.'

'And why that does that equal you messing up?'

'Because he's now on the top of a multistorey car park, threatening to jump unless the Hartley family agree to tell him whether Gemma's baby is his or not.'

'Jeez.'

'The car park in Lakes Lane. Meet you there?'

'On my way.'

The traffic's bad and by the time Matthew turns the corner into Lakes Lane, there's not only all the expected police activity – cordons and uniformed presence – but ominously two satellite TV trucks.

As he turns off the ignition, a new call comes in. Amanda at the university press office.

'Sorry to intrude, Matthew. But you said if I needed a return favour?'

'Shoot. But you'll need to be quick. Crisis here.'

'I'm getting media calls about Gemma Hartley. Or rather her boyfriend. Suicide attempt. I'm saying nothing, obviously, but do you know what the hell's going on? I'm just going in to see the chancellor. Can you help?'

'At the scene right now. Can't talk, Amanda. I'll ring you back later. You know the drill. Say *nothing* to the media, please. Although—' He lets out a breath as the camera crew get out of the van directly in front of him. '—you may want to switch on your TV.'

He hangs up and marches to the barrier, showing his ID to the PC who checks on his radio before letting him through. He's quickly met by one of Mel's sergeants who leads the way to the car park's main stairwell.

'He's on the roof. Six floors up. You can't see this side but on the other side, he's got quite an audience in the office block opposite. We're working on getting that cleared. He's got a banner and loudhailer. Oh, and he's been in contact with the media.'

'So I see.'

'Mel's up there already but she's waiting for you. So I'm guessing you're our official negotiator then?'

Matthew feels a surge of surprise; it hadn't occurred to him that Mel would cast him in this role. Sure, he did a course once. Sure he's had a lucky break here and there but the police normally use their own people. Also – the media wouldn't normally dream of covering a suicide attempt. What the hell's going on here?

His mind's suddenly in overdrive, shooting back in time. To that conference centre. The course.

You need to separate yourself from the team on the ground, especially the police. You need to connect with the target. Just you two.

Don't be a part of 'them'.

At the top of the stairwell, he finds Mel barking instructions into her mobile. She hangs up on seeing him.

'I need to approach him from the other side. Away from your team.'

'Why?'

'Trust me, Mel. Can I get round?'

She glances about. 'There's a route round there. You can skirt the top floor and approach from the west.'

'Comms?'

'No need. He can hear you fine. Be warned, he has a loudhailer. Small crowd. We're moving people back.'

'And the TV crews?'

'I've spoken to the newsrooms. Warned that if they go live, it could trigger him jumping. Strictly between us, my gut says he's doing this for the coverage and is unlikely to jump. But no way can we assume I'm right. We play this by the book, assuming he's one hundred per cent serious. Understood?'

'Of course.'

'For now TV coverage is running edited footage only. We'll see if that holds. He emailed widely so in theory he invited the media.'

'Right. Let's see if he'll listen.'

Matthew sets off, sweeping around the row of cars on the western side of the top floor. He moves quietly from pillar to pillar. As he nears the front of the other side of the car park, he sees Alex, sitting on the concrete outer wall. There's some kind of banner spread out, with bricks positioned on the wall to keep it in place. It's hanging over the edge so Matthew can't see what it says. Alex has a loudhailer.

'Hey there, Alex. Hello. My name's Matthew and I'm here to see what I can do to help you. So what's all this about? What's it you want today?'

'You police?' Alex swings his head, his eyes glaring.

'No, I'm not. But the police are here so I can pass on messages to them if you like.'

Alex turns his head back to the front. 'I have nothing to say to the police.'

'Fine. That's absolutely fine. So what's going on, Alex? It's very windy up here. You look cold.'

Alex frowns. He moves his shoulders as if he's only just registered how cold he is.

'Would you like a blanket? A coffee. Shall I ask for that? Keep you a bit warmer and a bit more comfortable while we talk?'

Alex looks confused. Matthew is remembering his training. To keep the focus on the future. On normal needs.

'I don't want anyone coming near me. I don't want tricks.' Alex's voice is clearly affected by the chilly wind. He's wearing just a shirt and jeans and is shivering. Matthew is worried that even if Mel is right and Alex isn't planning to jump, the cold could trigger an accident.

'I'll tell the police not to come anywhere near you. How about I send for that blanket and coffee and I put it where you can reach it? I won't come too close, I promise. You'll be able to think more clearly if you're warmer, Alex. Then we can talk properly. Work out exactly how I can help you. Yes?'

Alex thinks for a while and then nods.

'OK. I'm going to take out my mobile and get those things for you. It's not a trick. OK, Alex? Just my mobile.'

He nods again.

Matthew takes out his mobile and rings Mel. 'A large blanket and coffee with sugar, please. Fast as you can but leave it by the pillar behind me. Don't send anyone close. No uniforms.'

'Understood.'

Matthew puts his phone back in his pocket. 'Right. The police have said yes but I've told them to stay back. OK?'

Alex nods again. Good. Whether he's acting or whether he's serious, Alex is starting to see Matthew as an intermediary.

'So what do you want here, Alex? What can I do to help you?'

'A father has rights.'

'Of course. So is that what this is all about? A child? Is this about a child, Alex?'

'You know it is. The Hartleys won't talk to me. They won't let me see Gemma. And they won't do a paternity test.'

Matthew has to think fast what to say here. No way could anyone sign off a paternity test while Gemma is in a coma. Alex is being totally irrational.

'It must be very frustrating for you. Not knowing where you stand.'

There's a long pause. Alex puts the loudhailer down alongside him on the wall and shuffles forward a little.

'You don't want to go nearer the edge, Alex. We need to talk some more. Work out what I can do to help here. You can't get what you want unless we talk, now can you?'

A few moments pass. Matthew's heart is beating very fast. Is Mel's gut instinct right? Or is Alex serious here? Matthew hears a noise behind him and turns to see a uniformed officer place a blanket two pillars back.

'Right. The blanket's arrived. I'll fetch it. I expect the coffee will come soon too.'

Matthew retreats to pick up the blanket and moves back to his position near the front wall but several feet from Alex. 'I'm going to throw this on to the wall to your left, Alex. Don't try to catch it. Sit very, very still where you are. I'm a good shot. Don't move. Do you understand?'

Alex nods again. Matthew throws the blanket so it ends up over the wall, an arm's length from Alex.

'I don't want you to reach out, Alex. I want you to shuffle back, away from the edge. And then you can move more safely towards the blanket to your left. Is that OK with you?'

'Yes.' Alex does as he's asked. He shuffles back a little and then moves, bit by bit, to the left to reach the blanket which he quickly wraps around his shoulders.

'Good. That's good, Alex. Stay like that and warm yourself up a bit.'

Alex is now in a much better position, nearer the back of the ledge, but Matthew's heart is still pounding. He glances at the office block opposite.

If he says the wrong thing or gets the tone wrong . . .

CHAPTER 33

THE FATHER – *NOW*

Ed expects DI Sanders to be waiting for him with Rachel at the hospital. Instead he finds the ward in a strange state of heightened activity. There are several huddles – nurses and visitors – each grouped around the various TVs set at intervals along the opposite wall. Several heads turn as he walks in.

All he can make out on the televisions are different shots of a car park. He can't read the scrolling headlines from where he's standing, yet all the faces look sheepish.

'What's going on?'

More heads turn to him.

'You should go through and join your wife,' a nurse says finally.

'I need to know what's happening.' Ed directs this at the policeman on duty outside Gemma's cubicle, but the guard just stands to open the door into Gemma's space.

Inside Rachel has her hand up to her mouth, watching the TV above Gemma's bed on mute, tears rolling down her cheeks.

He was expecting an immediate row over Laura. A scene with DI Sanders.

'It's Alex,' Rachel whispers. 'He's on the top of a car park, threatening to jump.'

'What? And they're showing that on live TV?'

'No. Not live. But they're showing pictures. He's got a banner, Ed. And a loudhailer. He's making demands. Saying things about Gemma.'

'Gemma? What the hell . . .' Ed moves deeper into the room so he can read the screen.

A rolling headline says, 'Rooftop protest linked to coma student Gemma Hartley'.

'He's told everyone she's pregnant, Ed. The whole world.' Rachel is sobbing now. 'Why would he do that? Why would he do such a horrible thing? Is this because we refused to see him? Ignored those notes?'

Alex sent a second note, asking for a paternity test. A ridiculous request. They gave the note to DI Sanders. She said not to engage.

Ed moves across the room to put his arms around Rachel's shoulders – the chasm and confusion over Laura temporarily forgotten.

'The absolute bastard. Why are the media allowing this?'

'He contacted them through some campaign groups. Pro-lifers and fathers' rights groups. He says he has a right to know if it's his baby. He's going on about wanting the test; he says we're refusing to see him and the police won't tell him anything either. He's saying that he wants to bring the child up himself.'

'The man's completely off his head. This is monstrous.' Ed feels furious. Also helpless. He was resigned to the possibility of Gemma's news becoming public eventually. But not like *this* . . .

He glances at their daughter, silent and still in the bed. She has on the headphones that Rachel now uses to resolve their disagreement over whether Gemma can hear. They're his expensive noise-cancelling ones. Rachel plugs them into her iPad, linked to a relaxation or meditation app, playing gentle sounds of running water. A soft breeze. It normally annoys him that Rachel still insists on this. He doesn't think Gemma can hear. But at least they've stopped arguing about it and today he's surprised to feel grateful for the precaution. He could not bear for his daughter, trapped wherever she is trapped, to know what's going on today.

Just a week after someone sank a bullet in her leg.

'Do we still need to talk about Laura?' Ed's staring at Rachel.

'Yes. But *not now. Not now*. DI Sanders is dealing with all this first. Oh – what the hell do we do?' Rachel's tone is desperate. 'Should we get a lawyer, do you think? Is there some way we can stop the media running this? Letting him say these things?'

'I don't know, love.'

'What about Helen's sister? She deals with the press all the time. Maybe she can advise us?'

'No, no. We don't really know her, do we? And we need to be careful who we talk to.'

But Rachel's already taken out her phone and is typing.

'What are you doing?'

'I'm just sending a text to Helen. Telling her we need media advice.'

Ed lets out a huff of air. This is not favour territory. 'What about the police guy? In their press office?'

'I don't like him. I'm not even sure I trust him, Ed.'

'Well – I'm going to ring our lawyer. We need proper, sound advice, not favours.' He stands just as the picture on the TV changes. There's a close-up of Alex, sitting on the outer wall of the car park's top storey. A headline says 'These are not live pictures'. There's some kind of home-made banner strung out from the wall. The other channel's pixelating it. But not this one. Ed leans forward to read it properly. Rachel follows his gaze and does the same.

'A father's rights'.

'Why do they say it's not live?'

'They probably don't want to get blamed if he jumps.'

'Jumps?' Rachel looks horrified. 'You don't seriously think he'll jump, do you?' She looks back at the screen. 'No, no. He's doing this for attention. To ruin Gemma's life. Like when he came here and caused the scene. He's just bitter because they split up.'

'And what if he *is* the father?' Ed looks at Gemma. 'What if he actually did this to her?'

Rachel looks confused. 'You're just saying that because you don't want to believe it could be Laura.'

He doesn't answer at first. Doesn't want to fight over Laura while all *this* is going on.

'What if he meant to kill her, Rachel, but didn't know about the baby? And now he's doing this out of guilt – because he realises he nearly killed his own child?'

Rachel turns back to the screen, tears still rolling down her cheeks.

A male reporter, his hand holding his earpiece in place, is now giving an update live. He says that the rooftop protester is understood to be the boyfriend of Gemma Hartley who was shot during her graduation ceremony at Maidstead Cathedral.

'*Ex*-boyfriend,' Rachel barks at the screen.

The reporter continues to say the protester has emailed local media to claim that he and Gemma are expecting a baby together and he wants a say in the child's future. And information on Gemma's condition in hospital which he's being denied.

'How are they allowed to say this?' Rachel's tone is utterly distraught.

The phone at their legal team's office is finally connected but goes through to answerphone. *Damn.* Ed asks for his lawyer to return his call urgently but checks his watch and realises it's unlikely. They've only used the firm for wills and moving house.

He has no idea if they do out-of-hours work or will even be able to advise him within standard hours.

Rachel's phone buzzes. 'It's a text from Helen. She's watching the news too. The national bulletin must be running a summary.' She pauses to read some more. 'She's sent her sister's number. So what do you think? She's experienced with the media. Shall I ring her?'

'No. I don't think that's a good idea at all. The fewer people we speak to the better.'

Rachel hesitates and then Ed can see a male reporter, just finishing his live update on the TV screen above Rachel's head. The journalist suddenly turns towards the car park, which is behind him. It's not possible to see Alex from the reporter's position. Ed suspects that's deliberate in case something awful happens.

'Wait a moment. I'm just hearing something . . .' The reporter seems to be listening to someone out of shot. When he turns back, his eyes are at first difficult to read.

'OK. The police are just sharing an update.'

CHAPTER 34

Black and white

Shouldn't it always be what's best for the child? Isn't that always the bottom line?

Here is the way I see it. I have everything ready. Everything set up. I am prepared to do this properly. To put everything else on hold for this. That's what a child needs. Absolute dedication. Unconditional love.

A person who doesn't want a child shouldn't have that child. The child would be better off somewhere else. With someone who wants them.

Being wanted is the most important thing of all, surely.

It's not rocket science. It's simple.

I am ready to do this. Make the sacrifices. The child should be with me.

People are not always what they seem to be. And sometimes people just will not listen. Or believe. Or face up to the truth.

But I know the truth. And I see things clearly here. I see things that other people cannot see. People just need to listen to me now . . .

I feel completely sure that I know what's best here.

CHAPTER 35

THE FATHER – *BEFORE*

Ed Hartley was certainly not looking for love the night he met Rachel.

He'd given up on love – in fact had pretty much given up on life. Back in England after the nightmare of Laura's illness, he'd told no one the truth of what had happened in Canada. Without parents to take an interest and no siblings, there was just a small circle of friends who were all surprised to learn he was back so soon.

So what happened?

At first Ed hedged his bets, imagining he would eventually be returning to Canada. That a treatment programme would be found for Laura. Given this, he dodged all the questions out of loyalty to his wife. He didn't want her to be judged and he didn't want to be judged himself for seeming to have abandoned her.

But as the weeks stretched to months with Laura's condition getting worse rather than better, his strategy came undone. He felt utterly isolated.

His circle of friends was the usual mix of old and newer via work. There were a few university friends who kept in touch and a couple of boarding-school friends who knew him a little better, being aware of his childhood trauma. There was also Mark, who'd worked alongside him at the agency before Canada. Ed liked Mark. A laid-back kind of guy with a dry wit and a warm smile. He wasn't as blokey and showy as some others in marketing. They often had drinks together on a Friday. He and Laura had invited him for supper a few times and she'd liked him too. They'd issued an open invitation for Mark to visit them in Canada. They'd even exchanged letters over possible dates but of course the trip never came off.

Mark was one of the first to get in touch with both curiosity and concern when Ed was suddenly back in the UK. Ed played it cool. Put on his brave face. He shared only that he and Laura were sadly trialling a separation. He let the assumption of an affair hang in the air, neither confirming nor denying leading questions. He got sympathy and curiosity and handled both from his dazed state with a mixture of detachment and annoyance.

Still Ed was hoping to keep Laura in his life. What he didn't realise at the time was he was already slipping slowly into a depression. He had some savings and set himself up initially in a budget hotel near Bristol. He spent his days filing his CV with recruitment agencies, stressing that he didn't mind where he worked but he needed something fast. He didn't want to commit to renting anywhere to live until he knew where work might take him.

His CV was thankfully sound. And in the end it was Mark who came up trumps work wise. He'd moved and was now in a senior role in a marketing agency in Manchester; he offered Ed some freelance contracts with clients in the sector he knew well. Drinks and hospitality. Ed did so well he was offered a contract, which Mark hinted was very likely to turn into a full-time job. So Ed took the plunge and got himself a studio flat with river views.

He couldn't say that he was happy but he found a way to function. The hermit life. He phoned Canada every week at first, pushing for permission to visit Laura. But there was no change in her condition and no change in the advice for him to stay away. Slowly her parents became more distant on the phone. The gap between calls became greater. After six months they raised the 'D word', believing it better for Laura. Better for them too. *Get on with your life, Ed. This is the best way to help her. Let her go . . .*

He resisted. He investigated therapies in the UK. But it was like pushing water uphill. And there was no way Laura could travel. Or even see him.

After nearly two years, he caved. Signed the divorce papers. He had never felt such a failure.

In sickness and in health . . .

He'd let Laura down and he'd let himself down.

Through all this, Mark coaxed him out when he could. Drinks here and there. A movie. He tried to get him to talk properly about what had happened with Laura but Ed said there was nothing much to talk about. *We got married too quickly. End of.*

And then one cold week in November, Mark and his girlfriend Lottie invited him to dinner. *Just a few nice people. Please come.*

It was all very last-minute – a call just a couple of hours ahead of the meal. He doesn't even remember why he said yes in the end. Maybe precisely because it was late notice. No big deal. But suddenly he was 'out' on a Saturday evening, freshly divorced and freshly showered in a clean shirt, and there *she* was. Rachel in her red dress with her big, broad smile and her sparkly eyes.

'I hear you were in Canada. So what's Canada like?'

'I don't really like to talk about it to be honest.' He looked into her face and waited for the wary expression. He waited for the follow-up questions and the narrowing of eyes. He waited for her to look bored; to excuse herself to the bathroom so she could return and talk to the guest on her other side without seeming rude. But to his surprise, none of that happened.

That night . . . or ever.

Instead Rachel leaned in closer and her smile broadened. 'Well that's fine by me. Let's forget Canada. So what *do* you like to talk about?'

CHAPTER 36

THE DAUGHTER – *BEFORE*

Revenge is not forced upon a person but is a choice.
Discuss in relation to A Tale of Two Cities *by*
Charles Dickens.

I still feel numb. I still feel angry. And I still feel a complete mug.

But I also feel just a tiny bit more in control, because at least I'm getting information together. Proper information on my options.

I finally got to see 'S' yesterday and I've spent most of the time since in bed or on the phone, trying to be more practical. I will not let that man ruin my life . . .

I now have an assessment booked. Apparently they can do a scan to work out my exact dates so I know exactly how long I have before I need to make a final decision. They're also offering counselling which I will definitely need because I honestly still have no idea what to do.

When I got back to my flat after seeing them together – 'S' and his very pregnant wife – I was so furious, I wanted revenge. I admit it; I wanted to tell everyone. I wanted to ring my friend Maddy. Post it on social media. Stuff his stupid job. I go cold thinking about it now – the fallout if I'd done that, I mean. But thankfully I calmed down quickly enough to realise a public showdown would reflect as badly on me as him. And it's not just me any more. I have to think of the baby. If there's even to be a baby.

So I sent a text to 'S', threatening to call round at his house for a chat if he didn't reply.

He replied.

We met at a hotel we've been to before in a small village. I had to take a damn train again, fuming all the way. This time he didn't book a room. He met me in a tiny alcove in the corner of a snug bar at the back of the place.

I can only assume he was planning to break up with me while securing a promise not to kiss and tell. So I decided to come out with it straight.

'I'm pregnant. I've been trying to contact you ever since I found out.'

The shock on his face was extraordinary. 'Pregnant? But I thought you were on the Pill?' He was whispering and glancing around.

'I am. I don't know how it happened. So why the radio silence? Ghosting me.'

He ran his fingers through his hair and I watched his face really, really carefully and it was like seeing him for the very first time. I honestly couldn't believe in that moment that I had been such a fool. He feigned all this concern. Tilted his head. And suddenly instead of seeing this man as mature and kind and genuinely into me, it was like watching him through this new lens; an actor rehearsing.

'Wow. Poor you. What an awful worry.' He leaned forward and touched my hand.

I pulled it back. 'Yes. Poor me. So why didn't you text me back?'

I wasn't ready to tell him what I already knew; I wanted to see what lies he would tell me. How he would try to squirm out of the hole. But I honestly had no idea just how callous he would be.

'I'll pay. You mustn't worry about the money.'

'What?' I could feel all this bile bubbling up. I was so shocked and so angry I wanted to hit him. I had to clench my hands into fists on my lap to stop them trembling.

'Well. You can't keep it. You won't want to keep it.' He paused. 'I do know it will be unpleasant. *Awful* for you. But I'll help you through it. You will get past this.'

'And what if I want to keep it? The baby. Our baby?' Until that moment, I honestly hadn't let myself even imagine this. I am terrified of a termination but kind of imagined I'd have no other option. But 'S' taking it instantly for granted I would do that, without a second thought, was too much.

'Well. You can't keep it. How can you keep it? Bring up a child?'

'I thought you were going to leave your wife down the line. That's what you said. That's what you made me believe. That we were going to be together.'

He blushed then. Those fingers through his hair again. 'Well, actually. That's why I haven't been in touch.' He cleared his throat. He cast his actor's eyes across the room and then back again, lowering his chin. I wondered if he actually practised this in a mirror. 'She's not been well.'

'What's the matter with her?'

'I told you. She's fragile. Ups and downs. We're in a down.'

I remembered them alongside the car with the picnic basket. The way he kissed her. The way he touched her bump. Cupped her face. Took the sunglasses from the top of her head and placed them gently back on her nose.

188

I took in a deep breath and was weighing up if what I actually wanted was a scene. To call him out there and then. Shout. Cry. Have it out with him in public. Hit him?

A part of me did very much want all that but another part of me felt such an idiot too. I mean, you read about this kind of man. You see him in the movies. The problem is that you think you will be able to spot him in the flesh.

I looked right into his face and spoke very quietly. 'I *saw* you. You and your *pregnant* wife. So you can cut the bullshit.' I stood and picked up my handbag. 'I came here tonight for one reason only. To warn you that I have your number. And you'd better watch yourself – because if I want to ruin your career, I can. And I will.'

And then I did something very childish but immensely satisfying. I threw the glass of wine he'd just bought me in his face.

CHAPTER 37

THE PRIVATE INVESTIGATOR

'You don't seriously think I'm buying this good cop, bad cop bol-
locks, do you?' Alex doesn't turn his head as he says this but there
is a distinct change, not only in his tone, but in his posture. He
just takes a sip of the coffee, sits up straighter on his little patch of
car-park wall and pulls the blanket tighter around his shoulders.

Matthew's thrown. A moment ago, he genuinely thought he
was getting through. Alex appeared to be listening. So was that just
an act? Was Mel right about Alex?

Matthew opts for silence, needing a beat to regroup. Alex waits
too but then swings his legs to and fro as if to taunt Matthew, turning to stare right at him. Like a dare.

'So – I'm right? They sent you over to pretend to be nice to me?'

'I'm not pretending. I am actually quite nice.' This makes Alex
laugh for the first time and Matthew feels another shift inside; the
guy in the blanket no longer sounding like or looking like a man
who has any intention whatsoever of ending his life.

It's risky but Matthew decides to push forward. Bull. Horns.
'Look. You watch the telly. You're a bright guy. You clearly know

the score here. The tactics. But I really do want to help. So we need to work out an exit strategy.'

'And what precisely do you suggest, Mr Nice Guy?'

'It's time to move to the next phase, Alex. To deal with the police. And yeah – that's going to be a pain in the arse but that's just how it is after a protest like this. But the media are also going to want to do more on this. And that's what you want, isn't it?'

'So we're still pretending you're not the police?'

'I'm not.'

Alex appears to be thinking about this just as Matthew's phone rings.

'I'm sorry, but I'm going to have to take this. You stay calm now. Are you OK to wait, just for a moment?'

Alex shrugs as if he doesn't care.

It's Mel. 'We have some more background info on Alex. Family issues. He's estranged from his adoptive parents. They say he has been trying to find his birth mother and has cut them out of his life. Behaviour issues going right back to primary school. Sounds like controlling behaviour to me. Possibly abandonment issues. We need to look into this more and tread very carefully, Matt.'

'Understood.'

'Who's that? What are they saying?' Alex narrows his eyes.

Matthew puts the mobile to his chest. 'They want to know if we need anything else. I'm going to tell them we're moving down. Is that OK?'

Alex shrugs again.

Matthew puts the phone back to his ear. 'No more coffee, thanks. We're coming down now.' He hangs up. 'That right, Alex, isn't it? You ready?'

Alex shifts his position. He looks at the office block opposite – no faces at the window any more. Moved out by the police. Then he turns his head back to look again at Matthew intently, again narrowing his eyes.

'OK. Yeah. I'm ready now.' Alex suddenly swings both his legs back over the ledge and turns his whole body to face the inside of the car park. He's still sitting on the wall but with his back now to the drop. He's glaring at Matthew and rocks to and fro.

'I could still do it, you know.' A pause. 'And you'd be in a lot of trouble, wouldn't you?'

Matthew takes in the new and sinister expression on Alex's face. They lock eyes – unblinking – and both keep very still. Silent.

And then Alex suddenly laughs.

CHAPTER 38

THE MOTHER

'What's happening?' I'm frowning as we both stare at the television. The TV reporter has turned his head to the side again and is pressing his earpiece in place.

'No idea.' Ed's eyes are wide. He sits down while we wait, crossing his legs and jiggling his right foot up and down.

I glance at Gemma, her face as still as ever, the headphones in place. A sweep of dread as I think of all the horrible things we have to tell her when she wakes up.

Suddenly the reporter is looking at the camera with the update. 'I'm being told the situation has been resolved safely.'

I feel my shoulders slump. We wait in silence as words scroll across the screen, confirming that Alex is now in police custody. The news feed immediately updates to live pictures and we watch as uniformed officers remove the banner Alex hung from the top ledge of the car park.

I can feel my heart still beating too fast as my phone goes. I pick it up from the side table to see an unknown number.

'It's probably the media. Don't answer.' Ed sounds nervous.

'How would they get my mobile number? I'll just listen. See what it is.'

I don't know what to expect but the voice is measured and calm. 'Hello. It's Amanda here. Helen's sister. Helen got your text and asked me to ring you, but please say if it's a bad time to talk.'

'Oh, no. It's fine. I'm grateful Helen passed on the message.'

'I was just wondering if you knew the latest? That Alex is in custody? Literally this minute. I'm watching it on television.'

'Yes. We're watching it too.'

'Look, I'm not really sure what you were hoping. Helen said you were worried about the media? That you needed help?'

'Yes, we are. We're beside ourselves to be honest. We can't understand how this was allowed. All over the television?'

Ed's staring at me, frowning, and so I hold the phone away from my face for a moment to mouth that it's Helen's sister.

'Be very careful what you say.' He's whispering, eyes wide. 'I'm not comfortable with this.'

'We were just after some advice about how to handle this. The media, I mean. We're taking legal advice too but it's all a bit over-whelming. The coverage of the shooting was bad enough. But this . . .'

'I'm just about to go into another meeting at the university.' Amanda's tone is guarded and I feel a wave of disappointment. 'We'll be liaising with the police. They have a good press office. Have their people not been advising you? They're normally very helpful in situations like this.'

'Sort of. But through DI Sanders.' I don't add that I don't much like the police comms guy. 'We feel a bit exposed, to be honest. A bit helpless. We just wondered if you could give us some advice? You know – independently?'

There's a pause. 'Please know that I feel for you and I want to help. Of course I do. But it's just a little bit tricky, given my role here, I mean.'

There's another pause and I realise Ed was right. She's not going to help us.

'Listen, Mrs Hartley—'

'Rachel, please.'

'Rachel. We're all so devastated about what's happened. We think of Gemma all the time. How is she today, by the way?'

'The same.' I glance again at Gemma. 'I'm with her now. She's just the same.'

'As I say, we're all thinking of you. And I will get back to you, once I've got a stronger picture of what's going on. Does that sound OK?'

'Yes. Thank you. I appreciate it.'

'You're welcome.'

I hang up. 'Helen's sister. She works in PR for the university.'

'Yes, I know. But they will be more worried about the university and its reputation than Gemma. You do realise that?'

'I think that's a bit harsh. She sounded nice. And she didn't have to ring.'

'She's paid by the university, Rachel.'

'Yes. I did get the feeling it's tricky for her.'

'Told you.'

My heart sinks. I feel that I need *someone* on our side. My side. I don't know what we should be doing next. Or not doing. To speak up for our daughter while she can't.

There's a knock on the door to the cubicle and the police guard then leans in to check that we're up to date. We nod. He says that the team have been in touch and DI Sanders will talk to us as soon as she can but she'll be tied up with interviewing Alex first.

'Thank you. Good.' I try to find a half smile. He meets my eye, closes the door again and retreats.

And then Ed and I just sit in silence for a bit as the television screen moves to a shot of DI Sanders, who is making a short statement. We watch the words scroll below her, summarising. Ed reaches for the remote control and puts up the volume, just a little. DI Sanders is saying only what we know already. The situation has been resolved safely. No one was hurt and a man's now in custody. She thanks everyone for their cooperation at the scene but says it's too early to comment further.

I can see a number of reporters moving forward with microphones, all talking over each other, trying to pose questions, but DI Sanders just smiles and steps aside, ushered swiftly into a waiting car.

And it is the sight of her, DI Sanders, that suddenly pulls me back to reality.

Laura. Ed's first wife . . .

'I'm pretty sure she followed me. Stalked me,' I say suddenly, turning to Ed. And even as the words leave my mouth, my mind is shooting through time. To the moment the photograph pinged into my phone from Ed's at the house. Before the horror of all this nonsense with Alex. And I can no longer make any sense of any of this. I don't know whether to still suspect Laura. Or whether this has all been Alex all along.

'Who?'

'Laura. Your first wife. That's why I needed to see the photograph.' I put my hand up to my head, realising that I should have said something to the guard. I shouldn't have let this business with Alex distract me so completely.

'But she could look entirely different now.' Ed's face is flushed and I feel a coldness inside. Anger at him again. The fury at Alex switching back into this room. The confusion returning that my own husband kept so much from me. *Lied* to me.

'What do you mean? Stalked you?' Ed glances back at the TV screen as if, like me, he can't compute these two very different strands to this horrible nightmare.

'I have to speak to DI Sanders. It can't wait,' I say, standing. 'Turn the television off and get the guard back in here.'

'No. Tell me first. What on earth do you mean? Laura's been stalking you?'

CHAPTER 39

THE DAUGHTER - *BEFORE*

Discuss how Mary Shelley's troubled family life is evident in her writing.

There's so much going on, I'm exhausted. I've worked out the dates after seeing the counsellor at the clinic and I can technically bump the decision about the pregnancy until after graduation, so that's what I've decided to do.

I'll get the ceremony done and then I'll tell Mum and Dad. Try to get them on board, whatever I decide to do. It will be horrible and I'm dreading it. I keep imagining Mum's face. But the counsellor reminded me I'm lucky to have a family who could support me. She says I shouldn't assume I know how they'll react, so I'm doing what she recommended. One step at a time.

Results come in three weeks today. I've got everything crossed for a first but am worrying now whether 'S' will do anything stupid to interfere with my result. Surely he can't do that? I've checked all the grades online. It's looking good and the last exam went well. I worked really, really hard for it. Whatever. If 'S' tries to interfere, I'll demand an investigation.

The counsellor's right: I need to stop worrying about things that haven't happened yet and concentrate on the things I can control. So – I need to wait for the result. And I need to get through the ceremony. At least I'll have my degree. I'll be going home.

I've spoken to my landlord and I can stay on in the flat until the end of the summer if I want. The other two girls are going home a bit early and travelling to graduation with their parents. I don't want to do that. Mum will fuss, fuss, fuss and I'll struggle to look her in the eye. I'll have to make up some excuse to stay on; something to do with sorting the flat out.

The only thing on my mind now is getting a job. Earning a living. If I do decide to keep the baby (I really can't picture that, to be honest, but I'm keeping it on the list of options), I don't want Mum and Dad to think I expect them to bail me out financially. I have no idea about stuff like childcare, but I'd need to get a job after the baby arrived and work all that out.

It sounds impossible, right?

I've only got retail on my CV. Working in chemists and book shops. That's not going to earn enough to pay for childcare, is it? A while back I sent an email to the university comms department, asking for some work experience. Just a week. Something to put on the CV. So that it looks better when I apply for proper jobs later on.

But get this. The head of comms said her office was way too busy. *Sorry. I wish you well.* I can't believe it. You'd think university staff would want to help their own . . .

And on top of everything – the problem with 'A' is back.

I thought he'd finally accepted it was over and would leave me alone. But I think people starting to talk about the graduation has stirred him up. Months ago we'd talked about getting the two families together for a joint celebration. Dinner out. Feels like a different life to remember that now.

Today and yesterday, I've had two more weird direct messages via Facebook. *He's not who he says he is.* I've checked the profile – I must have accepted the friend request without checking. I do that sometimes. I've got hundreds of friends. That's just how it is at uni. But I'm worried now that it's 'A'. The profile has no friends. Just me. It had a picture up of a bar in town which is why I probably accepted without thinking. That picture's still there but it's nothing to do with the bar.

My first thought was to unfriend the profile or report it, but I'm holding off because I want to investigate. See whether the messages stop if I ignore them.

Most of all, I'm worrying that if this is 'A', he's somehow found out about 'S'.

He's not who he says he is.

The truth? This may sound paranoid, but my biggest fear now is that maybe 'A' has been following me.

CHAPTER 40

THE PRIVATE INVESTIGATOR

Mel has put Alex in the interview room early so they can watch him on computer screen via the live camera feeds.

He looks cocky. Almost bored.

'What do you make of him, Matt?' Mel leans in closer to the screen.

'Hard to read. He's arrogant. Manipulative. Likes to have the upper hand.'

'Capable of shooting Gemma?'

Matthew lets out a long breath. It's so hard to call what people are capable of. So many with dark minds live perfectly ordinary lives, holding down demanding jobs. Matthew's learned to keep an open mind. Always.

'He's controlling. So possibly. Who knows what went on between them over the break up? Do we have any more from his family?'

'Yes. Very interesting. They're here but he's refusing to see them. Adoptive parents. They're in bits. Seem genuine. Their story is that the relationship's been especially bad since Alex went to uni.

He's become obsessed with finding his birth mother but hasn't been able to trace her yet.'

'Could be why he's so fixated on the baby.'

'What I was thinking.'

'Wish you'd let me interview him, Mel.'

'He's our prime suspect for sending the dolls, including the one to your house. Best not.' Mel pauses. 'But I'm going to lead myself.'

'Won't that put more noses out of joint?' Mel's sergeant will be expecting to take the interview.

'I think that boat's sailed.'

Matthew laughs. Mel has a reputation for doing what works rather than what's popular, especially when she's under pressure from the suits upstairs. She leaves the room and a few minutes later appears on the screen as she enters the interview room, with the sergeant alongside her.

As Matthew puts on the headphones, Mel starts the recording of the interview and dives straight in. 'Recognise these, Alex?' She slides pictures of the dolls across the desk.

Alex glances at them, then shrugs. 'Never seen them before.'

It's hard to read his eyes, but Matthew remembers the car park. Alex's ability to play games.

'Someone sent these dolls to Gemma Hartley's parents, among others. Someone with a very nasty mind. Was that you, Alex?'

'Um, no. Why would I do that?'

'For the same reason you caused a nasty scene at the hospital. And in the centre of town. Because you can't accept that Gemma ended your relationship.'

Alex looks up to the ceiling. He doesn't reply. Mel waits.

'I understand you've had some family issues lately. This past year. Is that what this is all about?'

'My family is none of your business.'

'Well, I beg to differ. Is that why you're so wound up over Gemma's pregnancy? The baby? Because of your own background, Alex?'

'I want a lawyer.'

'I thought you said you didn't want a lawyer. That you'd done nothing wrong and you didn't need one.'

'Well, I've changed my mind.'

Matthew narrows his eyes and leans in to take in Alex's expression. So the uber-confident Alex is feeling the pressure after all.

CHAPTER 41

THE FATHER - *NOW*

They've had a message that DI Sanders will be with them in half an hour. Rachel's refusing to leave Gemma so it's not an option to go to the police station together.

They've been sitting in silence, each pretending to read again. Gemma has the bloody headphones on still. Ed wonders if he's wrong – if she really can hear the running water and the wind through the leaves. All that meditation stuff Rachel loves.

His own mind is all over the place, darting between theories. He glances up to the blank TV screen – switched off since Alex's arrest. He's still struggling to understand why on earth Laura would be in the country. He simply can't make the leap to see her being capable of violence, but none of this is making sense. Why would she follow Rachel?

Of course her illness makes her irrational and it could make her *seem* alarming; he of all people knows that. But she's unwell; she's not a bad person. His heart is telling him there has to be some *other* explanation. She wouldn't harm Gemma.

He's confused – much more inclined to put this whole dreadful business down to Alex. I mean – just look at his outburst at the hospital. And the car-park fiasco. It's hard to believe they didn't see through him earlier; that they actually welcomed him into their home. Their lives. How the hell could they have missed the signs?

Ed took Alex fishing once on a weekend trip away while Gemma and Rachel went shopping. It was a bank-holiday weekend and they rented a cottage near a river. It had spectacular views and Rachel was mesmerised. She would stand for ages at the folding doors from the kitchen extension. *Maybe we should think about moving, Ed. Somewhere with a view. What do you think?*

It was back in the days when Gemma was insisting that she and Alex were 'serious'. Personally, Ed took this with a pinch of salt. They were kids still. But he wanted his daughter to learn her own lessons and wanted above all for her to see that he trusted her. And so yes – he played along and took his daughter's boyfriend fishing. It was a little awkward at first but Alex wasn't bad company. They talked music mostly and discovered an unexpected mutual appreciation of jazz; in the end, Ed rather enjoyed the couple of hours at the river together. They didn't catch anything, but it was fun to share the stories of the bites when the girls returned laden with shopping bags. And he loved Gemma's smile when she caught his eye and he gave her the thumbs up.

Later in bed Rachel had said she was grateful too as she'd had a lovely time with Gemma, just the two of them. But then she paused and added in quite a serious tone that she found Alex a little bit *too good to be true.*

What do you mean?

Well – bringing me presents each time. Don't you find that a little bit much? A bit creepy?

He had to think about it for a bit. Most people would be grateful for a young man who bothered with gifts but she was right, actually. It was a little bit weird. As if Alex wanted to ingratiate himself with Gemma with a show of consideration towards Rachel.

It would have been fine and understandable if he and Rachel were close but they weren't at all. When left alone together, Alex struggled to find anything to say to Rachel. He would immediately get his phone out, she said. Borderline rude. It was almost as if he only wanted to make an effort if Gemma was watching. Ed hadn't liked this about Alex, but at the time he put it down to his youth.

The truth was, Ed had always seen Alex as wanting to impress Gemma and that hadn't seemed such a bad thing in a boyfriend. He had honestly not seen any sign in Alex that he was capable of *turning* on Gemma. Was that a lack of judgement on his part as a father or was Alex just a very good actor?

Whatever the case, Ed now sees Alex as someone deeply troubled – maybe even with some kind of personality disorder. His thinking is that anyone capable of staging that horrific nonsense at the car park is capable of the shooting at the cathedral.

He shudders at the thought of it. Him alongside Alex fishing. Alex in the cathedral with a gun?

What Ed still can't contemplate is that Laura would be involved. He's desperately trying to work out why the hell Laura might travel to the UK. There's been no contact in years so it really shook him when DI Sanders said she was no longer at the clinic in Canada. But the greater leap is Rachel's new suspicion that she's here in the UK and has been following her. That could be mistaken identity, of course. Paranoia even? But what the hell is the postcard all about? He presses his hand against his pocket – the rectangle of cardboard inside a plastic bag in case the police need to check for prints. He's planning to hand it over to DI Sanders, but all of a sudden a crazy thought circles the room and lands in his brain.

Is there a chance the postcard could actually be down to *Rachel*? Getting back at him? For the secret over Laura . . . He glances across at his wife. This woman has not a bad bone in her body. No, no, no.

He's going mad. She wouldn't do something like that – not Rachel. Not in the middle of all of this. *Would she?*

'What?' Rachel has looked up from her book.

'I didn't say anything.'

'You made a really weird noise. Like exasperation. Or shock or something.'

Ed wasn't aware that he'd made any noise at all. 'Sorry. Mind in overdrive here.'

'Me too.'

'I know I've said it already but if I could go back in time—'

She puts her hand up to stop him. 'Please. Don't, Ed. Just don't.'

He stretches his arm to put his book down on the end of Gemma's bed, conscious only as he stares at it afterwards that it's in the very place her foot should be. Rachel follows his gaze and he can tell by her expression that she's acknowledging the very same thought.

They don't say anything. Neither of them are ready to talk about how they're going to tell their daughter. The prospect of rehab. What it will be like – all the physio and the reality of some kind of prosthetic limb. They don't talk about it because even that horror – the adjustment that their beautiful daughter has to face – is an assumption too far.

Gemma has to make it out of the coma first.

He checks his watch again. DI Sanders is running late.

'It could have been someone else with the same colour hair.' This again is thinking out loud.

Rachel looks up at him. 'And why would she say such an odd thing? *He's not who he says he is.* Something which completely fits with Laura. The whole, bizarre story that is . . .' She pauses. 'Laura.'

He's trying to think how to counter this when there's a tap at the door.

Ed stands as he announces to DI Sanders that she can come in.

'Do you want to find a quiet room? An office?' Mel Sanders is taking in Gemma's headphones, looking a little puzzled.

'I would prefer that,' Rachel says. 'But I'll ask if a nurse can sit with her. They'll probably let us use the corner office if it's free.'

Rachel leaves the cubicle to liaise with one of the nurses and DI Sanders lets out a long sigh.

'I can't believe the media were allowed to cover it the way they did,' Ed says. 'Alex's show.'

'Some outlets held back. Our comms unit put out direct appeals to news desks. Some edited a lot out.'

'But not all.'

'No. We did our best but I'm sorry you had to go through that.' DI Sanders again looks at Gemma. 'I understand that your wife wants to speak to me on her own first. We'll send the nurse in when we're ready for you.'

Ed is shaken by this. Rachel didn't spell that out. He knows she's really upset over the shock of finding out about Laura and he expected her to be. Who wouldn't be? But he hates the thought of not knowing what she's going to say to DI Sanders.

The police officer pauses, but he has no idea what to say by way of protest.

'It can't be easy for your wife,' DI Sanders says finally as she heads for the door.

'No. And that's my fault. I do know that.' Ed sits down and leans forward to put his head in his hands as the inspector leaves.

He checks his watch every five minutes and it's fifteen before a nurse finally comes into the room to tell him they're ready for him in the corner office. He tries to find a small smile of thanks but his face muscles aren't working properly. He presses his hand once more against the hard rectangle of the postcard concealed in his pocket. The hypocrisy. He was going to show it quietly to the inspector, hoping Rachel would not see it, but he will need to hand it over in front of Rachel now. He thinks of his bizarre suspicion, wondering if Rachel might have sent it in anger. A little dig. But this suspicion feels like yet another betrayal she doesn't deserve.

He honestly doesn't know what it means or what to think any more. His head hurts. Did Laura really send the postcard to him? If so – why? Still he cannot think of her as anything other than unwell. But what if he's got this all wrong? What if Laura is now more ill than he realises and he's allowing his own guilt to cloud his judgement? Ed feels a terrible weight as he pulls himself up to standing and weaves through the door and the centre of the main ward towards the corner office that the nurses use for coffee breaks and admin during the night shift.

Rachel is sitting next to a filing cabinet, drying her eyes. DI Sanders looks up and glances between them, and Ed worries there may be even more to this private meeting than he realised.

But what exactly?

'Why didn't you want me with you?' He says this to Rachel but she won't look at him. 'What have you been saying? What's going on?'

CHAPTER 42

Black

I am watching an ant. It is tracing a line directly along the grout between the floor tiles. Black. Bold. And to me rather beautiful.

I have never minded insects the way others do. Spiders. Woodlice. Ants. When I was a child, we lived in a house that seemed positively infested with spiders. My friends hated them, creating all sorts of scenes. But I was always fascinated by their endeavours. Their secrecy. Slipping in and out of rooms and weaving their magical webs. Works of art, catching the light.

I had a friend who had a large dog that was petrified of woodlice. The dog would cower across the room, sometimes stress-weeing right on the carpet. My friend was mortified and her mother was furious. But I thought it was hilarious. A tiny woodlouse versus a large dog.

As for ants – what little miracles. All they do is work. Busy, busy, busy. I like that. I understand that.

What appeals to me about insects is they have it tough, but they don't let that stop them. I'm exactly like that. I focus on what I want and I work towards it. Like a spider. Like an ant.

Take this one, now halfway across the room. It's on its own, which is rare, so it must be some kind of scout. But is it afraid? No. Is it focused? Yes. It probably has a nest of baby ants waiting for it to return with news of a new food source.

This place is clean so it won't find much, but top marks for trying. I like a trier.

I put my hand up to my head and wish it did not hurt so much. Too much thinking. I am wondering what exactly the police are thinking. How much they really know?

I need to be like that little ant. Keep focused. Keep my thoughts on the road ahead. On the baby ants back in the nest. On the future and the task in hand.

I bet you didn't know that the worker ants are actually female. That surprised me too. I looked it all up when I was a kid. The queen ant lays the eggs and the male ants die very soon after mating. Then the female worker ants take care of everything.

I remember putting the book down after learning all that and thinking – wow. Realising that you need to look out on the world in an entirely different way.

It's like my USP now. Knowing all this. Knowledge is power. Once you realise that the females can be in charge and the males had better watch out, you look at everyone differently. You behave differently. You know.

It doesn't frighten me because I realise that most other people don't realise all of this. So I have stored the secret away and made myself stronger.

So let me tell you this. I know about the worker ants and the dead male ants and I am not going to let the system beat me.

I am not giving up. I am not letting them win.

I have come this far and I swear on that little ant's life, I am not giving up now.

CHAPTER 43

THE PRIVATE INVESTIGATOR

Matthew checks his watch. He's spent more than an hour on campus and has drawn a complete blank. Ahead of him is a large, red-brick building with an impressive first-floor terrace. It has smart glass edging the whole area, and he can see a waitress delivering food and drinks. Good. He skipped breakfast and is starving.

It's well signposted inside and soon he's sitting at a table, enjoying the view across the parkland that divides the study halls from the student accommodation. It's an appealing environment and he wonders if Gemma and her friends have ever sat here. Probably. Almost certainly. Seems a prime spot.

The thought chills him. Gemma in the past – carefree and complete with no idea of what lay ahead.

He closes his eyes to regroup, then opens them to look around properly. He's surprised at the age range. Mostly mature – clearly not students. He's just processing this as a waitress appears and he orders coffee, water and a panini.

'I'm surprised you're so busy?' he says as she sets out his cutlery and napkin. 'I thought everything would be winding down.'

'Far from it. Conference and summer-school season straight after the graduations. Busier than ever.' She tucks her order book into the pocket of her black apron. 'Just as well. I need the over-time.' And then she's gone and Matthew realises there's much he doesn't know about the rhythm of university life and finances. No wonder the chancellor's paranoid about the bad press. The question mark still hanging over the inquiry. No wonder she wants tomorrow's final ceremony. The confidence boost. The signal that life must go on . . .

Across the courtyard in front of the building, Matthew watches a small group of teenagers following a woman wearing a university tabard. She has a clipboard and is pointing out various buildings and then waving her hand towards the blocks of accommodation in the distance. Some kind of open day? Summer course?

The teenagers are asking questions just as his waitress reappears with his order. Matthew leans back as she puts the panini down, thanks her and is just reaching for his cutlery when he looks up to see Amanda staring at him.

'News travels fast.' He tries to make his tone light. She's been very helpful, recommending the counsellor for Amelie, and he doesn't want to fall out with Amanda. But she won't be pleased. Him poking around the campus. 'Do you fancy a coffee? I'm treat-ing myself to brunch.'

'No time, unfortunately. Just wondered if I can help you?'

'Oh dear. Am I in trouble?' Matthew bites into his panini to find it too hot. Melted cheese scorches his tongue and he takes a gulp of cold water. 'Sorry. Always do that. My wife says it's because I'm greedy. No patience.'

Amanda smiles and sits in the chair opposite. 'Some members of staff contacted my office. Said you'd been asking questions again. Just wondered if I can help?'

'No. I'm fine. Just routine stuff. Still trying to find out if the rumours are true: about Gemma having a fling with one of her professors. I don't suppose you've heard anything more about that?' Amanda will know that all the tutors have been interviewed formally. That's drawn a blank but Matthew is now looking for *informal* tips.

Amanda shakes her head and her expression falters. Matthew is well aware that the last thing the university needs is a scandal involving the shot student and a member of staff. He doesn't want to make Amanda's life difficult with the chancellor but the bottom line is they have very different priorities professionally. She's here to warn him off.

'It's unsettling people. All these questions.'

'Yes, I know. And I'm sorry. But it is an attempted-murder inquiry.'

'Of course.'

The truth is he's found out nothing on any of his trips to campus. It's Thursday – eight days since the shooting. The students are no longer around and, while sympathetic about Gemma, staff are either wary or openly hostile when he tries to question them about her relationships. He's spoken to just a handful today – most winding down admin in their offices. He wonders who alerted Amanda. Probably that guy in the politics unit. *Do you have permission to be here?*

'I had no idea the summer's such a season for the university. I thought the campus would shut up shop.'

'Quite the opposite.' Amanda takes in a long breath.

'So have there been cancellations? Summer conferences, I mean?'

'A couple.'

'Which is why the chancellor's so twitchy.' Matthew tries his panini again and is relieved to find it more manageable. Good too.

'So are you allowed to say if Alex is going to be charged? Do you think it was him?' There's a hopeful look on Amanda's face. 'We're all longing for this to be over. It would be such a relief to see a charge before tomorrow's ceremony.'

'I'm sorry. You know I can't say. But trust me, we want this over as much as you do. Which is why I need to find out if Gemma really was having an affair with someone on the staff. However uncomfortable for the university.'

Amanda looks down at the floor and then back up. 'Actually, seeing as you're here, there's something I wanted to bounce past you.'

'Fire away.'

'The Hartleys have been in touch with me via my sister. Looking for some advice about how to handle the media – especially tomorrow. A bit awkward for me, if I'm honest. I feel a bit compromised. Tried to steer them to the police comms team but the mother, Rachel, sounds quite at sea.' She pauses. 'I mean – I'd like to help them in theory. To be honest, I still feel guilty for fobbing Gemma off about the work experience. It's tricky.'

Matthew thinks for a moment. 'I'll mention to Mel Sanders that they may need some more support. They've said no to a family liaison officer for now. Don't want someone else with them at the hospital. Privacy, I guess. I don't see why you shouldn't speak to them but steer them back to us if you can, please.'

'OK. Thanks. I'll talk up the police support.'

'Good. Thank you.'

Amanda stands.

'Lovely view from here.' Matthew turns to take in the panorama. 'It's a beautiful campus.'

'Yes. How's your daughter doing, by the way? I meant to ask.'

'Oh, much better actually. The counsellor you recommended was really helpful. Thank you.'

'I'm pleased to hear that.'

'So do you normally take a break yourself? Over the summer? Do you have family? I never asked.'

'No, not me. Married to the job.' Amanda smiles.

Matthew sips at his coffee and raises his hand by way of farewell as Amanda makes her excuses and retreats. He watches her walk back across the terrace and takes in her smart navy suit and expensive handbag. He thinks fondly of Sally, who juggled part-time work with days in jeans with playdough under her fingernails. He hopes they're having a good day today. Not too many worries for the jar.

And then as he turns, Matthew's surprised to see a woman he recognises, checking her watch on the concourse below. He leans closer to the glass barrier to make sure he's not mistaken. No. It's definitely her. Wendy March. Another private investigator he's come across at a couple of networking functions. She's a very different kind of operator and he doesn't much like her. Matthew frowns, wondering what the hell she's doing on campus.

He stands, finishing his coffee, and is planning to head down to speak to Wendy as his phone rings. The display confirms it's Amelie's nursery school.

'Matthew Hill.'

'This is the school office. I'm sorry but we couldn't get hold of your wife.'

'Is Amelie OK?' He can feel his heart racing.

'Please don't worry. She's fine. She's with a member of staff but there's been an incident and I'm hoping you can come to collect her so we can explain properly. I'm afraid we've had to call the police—'

CHAPTER 44

THE MOTHER

I watch the two nurses giving Gemma her bed bath. Sometimes I help but just now they're doing all the extras – checking her catheter and her feeding tube – so I'm letting them get on with it.

It was quite a shock at first, facing up to the day-to-day reality of Gemma's care. In the movies a coma looks just like sleep. In the real world, there are these endless checks and the constant fear of bed sores. Physiotherapy.

The best times are when they bring the fetal monitor and we listen to the baby's heart. Strong. Surreal. The strength of the rhythm reassures me and yet it's still so hard to take in – a new life in the midst of all of this.

Today I watch them turn Gemma on to her left side, gently moving each arm in turn. Up. Down. Up. Down. Sometimes they ask if I want to take a break while they check everything. They mean – do you really want to be here while we clean her?

But I always stay. I saw her through all that as a baby. And she's still my baby girl.

I can feel tears coming and so, to distract myself, I reach for Gemma's laptop. I click through the files that have become so familiar and return to the essays, wondering just what it takes to get a first. Gemma always wrote so brilliantly.

There's one on Hardy – *Is Tess in* Tess of the d'Urbervilles *portrayed as being responsible for her own demise?* I've always loved Hardy so I open the file and start reading. But a shiver goes instantly through me. Because it's not an essay at all . . .

> *I don't believe it. I am sitting on my bed, staring at the test stick with tears rolling down my face and I still don't believe.*

> *Two blue lines. Pregnant. How? HOW?*

I read on, my mouth gaping. It's Gemma talking. Like a diary. I'm so shocked I must let out some kind of strange noise because one of the nurses turns to me. 'Are you OK, Mrs Hartley?'

'I'm fine. Sorry. I'm fine.'

I'm not. I race through the paragraphs. My poor Gemma agonising over what to do about the pregnancy. I glance up at her in the bed and it's so unbearable. To hear her voice through the screen of the laptop. So distressed.

And then I reach a paragraph which is like a knife.

> *Mum would never cope – it would literally kill her and I just can't talk to her about this kind of thing.*

I put my hand up to my mouth. It's as if the room has changed shape. The distance between me and the bed distorted. Stretched. I feel almost faint.

I read on – the words like bellows on the fire of my failings. Gemma didn't talk to me because Gemma *couldn't* talk to me.

I didn't let her. I was too closed. Too afraid.

I skim through the rest of the file. She mentions the father – the married man – but there's no name. Why so careful? In her own computer? And why the fake title?

I finish the piece and feel for my phone in my pocket. Should I ring DI Sanders? I don't understand how they missed this.

No. Not yet. I need to try to find a name. Something concrete. I need to see if it's just the one piece. And, although I can hardly acknowledge it, I need to see what else she's written about our family. About me.

I watch the nurses finishing their care. One of them marks up the charts before leaving. I thank them and as soon as Gemma and I are alone, the tears come. I cry for what feels like quite a long time and then I feel ashamed. Self-indulgent. What right do I have to tears?

I put the laptop back on the bedside cabinet and put the headphones back on Gemma, wondering how long before Ed gets back from the cafeteria.

I'm dreading talking to him.

I check Gemma's ears, first the left ear and then the right to make sure the soft cups are not pinching the flesh. I flip through the iPad selection and pick 'seashore'. She's always loved the sea.

'I'm so sorry, Gemma. For how I've been. What I've been.' I brush my face dry. 'There's so much I have to tell you, Gemma. When you're better. When all of this is behind us.' I'm whispering, playing with the ends of her long hair. Golden brown. The shade that catches the light and glistens like a conker or a burnished nut.

I remember watching her in the sunshine in the garden when she was little, running in and out of the sprinkler on a hot day. The sunlight caught her hair and I thought how lucky she was to have that shade. Not like mine. Flat brown. Boring brown.

I can feel tears pricking my eyes again but fight hard to stop them.

'I'm angry with your father for telling so many lies. But the truth is I'm a complete hypocrite, darling. And a terrible coward too.'

I'm aware that I'm only saying this because I know she can't hear me – the words an empty echo in my head – wondering when I will find the courage to tell them both the whole truth. Out loud. No headphones.

That my father was a drunk. That he beat my mother and I have always been terribly ashamed of that. It's the wrong reaction; I do see that now. I should be angry, not embarrassed, but I've never worked it out properly in my head. I was the one who caused the biggest showdown – over the tea bags in my sandwiches. When she had to call the police and we had to leave. *We can't take all your things, Rachel. Just your favourites. Get your bear and your pyjamas* . . .

And so I closed it down and pretended I had a different childhood. And I've tried to gift that childhood to Gemma. The better version. The perfect version. The version with no rows. No conflict at all.

Only I've stuffed it up, haven't I? Because nothing's ever perfect, is it? And all I've done is push her away from me. Been a mother she can't even talk to.

I'm losing the fight against the tears as the door clicks open. I can smell the coffee but turn away to wipe my face before I look at him.

'I'm still struggling to believe it.' He hands me my cup. It's very hot and he's forgotten the cardboard holder so I put it on the floor, not wanting it next to the laptop on the bedside cabinet. I need to keep that safe. Read what else she has to say.

'You actually hired a private detective. To see if I was having an affair?'

'I've already said I'm sorry. I wish I could take it back.' I look up at him and then at Gemma, wishing I could take *everything* back. And to my great surprise, I find that I've simply had enough.

219

Mum would never cope . . . I just can't talk to her about
this kind of thing . . .

It's like stepping on a twig and making a noise when you're trying not to be seen. I can't help it. The noise is out there and I simply don't have the energy any more to hold in all the lies.

'My father was an alcoholic, Ed. And violent too. The version of my childhood I told you was a complete lie. I didn't push you about Canada or what happened there because I didn't want you to push me about my past.'

When I turn to him, the shock on Ed's face is all-consuming. It's like he's looking at someone he doesn't even recognise.

He opens his mouth to speak but then changes his mind and just puts his coffee down on the floor too. For a moment, I'm afraid he's either going to storm off or try to hug me. I don't honestly know which would be worse but I do know that I don't want to be touched.

In the end he stays in the chair and his gaze moves around the room and then back at me. 'Did he hurt you? Your father?'

'Not me physically but he beat my mother. Many times. And quite badly the final time.'

'He *beat* her?'

'I don't know why I couldn't tell you. I didn't tell anyone. I was actually quite ashamed. And as a child, I thought it was my fault. So I just kind of pushed it down.' I find that I am touching my stomach for some reason. I feel this knot of familiar anxiety and recognise the matching desire to deal with it. Stop it. To go into the kitchen to bake something lovely. To smooth things over with cakes and flapjacks and the warm smell of home-made jam. But here, trapped in this room with the machines and the bleeps and the smell only of sanitiser and bad coffee, all I can do is reach across to check the iPad to make sure that Gemma's headphones are still playing the sounds of the sea. Waves and seagulls. I need to at least be sure that none of this is seeping through to her.

Ed reaches up to put his hand on his forehead as if processing. Thinking.

'So that's why you can't bear arguments. Won't work things out. Why you won't—' His voice trails away and he sits up straighter. 'But I don't understand. Why the change these past months? Why the sudden questions about Canada after all these years? Why the suspicion? Why did you start to doubt me?'

'I don't know, I don't know. I suppose the thought of Gemma leaving. Finishing university. Leaving for good. I started to worry about what it would be like. Just you and me, and I started to think about Canada. About my lies. Started wondering about your past a bit. And when I asked you, you were really weird with me. Avoiding me. And so I thought—'

'But a private detective?'

'I know, I know. It feels mad now. And terribly hypocritical, given my own lies. But it was the thought of Gemma leaving us for good. Starting a job. Just me and you in the house, not just during term time but all the time. And I'm getting older. And fatter. I started to worry that we might not make it, going forward. Without Gemma. I guess I thought, why wouldn't you have an affair? Everyone else seems to. You don't even know me. I'm a fake. A liar.'

'Oh Rachel.' Ed is looking at me with the eyes I cannot read. This man who was married to someone else once. This stranger? 'How the hell did we get here?' He stands and turns away for a moment.

I hold my breath and after a while he turns back, his expression softer.

'I do love you, Rachel. I promise that I've never even thought about having an affair. But all these lies? I don't know what to think any more.' He pauses and drops his voice to add something I can't make out.

'I'm sorry. I didn't hear that.'

'I said it was my fault, not yours. You can't blame yourself for what your father did but I have no excuse. I don't know what I was thinking not telling you about Laura. I suppose I just felt ashamed. For giving up on her. Walking away. I was so relieved when you didn't push me in the early days. It was like getting a pass. Permission for a fresh start.' He looks at Gemma now. 'But I've let my guilt blind me. I honestly didn't think she was capable of hurting anyone. Laura. I was sure the police were wrong to even suspect her. But I'm worried now that I was just hoping to let myself off the hook. I will never forgive myself if I'm to blame for what's happened to our girl.' His voice is terribly quiet again, hauntingly so.

I close my eyes. A myriad of scenes suddenly swirl through my mind. *Go away until you calm down, Gemma. I'm not going to have an argument . . .*

I can see her on the lawn again, running in and out of that sprinkler.

Next I am a child again in my rabbit slippers, watching my mother on the floor of the kitchen with blood on her face.

It's as if the temperature in the room has changed and I feel as if I'm not quite in my own body, also a little bit sick. I listen to the rhythm of the monitors. The bleeping. The beat getting louder and louder.

'Rachel. *Stop* that. You're hurting yourself.' Ed's voice. I don't know what he means and I don't want to open my eyes to find out. It's like I honestly felt until today that I was doing OK as a mother; that loving her with my whole heart was enough. And suddenly I realise that I've done a terrible job. No. Worse than a terrible job. I've done *damage* – and it's like a picture coming into focus and I can't believe I didn't see any of this before.

'Stop it, Rachel. Look at me.'

I open my eyes to find Ed is holding both my arms at the wrists. I struggle free and pound again at my head. Bashing each word into my forehead to match the bleep, bleep of the machines.

I've lied. And I've let Ed lie. I've let us build a whole family on *lies*, *lies*, *lies* to avoid anything uncomfortable.

Again, Ed grabs my wrists and holds them tighter this time so I have to stop the pounding. He looks into my eyes and I feel as if I am going to fall down. As if my skeleton is melting inside my body.

'No. This is *my* fault, isn't it?' I look right into his eyes but it doesn't sound like my voice. 'I've let Gemma down. Never taught her how to *deal* with things. How to face things . . .'

I'm crying again, my wrists still held tight away from my body so that I cannot check the tears rolling down my face.

'I'll let go if you promise not to hit yourself.'

I don't want him to let go. I am afraid that if he lets go, I will crumble to a pile of dust on the floor.

'Look at me, Rachel. Do you promise to stop?'

'What have we done?' I stretch out my palms like a plea. Finally he lets go and I wait to fall. Through the floor.

Through time.

'What have we done to our beautiful girl?'

CHAPTER 45

THE DAUGHTER – *BEFORE*

Discuss the theme of isolation as portrayed in Jane
Eyre.

I honestly can't believe how much has changed since I last wrote
in this file. Seriously. A whole new avenue has opened up for me.
Something completely unexpected.

The first big news is that I've found someone to talk to properly
about the pregnancy. It's been a bit surprising and I won't go into
detail as it will be tempting fate and, knowing my luck, will all go
horribly wrong.

All I can say is that this isn't through uni counselling or anything so it's not dangerous. I mean I know uni services are supposed
to be 100 per cent confidential but if I let slip anything that might
identify the father, they'd be bound to do something wouldn't they?
Suspend him or something. Anyway, this has all happened very
quickly. Off campus. Out of the blue. Safe. I've become friends
with someone who really *gets* me. Understands exactly what I'm
going through.

It's like having a weight lifted – to actually sit and calmly talk to someone about things that are so difficult and so serious. I keep thinking about my mum and how I couldn't in a million years have this kind of conversation or this kind of relationship with her. I had no idea this sort of calm support was even possible.

And suddenly I'm seeing not only that I'm strong enough to get through this but that I have more options than I'd realised. Apparently, you can do private adoptions. I didn't really know anything about this; I'd assumed it was just part of surrogacy or something. I'd discounted adoption as I know that Mum and Dad would completely freak out at the prospect of having a grandchild 'out there' with no proper contact. But get this. With a private adoption, you can write your own rules. Be as involved as you want in the child's life.

Like I say, it's like a weight has been lifted off my shoulders because it no longer feels as if it's a black-and-white choice. Have the baby (and put off all my dreams) or have an abortion (and possibly regret it?). I mean I'm not judging others here. Some people are fine having a termination and that's their business and their right but I just don't think that's me. It's been keeping me up at night. And I still feel fury that it was his immediate reaction – to get rid of the child.

But a private adoption? Maybe . . .

I'm not going to make any quick decisions, of course, as I've been swinging like a pendulum ever since I found out about the pregnancy. But I want to at least consider this properly.

And I don't have to decide until after the graduation ceremony so I just need to get my head straight, dig deep, and talk to Mum and Dad.

Results are in ten days. All I need now is to get that damn first.

Also – just before I sign off – I need to sort out my Facebook security settings. I've had another couple of weird messages. I'm trying to be calmer about it as it's hopefully just someone random. But I've been googling and I didn't even realise that you can check which devices have logged into your Facebook account.

Unbelievable. There have been loads of log ins on devices I don't recognise – an iPad Air (I don't have one) and a Mac (don't have one of them either). Obviously my money is on 'A'. I changed my password but if he was already logged in via some other device, I'm wondering if that is a loophole? No idea.

I can apparently disallow these other devices which might solve the problem.

We'll see. I just wish I was on to all this sooner. I'm always careful now about what I post on Facebook and I don't use DMs any more, just to be on the safe side. I wish I'd taken the whole security side of social media more seriously before now.

But I'm feeling a *tiny* bit better overall. Not crying quite so much. If I can just get results and graduation out of the way, and then get Mum and Dad behind me, hopefully I can make the right decisions and come out of this all OK.

CHAPTER 46

THE PRIVATE INVESTIGATOR

Amelie has paint all over her hands when Matthew arrives at the school. She's in the art room of the nursery wing with one of the classroom assistants, and beams as he walks into the room.

Matthew sweeps her into a hug, not caring about the paint, and closes his eyes with relief.

'You're hugging too tight, Daddy.'

'Sorry, darling. Sorry.'

'I got paint on your shirt.'

'It doesn't matter. Listen – I need to just have a quick chat with the head teacher and then we're going home early.'

'Am I in trouble?'

'No, no. Of *course* not.' He kisses her on the forehead, cupping her face.

'What about my lunch? They said it's crumble and custard today.'

'We'll have lunch with Mummy. Find you something nice. Ice cream.'

'With chocolate sauce?'

Matthew ruffles his daughter's hair, relief still sweeping through him. Trust Amelie to play the advantage card. He stands and looks towards the head teacher Mrs Lewis who's waiting in the doorway. She's in charge of both the main school and the nursery wing too.

'Yes to chocolate sauce. I'll be back in just a moment. You finish your lovely picture.'

Matthew follows Mrs Lewis into her office where a uniformed officer is waiting. The PC introduces himself and looks wary. Matthew's already explained on the phone that there are 'complications' but he'll need Mel to sort out the protocols. The head teacher gave him an outline on the phone and he's shared the bare bones with Mel. But they urgently need more details.

'My wife should be here in about ten minutes.' He checks his watch, thinking of his own frantic drive here. Sally was at the hairdresser's and is distraught to have missed the school's call, which went to voicemail while she was at the basin.

Mrs Lewis adjusts her screen so that Matthew and the police officer can see the footage from the school's security cameras.

'We had a problem a couple of years back with reports of a man hanging around outside. So we had these installed, covering the playground and the gates. As I said, Amelie came in during the morning playtime to say she had a letter for her daddy.'

Mrs Lewis presses play on her machine and Matthew watches the blurred image. Amelie is playing hopscotch on her own near the corner of the playground and then suddenly looks up. A woman is standing outside the playground railings. Amelie pauses as if listening and then walks over to the woman. Matthew feels his stomach muscles tighten.

Amelie and the stranger talk for just a moment and then the woman passes something through the railings. They seem to say something else to each other and then Amelie moves across the playground, out of sight of the camera.

'She came straight inside and told a teacher about the letter.'

'Wasn't there a teacher on playground duty for the little ones?' Matthew can't help his tone. The nursery has its own section of the playground. Closer supervision surely?

'Yes, of course. But the staff member with Amelie's group was dealing with a child who'd fallen over and hurt her knee. So she didn't see what happened.' Mrs Lewis straightens her back.

'Right. So was Amelie upset?' Matthew tries to calm his tone. He doesn't want Mrs Lewis to be defensive. Not her fault. But he can feel fury rising inside him that his daughter has been dragged into this . . . *again*.

'No. She said the woman told her she had an urgent letter for Daddy. That she'd missed the post. We told Amelie that she'd been a good girl to tell us right away. But—' The head teacher lets out a long sigh. 'Look, I don't want Amelie to feel she's in trouble, but we will obviously need to agree how we take this forward with her. And with the other children too. We'll need to be open that the woman was in the wrong; that children don't always have to do what an adult says. We'll need to reinforce the stranger rules. We can't have this happen again.'

'No. Of course not. We'll talk to Amelie carefully.'

Matthew rakes his fingers through his hair. They've warned Amelie not to talk to strangers but she's so young, she can't be blamed. How could she know what to do in this situation? She was in nursery; supposed to be safe. And the woman was crafty – implying she was helping her daddy. Wretched woman. What the hell was she really doing? He asks Mrs Lewis to play the tape again and leans in even closer. The image of the woman is blurred. She's wearing a pale mac with a belt and has long hair. Could be Laura. Could equally be someone else entirely.

Just this morning his money was on Alex as their man but now he's not so sure. If this *is* Laura, he wonders what might have triggered her to suddenly pursue Ed after all these years. And his family too? He must speak to Ed again – see if there's anything in recent times that might have upset Laura. Set her off. Stirred up her illness and made things worse?

'I'm involved in a major investigation at the moment. With DI Mel Sanders.' Matthew is directing this as much at the uniformed officer as the head teacher. 'There's a possibility this is linked. DI Sanders will want a copy of this tape to see if we can enhance it.'

The PC is looking worried now. 'So this is definitely being bumped? I'll still need to do a report.'

'Of course. I'll get DI Sanders to liaise with you. I can't say too much at the moment. A lot's confidential.'

The PC makes a note in his pocket book, still looking curious. Wary.

'Thank you, Mrs Lewis. And the letter. Did anyone open it?' Matthew's desperate to see it but is reluctant to push too hard; he doesn't want to clash with the PC in front of the head.

'No. We called the police straight away. Tried to keep things low key for Amelie.'

'Good. Thank you.'

'Should the school be worried, Mr Hill? We need to be fully in the picture if there's a threat. If this could happen again?'

Matthew feels his heart sink. This is the last thing he wanted for Amelie. And Sally too.

'I'll ask DI Sanders to speak to you as soon as possible, Mrs Lewis.'

'Right. Good. And what about Amelie in the meantime? I understand she's been having counselling. She's been much more her usual self in nursery these past couple of days but I'm concerned this will set her back.'

Matthew notices the police constable raising his eyebrows, clearly wondering what is really going on here.

'Yes. This is the last thing we all needed. May I see the letter, please?'

The PC puts his hand in his pocket, fishes out an evidence bag and puts it on the head teacher's desk. Inside the sealed bag, ready for forensics, is a white envelope.

'I'll need to log this myself,' the PC says, as if reading Matthew's mind.

'Sure.'

Matthew uses his phone to take a photograph of the evidence bag to show Mel while it's being processed. It's handwritten. Neat, sloping writing with quite a distinctive 'M'– shouldn't be difficult to get it checked against Laura's.

'As soon as my wife arrives, we'll take Amelie home and be in touch once I speak to DI Sanders again.' Matthew pulls back. He doesn't add what he's really thinking. That he's not even sure if it's *safe* to take his daughter and wife home.

He's thinking of the dolls. So where does *this* fit in?

Matthew's mind is spinning. Maybe his family should go away somewhere? Take a break while he and Mel try to figure out what on earth is really going on here. He looks away towards the door, spooling through the options. Mel's mum is a close neighbour so that's no good. Maybe an Airbnb. Tell Amelie it's a little holiday? He badly needs to bounce this past Mel; see what she thinks.

Also Sally. He checks his watch again, bracing himself for her arrival. He prays she's driving safely. She's going to be horrified. Frightened. And quite possibly angry with him too for dragging them into this. He remembers how upset she was when he left them in town that very first day. *There's a gunman in the cathedral.*

Sally's face in the summer house when he arrived – the bomb squad checking the doll in the kitchen . . .

'Do you want tea while you wait?' Mrs Lewis says at last.

'No. But thank you.'

'That would be very nice,' the PC contradicts. 'If it's not too much trouble.'

Mrs Lewis picks up her phone while Matthew and the PC both stare at the evidence bag on the desk, Matthew wishing he could just grab it and rip open the letter.

Desperate to know what it says.

CHAPTER 47

THE FATHER – *BEFORE*

There were several things about Laura that both puzzled and delighted Ed in the early days of their relationship. Long, long before he had any idea that their story was to end so badly.

They moved in together within just a couple of months. A few friends raised their eyebrows, but Ed had no doubts at all. They were almost ridiculously happy, they were spending nearly all their time together, so why not live together? It was an hour commute to the school in Wells where she taught music but Laura loved driving; she was only working three days per week and insisted she didn't mind. She played classical favourites at full volume and told him that she liked the space; the time to herself.

Sometimes he worried that she had made too many compromises, agreeing to be the one to move for starters, but it was all very spontaneous. And also a question of practicality. Laura had a tiny studio flat with very limited cooking facilities on the outskirts of Wells. The first couple of weekends he went to stay with her, but mostly they ate out because her oven and hotplate was broken and the landlord was ignoring all her pleas to fix it. They each confided that they actually loved both to shop and to cook, so Laura offered to visit him instead. She fell instantly in love with his much larger kitchen . . . and more significantly his range cooker. So very quickly they switched to spending nearly all their early weekends at Ed's flat. Then, while pouring wine as she ladled stock into a risotto one night, he just blurted it out. *Why don't you just stay? Move in, I mean. Forget the rows with your stupid landlord.* She just smiled. *I thought you'd never ask.*

And yes – in those early months, she was this extraordinary puzzle – constantly surprising him. He discovered very quickly that she rose ridiculously early, 6 a.m. every single day, to do her exercise routine before music practice. He had imagined weekends would be different as she relaxed into their relationship, that she would look forward to a lie-in with him at weekends . . . but no.

He would wake groggy and slightly disorientated, an image of sex from the night before bringing a smile to his face even before he opened his eyes. He would reach out across the bed, hoping for a repeat, only to find her gone. A glance at the clock would bring an involuntary groan. Seven a.m. and he was already alone. He would then tiptoe to the loo as a pretence to see what she was up to, and every morning would be the same. He would find her on her exercise mat, her strawberry-blonde hair piled into a messy, high bun.

Laura said the early rising was part nature and partly due to her short stint in the army. The discipline. That was a shock too – the whole military thing, but she said it was perfect, just a limited spell and mainly for the music. Financial independence from her parents after uni and a chance to play in some huge concerts. She'd loved it.

I played for your Queen once.

You didn't?

I bloody did.

But didn't you have to go on military tours? What if there had been a war?

234

Ed associated the army with violence. Killing. And Laura was the least violent person he'd ever met.

But what if they'd sent you into battle? That's the contract, isn't it?

Chill, Ed. I played fabulous concerts, I had access to the best gyms and I worked in financial admin. It was a breeze.

Sometimes he would just stand and stare at her a while, wondering at the contradictions. Her extraordinary energy. The differences between them. He liked to laze about on a weekend morning. She wanted to get out and about as early as possible.

Come on. Let's go for a walk. Get brunch.

Don't you ever feel groggy? Tired in the morning? Never? What is the matter with you, Laura?

My brain doesn't ever let me keep still, Ed. It's always buzzing. Too noisy. Music is the only thing that makes it quieten down. When I'm not playing music, I can't bear it. Come on. Let's go out . . . please.

Later, when everything went so terribly for them in Canada, he would look back on those conversations and wonder if he should have heard an alarm bell ringing. Ask her what she really meant about her brain buzzing all the time. Was it a factor? Was it some small missed signal for the trauma that was to come?

But at the time he just felt they had different biological clocks. An owl and a lark. Also – it was rather good for him to get out and about more than he would have chosen. Laura was the champion of finding quirky places to visit – forever checking out composers and singers and dragging him to see their homes.

He lost count of the number of times he was positioned outside a property to be told that a special piece of music had been written within its walls.

Something that will last forever. Isn't that amazing, Ed?

He wished that he could say it was; he wished that he could match that wonder in her eyes. But Ed was more practical by nature; a man who liked to see evidence. To feel a connection with wonder, he needed to see flints and golden coins and actual treasure dug up and displayed in shiny cabinets. Alongside Laura, he very often felt prosaic, despite his supposed creative career. *I write for a living*, he liked to tell people. He did not add that it was marketing and advertising copy.

So was he jealous of Laura the musician? Laura who could make the piano seem to sing? Laura who had played in a concert for the Queen? No. Very quickly he realised in those moments when he stared at her on her exercise mat at a ridiculous early hour of the morning, or gazing transfixed at the home of some composer or singer, that he was not only in love with her but in complete awe of her.

She's extraordinary, he would tell people who questioned how quickly they moved in together.

For him, the relationship did not move too fast. He had no doubts. For during that spell in Wells and the early days in Canada, they were genuinely very happy.

There was just one small piece of the puzzle Ed would forget until it was much too late.

Once, from her exercise mat, she made an aside as – groggy and half asleep – he was messing with the coffee machine. It was loudly hissing its disapproval, the water tank nearly empty, so he didn't quite pick up what she was saying.

We should make it our thing. Cathedrals. Don't you think, Ed?

Sorry. I can't quite hear you over this machine. What did you say?

We should go to a cathedral for all our special anniversaries. Ten years. Twenty years and so on. It would be romantic. To remember how we met.

Sorry, honey. Now he was running a tap to fill the water tank. *I can't really hear you . . .*

CHAPTER 48

Blue

It's 5 a.m. and I'm sitting in the new chair in the nursery. I still don't sleep – not properly – so it's become a habit to move in here to wait for the light. Though it's very hard, actually, sitting here and not knowing how things are going to map out.

It's cold, which always makes me feel more afraid and unsure, but that's probably natural. The tiredness. The quiet. The cold. I am tapping my right foot up and down, up and down, and try to still it. But it's so difficult to be still.

I just have to stay positive. Determined. For me. And especially for the baby. Everything will be different when there are two of us in here. Our little bubble away from them all.

If I'm perfectly honest, the chair is not as comfortable as I'd hoped. Another of my impulse buys. I fell in love with the design and the colour – sea blue – and I let that sway me. I've tried different cushions but I just can't get comfy. Oh well. I suppose I could get another one delivered.

Some people say it's bad luck to get everything ready too early but I find it exciting. It makes me feel in control and some days it's the only thing that keeps me going; to come in here and wind forward to the days when we will be here together. Just the two of us. All the stress and the hurt behind me.

There are a few things still to put together but it won't take long, so I'm going to wait until all the fuss dies down.

I've kept the blind down because I don't want anyone looking in. Watching me, I mean. They might get the wrong idea and meddle. People do that way too much. Meddle. Ask questions. Drives me mad.

Are you sure you're OK?

Of course I'm OK. Leave me alone.

And that's the beauty of this plan and the thing I hold on to when I can't sleep. The thought of being alone in the best possible way. In here. With the baby. Just me but not truly alone any more.

No one to misunderstand.

No one to let me down.

CHAPTER 49

THE MOTHER

'That's enough for today. I'm getting a bit hoarse, darling.' I close the book, marking the place with a postcard. This one's a much better choice. An old favourite of Gemma's – *The Mill on the Floss*. I put the book down on the bedside locker and glance at the laptop.

I am trying to resist prying. I am trying to concentrate on Gemma and to respect her privacy but I can feel my heart quickening every time the light catches the shiny surface of the laptop lid. The truth is I'm burning to know if there's any more diary stuff by Gemma hidden in those files. I've looked. Of course I've *looked*; the problem is there are a lot of real essays. It's like searching for a needle in a haystack. Lots of work on poetry and Shakespeare. Also some creative writing – very good, I thought.

I suppose it's possible there was only that one day that Gemma jotted personal stuff instead of writing her essay. I've no idea. The dates are all over the place and there are quite a lot of module headings as well as essay headings. But it's like a haunting, wondering if there's *something* in that laptop that might help us.

I reach over and put it on the end of the bed again, waiting for it to load. I suppose I should talk to Ed about that one piece I found. Maybe the police too? But DI Sanders said they'd checked for anything important. And I don't want them to take the laptop away again, not unless it's genuinely helpful. It makes me feel closer to Gemma. It makes me feel useful, and hand on heart I still want to know if she wrote anything else about me . . .

I click on a few files in turn. More creative writing. The beginnings of a short story. Unfinished. An essay about Virginia Woolf's work. Pages and pages on that one. I should have been more methodical. Made a note of which files I've checked already.

But hang on. What's this?

Discuss the theme of isolation as portrayed in Jane Eyre.

I open the document and can see immediately that it's not an essay at all. It's Gemma's voice again. Right in my head. It's like the other diary entry but she's sounding very different here. More positive . . .

> *I honestly can't believe how much has changed since I last wrote in this file. Seriously. A whole new avenue has opened up for me. Something completely unexpected.*

I'm desperate to know how long this was after the panic of the last entry I found. I read as fast as I can, devouring the words. And then it is like the air is being sucked from my lungs . . .

> *It's the most unexpected thing. It's like having a weight lifted – to actually sit and calmly talk to someone about things that are so difficult and so serious. I keep thinking about my mum and how I couldn't in a million years have this kind of conversation or this kind of relationship with her. I had no idea this sort of calm support was even possible.*

I sit back from the laptop and am stilled. I look across at Gemma and burn with the shame of what I'm feeling. I should be pleased that she found a friend – and I am. Sort of. But I am also feeling jealous; that we were so very far apart, she couldn't talk to *me*. That I'm not the kind of mother my lovely daughter could turn to.

I need to read on but first I move across to the bed.

'I'm so very sorry, Gemma.' I smooth her hair and kiss her forehead, leaving my lips touching her flesh for a few seconds. But there's something not quite right. I pull back.

Her skin feels especially warm which is unusual. She looks so still and so distant, I have come to associate her form in the bed with coolness. *Apartness.*

I could never in a million years talk to my mother . . .

I reach for her hand. It feels quite warm too. I wonder about calling a nurse and am trying to remember the temperature of her hand the last time I held it. Am I imagining this? Am I just upset from reading the laptop?

I feel Gemma's forehead with the back of my hand but it's not hot per se. Not like a fever or anything. It occurs to me that I find the hospital too hot most of the time so perhaps it's my own body thermometer that's struggling.

I feel my own forehead for comparison.

And then it happens. Gemma suddenly opens her eyes.

It's such a shock that at first I simply gape – frozen and silent, just staring at those beautiful blue eyes.

Then both joy and panic kick in. 'Gemma. Gemma. It's Mum. Can you see me? Can you hear me? I'm right here, darling. Squeeze my hand if you can hear me.'

I stretch out with my free hand to ring the buzzer for a nurse – all the while talking, talking, talking. Babbling about how wonderful it is to see her. That I've been here all the time. How sorry – so very sorry – I am about everything.

For a short while, Gemma's eyes are wide open, staring at the ceiling. But then they close again.

'Gemma. Open your eyes again, darling. You can do this. I'm right here by the bed. You can wake up now. You're perfectly safe.'

On and on I babble as a nurse appears.

'She opened her eyes. Not for long but wide open.'

The nurse looks at all the numbers on the machine and gently lifts Gemma's left eyelid to check the pupil.

'Hello, Gemma. It's your nurse here. Do you want to open your eyes for me now? You're in hospital. But you're perfectly safe. Can you hear me? Do you want to open your eyes again for me?'

We watch. We wait. Nothing happens. The nurse repeats her encouragement. Nothing. She looks at me.

'She definitely opened her eyes. I didn't imagine it.'

'Did she look at you? Respond to your voice?'

'No. I don't know. She was just looking at the ceiling. But this is a good sign, isn't it? She could be waking up?'

'Possibly. It's a good sign – yes. I'll let the doctor know. You should keep talking to her. Stay with her. Call us if anything else happens.'

'I will. I will.' I stroke the hair back from Gemma's face. 'I'm still here, Gemma. Right here. I'm not going anywhere. I promise you.'

CHAPTER 50

THE PRIVATE INVESTIGATOR

'It's nice, don't you think?' Matthew is standing in the conservatory off the kitchen with its view of the sea. Waves roll in the distance and a seagull watches them from the roof of the stone garage at the end of the garden.

'It's lovely. A good choice.' Sally's tone is flat, her eyes worried. Matthew puts his arm around her waist. The seagull tilts its head.

It's been a rush. Fixing this. The packing. The journey.

'I'm so sorry about this.' He tucks the hair behind her ear and takes in her profile.

'It's not your fault. I don't blame you.' Sally's still looking out to sea and Matthew wants to press rewind; to tell Mel – *No. I'm really sorry but I can't help with the case.*

The cottage in Porthleven has been booked for a week – to take them well past the final graduation ceremony tomorrow. It was a lucky find – a cancellation – and Mel's said he can charge it to the force. Not an official safe house but as expenses for his work on the case. Just a precaution, he told Sally. Until we wrap this whole thing up.

'When are we going to the beach? Mummy says we can make sandcastles.'

They both turn to see Amelie in the doorway, carrying a bright red bucket and yellow spade. They've told her it's an extra holiday. A treat for being such a good, brave girl.

'Soon, honey.' Sally brightens her tone for their daughter. 'Daddy has to go back to work but we can do a quick trip to the beach before supper. Go and find your flip-flops. They're in the pink bag.'

Amelie beams and then disappears into the hall.

'I don't deserve you.' Matthew kisses Sally's cheek but she still doesn't turn to look at him properly.

'This is true.' She lets out a long sigh. 'Don't worry. I'll come round. It's just – I'm so tired. I honestly thought I knew what I was getting into.' At last she turns. 'But I realise now that I didn't at all.'

She looks right into his eyes and there's something in her expression that he can't quite read. 'It's hard to explain properly,' she continues, 'because I'm still working it out in my head. I just get scared. I do really love you—'

He can hear the 'but' coming and wonders if he should just interrupt. Make his case? That he'll step back from the case. The job. Everything . . .

'—but I don't love what you do.' She pauses, looking at the floor, and anxiety is coursing through him.

Don't say it. Don't say it, Sally.

He reaches out to touch her cheek, as if touching her will stop her saying it.

'I do get that you're not who you are unless you do this. And I fell in love with you *because* of who you are.' She takes in another deep breath and he finds that he's holding his own. 'So – here's what I think. You need to get back to Devon and do what you do best. I badly want this one to be over. I want you to find whoever's doing all this.' She kisses him and relief sweeps through him so fast that he feels almost light-headed. 'Fast as you can. Promise me, Matt?'

'I promise you.' He holds her close.

'You're crushing me.'

'Sorry.' He eases the grip but they stay locked. Ten seconds. Twenty. And then Sally steps back first, her eyes glistening as she tilts up her chin to regroup. She's still very afraid; he can see that. And Matthew cannot remember loving her more than he does in this moment.

Finally, she signals with her head that they should move. They've agreed he'll drive straight back to Devon, spend a night at home so he can get some rest before liaising with Mel first thing tomorrow. Friday. The day of the final graduation ceremony.

Matthew walks back into the kitchen and Sally follows, calling to Amelie to come and *say goodbye to Daddy*. He picks up his keys from the kitchen table, trying not to focus on the worry jar which Amelie packed in her bright pink case and which already has pride of place on the windowsill.

He kisses them both again, promising ice-cream sundaes on the seafront when he returns and hurries away to his car, fighting the hard knot in his stomach and tuning into the local radio for traffic updates.

He makes good time back to Devon and attempts an early night. But it's impossible. He sleeps badly and wakes early. He's never known a week like it and is not looking forward to returning to Maidstead Cathedral today. A crack-of-dawn text from Mel suggests an early catch up at their regular café. Already showered, he leaves straight away, expecting to arrive before her, but she's already on her second coffee as he slumps into the seat in their regular alcove.

'So you didn't sleep either?' She shakes her head. It's D-Day, after all; the day they've both been dreading. Another ceremony.

'Why here?' he asks. 'I thought that now I'm officially on the case, we didn't need to sneak around.' Matthew raises his hand to catch the eye of the waitress and orders a cappuccino. He glances around the room. He and Mel have met here for years, discreetly liaising on cases beneath the radar of Mel's colleagues.

'Dave's nose is a bit out of joint. I didn't want to rub salt in. Especially today. I need him on side today.' Mel finishes her drink and stacks it with the stained cup and saucer from her first round, pushing all the crockery to the edge of the table, ready for the waitress.

Dave is Mel's sergeant who would normally lead on interviews. He's a good operator and is still irked that his boss took over to interview Alex, with Matthew watching.

'I can handle Dave.' Matthew smiles as the waitress sets down his drink, waiting for her to cross the room before continuing. 'So where are we at, then?'

'We're pretty sure from the enhanced CCTV that it was Laura at Amelie's nursery.'

'Grief.' Matthew had expected this but still feels a ripple of unease.

'I'm so sorry about the way this has hit your family. I would never have asked if I'd had any idea—'

'I know.' Matthew lifts his hand to signal she's not to fret. She looks away for a moment, then back at his coffee cup.

'I've got two of the team checking CCTV in Somerset after the Wells Cathedral postcard to Ed and we may have picked her up there too.'

'Wells?'

'Yeah. A few days ago. The footage should be ready for review when we get back to the office.'

'So – what are you thinking? Laura back in the frame as a real suspect here?'

'I don't know really. I'll be happier when we get her in custody. Get a proper evaluation of her mental health. But I'm struggling to understand why she'd suddenly target Ed and his family after all these years. It feels a bit extreme to me. To fly to England out of the blue. Shoot his daughter at her graduation. Why? And she wouldn't be able to get a gun through airport security.'

'True. But we can't let that rule her out. She could have a contact here we don't know about.' Matthew scratches the back of his head. 'And she may be too unwell for the motive to be rational. Do we have anything more on her medical condition?'

'Not much. There seems to be a suggestion that her Capgras Syndrome could be linked to schizophrenia but it's a theory rather than a fact in Laura's case. Her files say she may occasionally have hallucinations. They've tried a variety of treatments. Long spells at home. Then back in the clinic. But they've never managed to stabilise her completely. The notes say she's been fixated recently on never having a family; she blames the *fake Ed*. I'm hoping to speak to her mother about that if she'll agree. The parents are divorced now. The father's remarried with a new family.'

'That could be a trigger?'

'Possibly. I'll check the timeline.'

Matthew lets out a long, slow breath. He's thinking of Laura standing at the perimeter of Amelie's playground. Knowing she's ill should make it easier for him to be tolerant but he's struggling. He looks at Mel. Her son is still very small. Still not sleeping, apparently.

'If it had been George. If he were older and it had been him?' He holds Mel's gaze.

'I'd want blood.' She tilts her head. 'You don't need to feel guilty for being mad, Matt, but I need you to harness that anger. Control it. I need to know you're OK. To go forward, I mean? Wanting blood in theory is one thing . . .'

'I'm not going to do anything stupid.'

'I know.'

'I've promised Sally I'm going to see this through. Fairly. Properly. Get the person behind all of this.'

'Good. Then we're on the same page.'

'And what's the latest on Alex?'

'No more from forensics. We've re-checked the footage placing him at the other end of the cathedral when Gemma was shot and it seems genuine. No obvious sign of doctoring but that's always a possibility. Also – Alex could have paid someone.'

'That's a bit of a stretch, isn't it?'

'I agree. It would be unusual. But let's face it, this is a very unusual case.' She pauses and closes her eyes. 'I should have cancelled the final graduation, shouldn't I?'

Matthew doesn't answer. It's an afternoon ceremony and they're right up against it now. With hindsight, cancelling was probably safer, but he knows what the political pressure's been like. The suits upstairs and the tourism chiefs all wanting signals that people are safe. That life must go on.

And then Mel's phone goes and she lifts it from the table, mouthing, 'Dave.'

Mel's eyes widen immediately as she puts the phone to her ear. 'Right. Area sealed off?' She stands, pausing to take in the reply. 'And SOCO there?' Another pause. 'Good. Take charge until I get there. Text me the address. Reckon I'll be half an hour. I'll get Matthew Hill to meet us there.' She listens some more, frowning. 'Get a photo of the wife. And her car registration on the system. Check family and friends. I want her found. Soon as.'

She ends the call and puts the phone in her pocket. Matthew's standing, pulling a note from his wallet to leave for the drinks.

'So?'

All the colour has drained from Mel's face. 'Looks like we may have found the father of Gemma's child.'

Matthew waits, stomach tightening.

'Professor Sam Blake. One of Gemma's English tutors – been found dead at his home.' She fishes her car keys from her bag as Matthew widens his eyes for more details.

'*Shot.*'

CHAPTER 51

THE PRIVATE INVESTIGATOR

The pattern of the adrenaline is always the same. A surge on the journey to a crime scene and then another spike when you actually see the body. Matthew is both used to it and paradoxically surprised by it every time.

A professional gear has always seen him through – in the years he was in the force and in his new business since. But always, deep down, there's that other less predictable response; the *human* response. Face to face with what one person can do to another.

By the time he's suited and booted in the white crime-scene paraphernalia, Matthew is perhaps ten minutes behind Mel. From the hallway, he can hear her liaising with the crime-scene manager. She's requesting backup from the same people who worked at the cathedral nine days back.

Mel glances down at the body on the floor as he takes it in for the first time.

'Told you it was a nasty one,' she says.

Nasty is not the word in Matthew's head. *Rage* is the word. He takes in the blood and the Halloween horror of the eye socket. The person who did this was, in the moment at least, full of anger beyond anything most people could imagine.

Sam Blake has not only been shot, his head has been bludgeoned so that one side of his face is completely disfigured – the left eye socket smashed in. A truly grotesque mess.

'Sorry. Could you step left, please?' A SOCO holding a camera is trying not to sound impatient. Matthew moves. It's a large bedroom, thankfully, which makes this first assessment just a little easier. From the corner of the room, Matthew glances from the body and the blood-soaked rug beneath it to the bedside cabinet which has a photograph of Sam beaming alongside a woman – presumably his wife.

Matthew leans forward, narrowing his eyes. It's a holiday snap. Looks like Greece – olive groves in the background. Hummus and tzatziki on the table in front of the couple. The professor is, *was*, a good-looking man. Strong jaw line. Sandy hair. Grey eyes. His wife's attractive too. Blonde. Petite. And quite a bit younger.

'Shot first or hit first?' Matthew asks.

'Not sure yet. With so much blood, hard to be sure. Will have to wait for the postmortem.' Mel is looking at the far wall, the smart, expensive-looking wallpaper splattered with red.

Matthew's eyes move to the blood-stained statue that lies alongside the body – presumably used to strike him. It's chunky. Dark green. He looks around the room to see its partner still in place on a shelf just inside the door. Not a statue at all but a heavy bookend in the shape of someone sitting and reading. The books, minus one of their supports, are now sloping at an angle, two very close to falling from the shelf. So the attacker grabbed one bookend on the way in? But why do that if you had a gun?

Matthew is trying to work out if this was someone who knew about the bookends. Or would they catch a stranger's eye easily?

He looks again at the body. There's a huge patch of blood soaking the pale-blue shirt at the chest and the rug beneath. The gunshot wound. Sam Blake looks at least six foot. Fit. The position of the body suggests he was facing the door, so facing his attacker. Seems unlikely anyone would risk striking him first. No. Shot first, *then* hit.

Matthew spends a few more minutes appraising the bedroom and then steps through the hallway to the room opposite. A chill runs instantly through him. It's a nursery in the making. The cot assembled, complete with mobile. A chair is set up in the corner as if ready for nursing, but the rest of the room is a work in progress. In the corner there are two large boxes – the labels confirming flat-pack furniture. One's clearly a changing station with drawers. A mat covered in brightly coloured animals is leaning alongside, still in its plastic wrapping.

An image flashes into his mind of Amelie on her changing mat when she was tiny. Skinny legs kicking in frustration. Puce face furious at his fumbling. *Sally, help me. I can't get the new nappy on.*

He pushes the image away as Mel walks past him. 'Meet you outside when you're ready, Matt?'

'Sure. What do we know about the wife?'

'Lily Blake. Fifteen years younger. *Missing,*' she says. 'I've put the call out.'

'Pregnant?'

'Yes.' Mel pauses, staring right into Matthew's eyes. 'Six or seven months according to the neighbour. She's not been seen for a while. I've sent Dave round to the parents. They live nearby.'

Outside later, as he waits for the full update from Melanie, Matthew stands across the street, taking in the red-brick suburban semi with its hydrangea and cluster of rose bushes. There's a hanging basket – well kept. Watered regularly. He's trying to imagine it. What exactly went on inside here today? Mel is still liaising with the uniformed officers who arrived on the scene first. House-to-house inquiries have started and neighbours say the couple had been volatile in recent months. Loud arguments. But no one heard a gunshot. The cleaner found him. She's still in shock, having cups of tea in a neighbour's house, giving her preliminary statement.

Social media means news travels fast these days and Matthew's not surprised to see a car pull up behind the cordon with the logo of a local news group. He's never understood why the media do that. Label themselves. Wouldn't they want to be discreet? It occurs to him that maybe they use different cars for different jobs. Maybe this is from the advertising department? Who knows?

Whatever the case, he's remembering the car-park drama with Alex and suspects a local TV crew will be along very soon too. It's going to be a nightmare once journalists realise the victim's from the university. Today of all days.

Matthew feels his phone vibrate in his pocket and takes it out to see another text from Amanda. *Can you tell me anything yet? What about the graduation?*

Damn.

Sorry. Not yet. He presses send; he'll ask Mel to call the chancellor. They'll probably need to make a joint statement but it will depend if the wife's found quickly; whether she can immediately be ruled in or out as a suspect. In effect, whether they need to put out an appeal to find her.

Matthew's thinking again of that nursery inside the house. He remembers so well Sally's clucking and fussing and worrying in the final days of her pregnancy. She wouldn't put the mobile up above the cot; was worried it would be bad luck. Tempting fate. He presses the speed dial and puts the phone to his ear.

'Is everything OK?' Sally sounds alarmed but it's so good to hear her voice.

'Yeah. I'm safe. But things have changed. You mustn't share this yet, honey, but there's been another shooting. Someone from the university.'

'Oh no. Are you wearing your jacket? Your bulletproof jacket?'

'Yes, I am.' This is a lie and he feels a pang of guilt. It's in his rucksack in the boot. He finds it uncomfortable and had no idea today would take this turn. 'I'm at the scene. I'm safe but it will probably be on the news soon. But listen; they're bound to up security even more now. At the hospital, the cathedral. I'm wondering if we should rethink security for you at the cottage. Just as a precaution.' He tries to keep his voice steady but his heart rate is increasing, thinking of Amelie on that changing mat a few years back. Of the doll delivered to their house. The woman – Laura probably – at the school. Of the horrible way his family has been sucked into this.

'But we were so careful. The hire car. Surely no one knows where we are.'

Matthew pauses. Sally's right. They were incredibly careful and it should be fine.

Should be.

'My gut says it's fine but have a think and let me know how you feel about it. I'll talk to Mel after we've processed the scene. It's a bit hectic right now. I'll have to go. How's our princess?'

'I'll send you a picture. You promise you'll be careful? And keep that jacket on.'

'I promise. Love you.'

He hangs up and is about to put the phone back in his pocket when a ping signals a text. He opens it. A picture of Amelie, beaming on the beach – the bright red bucket in one hand, the yellow spade in the other.

From Sally: *Be careful! We love you. x*

He'll book the security. Sod it. He'll just book the bloody security and tell Sally that Mel insisted. *Sorry, love. Procedure.*

Matthew clenches the phone in his hand to feel the connection, all the while watching Mel on the drive of the house, talking to two of the uniformed officers. A huddle of neighbours just beyond the cordon is being approached by a reporter from the media car. Here we go, Matthew thinks – his brain sucked back from Cornwall. From the beach. From Amelie and Sally. He scans the scene, still gripping the phone as he looks up and down the road, checking for CCTV cameras, trying to process the surprising turn in this case before he gets a chance to properly talk to Mel. See what she thinks. So have they got it all wrong? Is this not about Alex or Laura?

Alex is still in custody and how the hell would Laura even know about Gemma and this professor?

So is this actually more straightforward? The jealous rage of a betrayed wife. Did Sam's wife find out about Gemma? Was it simply all too much with the pregnancy?

But would a jealous wife take a gun to a cathedral and shoot someone in broad daylight? Would she? *Could* she?

Matthew thinks again of the body in the bedroom. That smashed-in eye socket. The evidence of white-hot rage. Then he calls up the image of the holiday photograph beside the bed. The smiling face of the petite Lily. Tanned and holding up her glass of wine glinting in the sunlight.

He's not wondering if she could be capable of this. The heavy bookend in her hand. Smashing. Obliterating. He's seen enough of the darker underbelly of life to park any surprise quickly; to stop questioning what ordinary people are capable of.

What he's wondering about is the gun. If this really is down to a tortured wife, he'd expect something more domestic. A kitchen knife. A spur-of-the-moment lashing out.

But *a gun*? It's always been a puzzle to everyone on this case, Matthew especially, that Gemma was shot. Firearms are the territory of drugs crime and gangs, not domestics. And how the hell would nice, middle-class Lily even get a gun?

CHAPTER 52

THE DAUGHTER - *BEFORE*

Discuss the theme of parental responsibility and neglect in relation to the novel Frankenstein *by Mary Shelley.*

Don't know why I'm bothering with the fake essay headings. It's official. No . . . more . . . essays. And for a blink at least, I hardly care if 'A' is hacking me. Guess what?

I got my first!!! Results came through about ten minutes ago and for a blissful moment it really did make me forget everything. I've phoned home and Mum and Dad are over the moon. Neighbours must have heard Mum shriek for miles.

It was lovely, actually. For those few brief minutes on the phone, to hear Mum so happy. I've only ever wanted Mum and Dad to be proud of me. But when I finished the call, I just looked at the phone and the tears came again. And it's horrible, realising that the good feeling can't last. I've had to lie to them about why I'm hanging around until the graduation ceremony. I've told them it's to do with the flat lease and helping out to cover a mate's job in a coffee shop. Felt terrible, but I just can't face going home yet.

Look at me; a complete hormonal mess already. I'm afraid I'll just break down.

Can't even bear to mention what's happened with that adoption idea. Talk about a wrong steer. Not even legal, I've discovered since. And the advice I was being given? Very, very dodgy . . .

I'm distancing myself now but it's all going horribly pear-shaped.

And the worst thing of all is I think I may have been wrong about who's been targeting me. My social media and everything.

I've got this truly horrible feeling it might actually be someone connected with the snake's wife. There's been this woman watching me around the campus. Not his *wife* herself but someone a little bit older – and I'm starting to wonder if she's a friend of hers or something.

I had this sort of weird feeling of being watched a few times. I put it down to yet more paranoia at first, and then this one day I caught the woman's reflection in the glass door of the coffee shop on campus so I was able to watch her without her realising. I pretended to wave at someone inside the shop at the counter and she was definitely eyeballing me. And it's happened again since. She carries a magazine or a paper and sits on benches and stuff. But every time I move, she moves.

I'm sure I'm not imagining it.

So if it is someone, put up to it, I mean, by 'S''s wife, I really don't know what to do. Maybe I should just confront her. Walk up to her and have it out – *what the hell do you think you're doing? Why are you watching me?*

Problem is the messages are so weird. *He's not who he says he is.*

Is that really something his wife would write? If she's found out about us, I mean. I suppose she might mean he's not genuine. Maybe she thinks I believe he's single or properly separated. But

I can't help wondering – surely she'd just write something angry. Bitchy. More direct.

I'm trying really hard to just ignore it all, to concentrate on getting through graduation and how the hell I'm going to tell Mum and Dad afterwards. About the baby. But every time I pull myself together, I get more DMs.

More and more, I keep thinking about karma; that I've brought all of this on myself. I mean – a fling with a married man. What was I thinking?

Maybe the bottom line here is actually very simple.

I deserve all of this.

CHAPTER 53

THE MOTHER

My eyes hurt nearly all the time now. Ed says I'm not blinking enough; that I've developed the habit of staring at Gemma, afraid to close my own eyes even for a nanosecond, in case I miss her waking up.

The hospital atmosphere is dry enough, to be frank, so it's small wonder this is making it worse. I've tried putting drops in my eyes to soothe the itching, and I pointedly look away from Gemma as often as I dare to try to prove to Ed that I'm not obsessing.

It's wasted effort. I *am* obsessing and he knows it but we're trying to be kinder to each other. To get past the lies, the half-truths and the strain and to put all our effort into Gemma now. It's more than twenty-four hours since she opened her eyes and there's been no change since. The doctor came to talk to us last night. He confirms it's a good sign but there's no way of knowing if she's about to wake up for sure. They're monitoring her even more closely, but we just need to carry on waiting.

I didn't sleep much. Never do. So I've already read her two more chapters of *The Mill on the Floss* but my voice is croaky – the tiredness, I guess, so I've popped the headphones back on with some gentle music. I do hope she can hear it.

I reach out to sip my coffee, badly needing the caffeine, but it's still scorching. Ed's standing at the window of our cubicle, looking out on to the main ward. He has asbestos fingers and an asbestos tongue and is drinking his own coffee without even wincing.

'That's odd,' he says suddenly. 'Have you noticed they seem to be moving the other patients out?'

At first, I wonder what he means. We're used to patients being moved in and out. This has always seemed to be some kind of transitionary unit between theatre and the main wards. Maybe overflow? The number of other patients varies from day to day. I've even heard some visitors mumble complaints about being in the same space as Gemma, once they spot the guard. *Is it safe? Do we have to be here?*

The nurses always reassure them and no one seems to stay here long. But there tend to be two or three other patients overnight.

Ed looks really puzzled and so I stand up to get a better view over Gemma's head. He's right. The two beds opposite are already empty but the remaining beds – with patients in situ – are being wheeled out by porters with staff juggling the drips and paraphernalia. This much bustle hasn't happened before. So many moved out on the same day.

'You're right. There's something going on.' My voice is low and I can feel anxiety creeping back into my stomach. 'Ask the police guard. Or one of the nurses.'

We can both see that our guard's on his radio. Ed moves to the door, opens it and calls out to one of the nurses. 'Excuse me. Can you tell us what's happening?'

She looks flustered, glancing at the police officer. 'Probably best you speak to the police. Just a precaution. I'm sure it's nothing to worry about.'

The guard hears this and lifts his hand to signal for us to wait a moment before turning away to continue talking on his radio. Infuriatingly we can't hear what he's saying.

I'm remembering the horrible scene that Alex caused. The shouting and the smashed glass. But Alex is in custody. Surely they won't give him bail again?

'Do you think this is about Laura? They said she's in the country. You don't think they suspect she's coming *here,* do you?'

'I don't know. I honestly don't know.' Ed's still in the doorway, one arm now craned over the top of his head as he waits.

At last the police officer turns to us, gesturing for us to move back into the cubicle together. He shuts the door.

'Can I ask if you've let anyone know about Gemma's condition? About the fact she opened her eyes yesterday?'

'I texted a friend.' I don't tell him who. Wonder why he wants to know. 'Well not texted. I told her on WhatsApp. Why?'

'Can you please message her now to keep that confidential? Did you tell anyone else?'

'No. No.' I feel flustered and confused as I take my phone from my pocket and fumble a quick message, trying not to sound too desperate. Just an issue of confidentiality. Not wanting the media to know.

When I've finished, the officer signals for us to sit but I shake my head. 'Please just tell us what's happening. Is it Laura? Ed's ex-wife?'

'I can't say who's involved but there's been a shooting that may be connected to the attack on Gemma.' His expression is grave. 'It's procedure to up the security. They may be sending an armed guard. Just until they assess where we are.'

'They think someone might come here? With a *gun*?'

'No one's saying that. But it's a live situation. I'm just telling you what I know. You mustn't share this. Or any news on the possibility of Gemma waking up. You understand?'

I nod, my mouth gaping as my head moves involuntarily. 'Can we speak to DI Sanders?'

'She's overseeing things at the moment. But I'm sure she'll want to update you personally when we know more.'

'That's why they're moving the other patients. They think someone might come here. With a gun?'

'No, I didn't say that. But we want to lock this unit down as a precaution. Once the other patients are out, the unit will, in effect, be out of bounds. Staff passes only. DI Sanders' orders.'

'OK. Thank you.' Ed's tone is steadier than mine as he turns but I notice that both his hands are in tight fists.

I look at him and have never been so afraid. It occurs to me that someone mad enough to shoot Gemma in broad daylight might take someone hostage, like a human shield, to get in here. A nurse? A porter?

Suddenly no amount of security feels enough. Suddenly I have this horrible picture in my brain of a member of the hospital staff, gun to their head, being marched right down the centre of this ward.

CHAPTER 54

THE PRIVATE INVESTIGATOR

Everything's moving so fast that Matthew feels the familiar rush of blood and energy as he drives. He's praying this isn't another wrong steer. His gut's telling him that it's just too strong a coincidence and he has to drill down to the bottom of this as fast as he can, for Mel's sake.

She's still at the crime scene and they're up against the clock. He checks the time on his dashboard. Nearly 10 a.m. *Please be in. Please be in.*

The village near Exeter's an odd choice for a PI's office – a bit quiet – but Wendy March is an odd kind of PI. He's never much liked her – a maverick at best – and the thought of her being wound up in all this and failing to come forward is both infuriating and soul-destroying. No wonder PIs get bad press.

Wendy's card has just been found at Sam Blake's home, among the wife Lily's clothes. It was tucked in the pocket of a raincoat that looked as if it had been worn recently. Further inspection suggests the wife recently packed some of her clothes. This fits with neighbours' suggestions that she's not been around for a little while.

It was Wendy who Matthew saw at the university campus. As soon as he shared this with Mel, she was furious. Dispatched him to speak to Wendy face to face. *Bring her in if you need to. I want everything she knows.*

There's parking near the office thankfully and Matthew finds coins in the glove compartment to avoid a fine. The office is above a pasty shop of all things, with a separate entrance. As he rings the bell, Matthew wonders how it will compare with his own office.

Come on. Come on. Answer.

It feels strange to be turning up at a rival's place. Correction; not a rival. Wendy is a different kind of PI altogether. Her website is all about the money and all about the matrimonials – the very work Matthew hates. She even offers a lie-detector test. Classy.

At last the buzzer on the door sounds and he climbs stairs a good deal less steep than his own to find no second door at the top – just a small, open-plan office.

Wendy March is on the phone but stands the minute she spots him, making apologies to her caller and ringing off.

'Matthew Hill? What are you doing here?'

'I'm here on behalf of DI Sanders.' Matthew pauses, not wanting to give away too much yet about the new crime scene. 'We're investigating the attack on Gemma Hartley.'

'Mrs Hartley gave you my name?' Wendy looks shocked.

Matthew's equally shocked. 'No, she didn't.' His mind does a somersault as he tries to regroup. Rachel Hartley wasn't pressed for the name of the PI she used to investigate her husband Ed. As nothing was found, it wasn't important.

'So *you* were the PI that Rachel Hartley hired?'

'Isn't that why you're here?'

'No, it's not. What do you know of Lily Blake? Are you working for her too?'

'I might be. What's it to you?' Wendy now looks less assured, her neck starting to redden, the blush moving up towards her chin like colour soaking on litmus paper. 'My work with my clients is confidential. We aren't all in the pockets of the police.' She widens her eyes. Cocky expression, despite the flush.

'A girl's in a coma with part of her leg gone. Anyone with any decency and any information has a duty to come forward. I have no idea why you wouldn't see that, Wendy. And why were you at the university the other day?'

'I'm going to have to ask you to leave. If DI Sanders wants to speak to me, she can do that herself. You have no jurisdiction here.'

'No problem.' He takes out his phone. 'I'll get a uniformed officer here to arrest you. Marked car, flashing lights, all the neighbours watching?'

'On what possible grounds?'

Matthew looks away to the window and decides to gamble. Hell. It'll be on the news any moment anyway.

'There's been another attack. Linked to the Gemma Hartley case, we suspect. And so I'm going to ask you again. Are you working for Lily Blake?'

The colour from Wendy's neck moves right up to her chin. 'Has she been hurt?'

'No. But we need to find her urgently.' Matthew takes in Wendy's expression. She doesn't know, he's pretty sure of that. 'Her husband's dead, Wendy. Sam Blake's been shot.'

'*Dead?*' Wendy's shock is clearly genuine – the blush fading and her face taking on an altogether paler tone. All her capillaries apparently in overdrive. 'I'm sorry. I need to sit down.'

'So you found out her husband was cheating? Gave her the evidence?' Matthew moves closer to her desk.

'Yes. But this isn't my fault. This is what I do. What clients *ask* me to do.'

'Never mind about fault. Just start talking, Wendy. I need to know the timeline. What exactly you found. And where Lily might be now. She's not with her parents. Do you have any idea where she is?'

CHAPTER 55

THE FATHER – *NOW*

Ed presses the buttons on the coffee machine and watches, in a daze, as the sequence begins. He's so tired. His mind's still on the ward, taking in Rachel's exhausted face, and as the first cup fires into position and the flow of hot liquid begins he realises that he's got the order wrong. Too distracted. He's pressed for two cappuccinos. *Damn*. Rachel wanted black.

Truth is he didn't want to leave the unit at all but Rachel was getting in such a state. Another shooting? The day of the final graduation. They can't believe it. Rachel wants him to quietly check the corridor. The lockdown security. *See if there's an armed presence, Ed. See if there are proper checks on the door. Please . . .*

Rachel looks completely done in and he wonders how much more she can take. He's found out from the nurses that she never uses the relatives' room to rest. A lump forms in his throat as he thinks of what a good mother she's been – has always tried to be. Despite what she went through herself as a child; maybe precisely *because* of what she went through as a child.

He genuinely had no idea about her father – the drinking and the violence – and wonders why Rachel's mother has never said anything either. Their joint secret. All these years. Their blanked past.

He keeps rewinding scenes and watching through a new lens; all those times it drove him mad to see Rachel dismiss Gemma to her room to try to calm her down. Always shutting conflict down with her babbling and her baking.

Oh, Rachel.

The guilt over Laura is like this cancer growing inside him now. If he's wrong, if Laura is in any way connected with what has happened, he will never forgive himself.

Ed watches the second cup zoom into position beneath the second spout. He'll have to find somewhere to pour one away. Order a third? He badly wants to get back to the unit and feels a shiver of unease.

He waits for the drips to cease and then puts one of the coffees on the ledge to the side of the machine so he can order Rachel's black one. Again the machine revs into action while Ed takes his phone from his pocket.

He's already tried to speak to DI Sanders. That's the real reason he caved and stepped out. He's feeling angry on top of his guilt, seeing his wife so very upset. Never mind how busy DI Sanders is. Why hasn't she phoned? They need to know what's going on.

Ed starts to scroll for DI Sanders' number and for the first time notices the date in the corner of the screen. He pauses and stares – and suddenly it hits him.

Friday the twenty-sixth.

It's all been so much lately that he'd lost track of days, never mind dates. But as it dawns, he feels disorientated. For a second he's not here at all; he's transported back in time – Laura frowning as she places two alternative versions of their wedding invitation on the breakfast bar in front of them.

Which one do you think? I want classy. I think I prefer the cream with gold but I'm not sure. The printer needs a decision today otherwise we'll lose our place in his queue.

How could he forget this? Not think of the date. Notice the date.

'Excuse me, but have you finished?'

Ed turns to find a woman waiting behind him for the coffee machine. He almost tells her to push off but just stops himself. 'Sorry. Sorry. Distracted.'

He grabs the two coffees and casts around for somewhere to put them down safely, all the while frantically doing maths in his head. A chair's the only option. He huffs his annoyance, placing the two cups down near the centre of the seat, but it's not flat and one cup tips instantly, spraying hot coffee everywhere. *Oh, sod it.*

Ed leaves the mess, the woman at the machine tutting loudly as he takes out his phone to dial DI Sanders. It goes to voicemail so he rings Matthew Hill – the PI he went to see, who's now working as Mel's sidekick. Which Ed doesn't quite understand. Don't the police have their own people?

'Matthew Hill.'

'Matthew, it's Ed Hartley. I can't get hold of DI Sanders and something's just occurred to me. She asked if there might be a trigger. For Laura – my ex-wife.'

'I hope you're not going to just leave that.' The woman from the coffee machine has walked right up to Ed, leaning in to confront him.

'Look. Could you just mind your own—'

'What did you say?' Matthew's tone is confused.

'Sorry. Not you. Someone this end.'

'Oh right. Go on.'

'Well, there might be. A trigger for Laura. I don't know why I didn't think of it before.'

CHAPTER 56

THE PRIVATE INVESTIGATOR

Matthew punches in the search to his sat nav. An hour and a half. *Damn*. Mel will need to send a local unit but he wants to be there too. In fact he wants to *lead* on this. He'll ask them to wait for him.

'I'm sorry Wendy but I'm going to have to make a detour. Emergency.' He carries on round the roundabout while the sat nav recalculates and then takes the right exit.

'So where are we going now? I thought we were going to the station to wait for your boss. I have work I should be doing, you know.'

Matthew doesn't answer but instead is doing the calculation in his head. He should make it to Wells just after 11 a.m. if the traffic's OK. Doable. It's a long shot but the best use of his time while Mel focuses on finding Sam's wife. And he wants to be the one who brings Laura in.

He thinks again of her standing at the railings by Amelie's school, handing her the note.

'I asked you a question.' Wendy's curt, her arms crossed.

'OK. Start talking and I might answer. Tell me everything you told Lily about her husband. Everything. We need to find her.'

Matthew's head is practically bursting with the possibilities. Laura, or Sam's wife? Or Alex hiring someone? What the hell is really going on with this case?

'Tell me first where we're going.'

'Detour to Wells.'

'That's bloody miles. You can't just kidnap me. Let me out.'

'Sorry. No can do. We're on a dual carriageway and it'll take too long. You need to help me out here so cut the victim act. You know full well you should have checked in with the police the minute Gemma's name was released.'

Wendy stares again out of the passenger window. 'People don't trust you if you go running to the police. My clients like to be sure everything we do is confidential. I have the right to make a living.'

Matthew bites his tongue; Wendy was never in the force. She came to PI work via security. Has a whole different take. It's a waste of time arguing with her. Outcome's the issue now. Also time. Wendy's another pair of eyes; he might not rate her moral compass, but word is she's very good at what she does. She probably has more undercover hours under her belt than any backup he can get at short notice for this. Fact is, she just might be useful if he can get her to cooperate.

It's all a long shot, but if Ed *is* right and Laura's going back to the cathedral for their anniversary, they're going to need a very careful approach. They have no way of knowing if Laura is armed. Just how dangerous she may be. Mel might want to clear or close the cathedral but Matthew doubts they'll have time or a mandate for that at such short notice on a hunch.

He'll just have to keep this as low key as possible. Bad news is Laura knows what he looks like. Must have checked his website and address to reach him through Amelie. He could request an undercover female officer to assist but – no time. The fallout will be horrendous if they get this wrong. Last thing they need is another scene in a cathedral.

'How do you fancy helping me bring in a key suspect? It's a long shot. Might be a wild goose chase, but if it comes off, you'll get all the brownie points from the DI. She'll probably stop talking about charging you for obstructing the inquiry.'

'She can't charge me. Don't be ridiculous. I haven't *done* anything.'

'You failed to tell us that Gemma Hartley was key in one of your marital cases. DI Sanders is not happy.'

Wendy narrows her eyes and then turns to him. 'OK. I might help.'

'Good. But first tell me again about what you passed on to Lily.'

Wendy talks him through it. How Lily Blake was sick of rumours about her husband and wanted to know one way or the other. She hired Wendy to find out. It didn't take long.

Wendy discovered he was seeing two students: Gemma Hartley, and more recently a mature student, late twenties, studying politics. That's why she was back at the campus – updating on the latest affair. She supplied picture evidence to the wife weekly, got paid and thought no more of it until Gemma Hartley was shot. She said, even then, she was sure it couldn't be anything to do with Lily. A timid personality. Also heavily pregnant. Matthew remains shocked that Wendy didn't contact the police.

He turns briefly to her but parks his outrage. Needs must. She'd better be as good as he's heard.

'Right. This long shot. I should be completely transparent here.' He pauses. 'I'll request backup but we may not get it and there's a small chance our target could be armed.'

CHAPTER 57

THE DAUGHTER – *NOW*

She's tired of it all. This strange place. This unending sleep – stuck by the ocean.

She wants so badly to wake in her bedroom at home with the fairy lights wound around the bedhead and all the books on their shelves on the opposite wall. Colour-coded. Spines aligned. She can picture the room so clearly in her head but she can't *make* it there; can't even make herself dream about it.

Instead she 'wakes' always to the sound of the sea. Soft and whispering. But she's not awake, is she? That's the cruelty of it here. Every time she opens her eyes, she's trapped in the same limbo. The same dream? The only new thing is that sometimes now there are distant voices too, as if coming from the sky.

One time, it was like an audio book playing on the breeze. When she listened more closely, it sounded like her mother's voice as the narrator. Strange. Impossible. She felt her ears for earbuds and her pocket for a phone to turn up the volume but there was no phone. So where was it coming from?

She called out – *turn it up; I can't quite hear* – but no one answered so she closed her eyes and strained to keep very, very still to listen. Familiar words. Familiar names. Maggie Tulliver. *The Mill on the Floss*. It took her back to school, reading in the library at lunchtime, and she felt a shiver, remembering how the story ends so badly. So sadly.

She thinks again of the sea, always stretching so far in front of her in these dreams. Waves rolling in the distance. Sometimes she wonders if she's supposed to swim. Is that it? But she's afraid of the currents and the rip tides. She remembers her mother at the beach when she was little – *watch the flags; there are rip tides*. And she thinks again of Maggie Tulliver. The water. Sinking *down, down*.

She wants so badly to go home but she just can't work out how. She still can't feel one of her legs properly, as if she's slept on it awkwardly. She waits for the feeling to return but how can she swim meantime? Will her arms alone be strong enough?

In the last dream or waking, or whatever this is, when she opened her eyes there was this huge flash of light in the sky. Not blue. No clouds. Just this huge expanse of blinding light. She must, by mistake, have looked straight into the sun. It hurt and so she closed her eyes.

And then, in the darkness, she felt that lovely thing again. Warmth on her skin. Like the soft spray from the sea on to her forehead. Only somehow she knows that it isn't the sea mist . . .

Suddenly she aches for her mother. For the voice on the breeze. And she misses her so very, very badly that it physically hurts deep inside her. She wants to cry but can never find any tears.

CHAPTER 58

THE PRIVATE INVESTIGATOR

Nearing the cathedral, Matthew pulls into a parking space as his phone rings. Mel.

'I've got a uniformed team there but no armed response. I'm not happy. Think we should leave it to the locals. They can liaise with the cathedral.'

'Wendy and I have a plan. We can do this, Mel.'

'Wendy? No way. I don't want that woman anywhere near this, Matthew. Have you gone mad?'

'Mel. You have to trust me. We've talked it through on the drive. If Laura *is* there, she'll respond to her. I know she will. This will work. Laura must know what I look like. Wendy's our best bet. If Laura sees uniforms, she could panic.'

Matthew thinks of the message in the note given to Amelie, now in the forensics lab. *You have to help me, Matthew. No one believes me. He's not who he says he is.*

'Did you get through to Laura's mother?'

'Yes. And she confirms that Laura's been talking about the anniversary – silver wedding. Obsessing again about finding the real Ed. But she didn't take it seriously.'

'Right. So this could be more than a hunch?'

There's a very long pause during which Matthew gets out of the car and moves to his boot. He signals to his backpack and Wendy nods. He watches her take out his bulletproof vest and take off her jacket to put it on underneath. He's worried it will show but thankfully Wendy's jacket has a high collar.

'Any progress with Sam's wife?' Matthew checks his watch as he moves off, Wendy following as she buttons up her jacket. Eleven o'clock. They need to move.

'Her car's been picked up on motorway cameras. We're on it. Local car tailing.'

'Good. That's good. So will you message uniformed to let me take charge of this here? Please, Mel. I've got this.'

There's another pause.

'I want you both in vests. Do you have a spare?'

'Yes.' Another lie. But he needs to be there too, albeit out of sight. He's thinking of Amelie. The doll with the bleeding eyes. Laura at the school boundary. He needs this to be over.

'We need clearance from the cathedral.'

'There isn't time, Mel. Laura could get away.'

'I can't have the public put at risk.'

'If Laura's about with a gun in her bag, they're already at risk. I can handle this, Mel. I'll keep everyone else away. Keep it nice and calm.'

'It's risky, Matt.'

'Look. You need to trust me. Message uniformed to stay out of sight – and let me know where they are. And can you tell them they answer to me? Can you do that?'

'OK.' She pauses. 'Matt. Good luck.'

Matthew releases a breath and can feel his adrenaline pumping. Wendy has a good plan but if it backfires, it will be Mel's head on the block.

He puts his phone back in his pocket and updates Wendy as they head to the cathedral. There's a market en route; a lot of people about. He remembers the chaos at the graduation ceremony. Everyone running . . .

'So our target wanted them to come back here for their anniversary?' Wendy is now taking in the cathedral.

'Yes. As I say – a long shot. But if she turns up, we need to keep her inside the cathedral. Until we're sure she's not armed.'

Wendy nods.

'Not too late to change your mind.' He turns to look at her, to be clear he means this.

'I'm fine. Let's get this done.'

Matthew moves off again. 'I wish to God she didn't know what I look like. I'll have to keep back with uniformed. Keep your phone line open in your top pocket – I need to know the moment you have her bag.'

'I know what I'm doing.' Wendy sounds a little cocky but Matthew can see that in truth she's a little nervous which is no bad thing. She needs to be cautious, not overconfident.

Once they reach reception and the shop, Matthew moves behind a display and Wendy directs a member of staff to speak to him.

'Are the police on the premises? My name is Matthew Hill. You should have had a call from my inspector?'

'Yes.' The woman looks very worried. 'We're trying to get hold of the verger to handle this. I don't have the authority—'

'Please don't be alarmed. We haven't got much time. I'm going to keep everyone safe but we need to make an arrest as discreetly and as quickly as we can. Have you cancelled the midday tour?'

'Yes. We're telling people he's off sick. But like I say, I need to speak to someone more senior—'

'No time. Just don't allow anyone else through. Unless there's a woman with long, curly hair. Like this.' He takes out his phone to show her the picture of Laura. 'She can go through if she turns up. No one else. Understood?'

The woman picks up the phone, clearly concerned about protocols.

'Where are the officers?'

'Through there.' She points.

'Thank you.' Matthew turns to Wendy. 'I'm going to speak to them. Keep your phone line open like I said. You got enough battery?'

'What do you think I am, an amateur? Of course I've got enough battery. Does the vest show?'

Matthew shakes his head, still wishing he could step up himself. 'She may not even turn up.'

Wendy shrugs and heads off through the cathedral to get in position near the clock. Matthew retreats to the centre of the cathedral, out of sight, to brief the two uniformed officers who've been discreetly asking visitors to leave – allegedly for a staff fire drill. Fortunately, it's quiet. Just a few tourists who leave without a fuss.

Now they just have to wait.

CHAPTER 59

THE FATHER - *NOW*

Ed puts the two coffees on the bedside cabinet and turns to Rachel.

'Sorry I was so long. Spilled the first coffees. Stupid of me. But I just spoke to the police. There's a lot going on, apparently. They hope it will be over soon. Ahead of the ceremony, I mean.'

Rachel still looks terrified. 'Did they check you coming in? Was the door security good?'

'It was fine. They checked.'

'Good. Good.' She's sitting on the chair alongside Gemma's bed, her right foot flipping up and down furiously with the tension. She seems to notice him staring at it and uncrosses her legs, putting both feet on the floor, clearly struggling to sit still.

'So what exactly's going on? What did they say?'

'No specifics. Just that there's a live operation. More arrests imminent, by the sounds of things. It's going to be all right, Rachel.'

'Is it?' She looks out on to the now empty ward. 'Why's there no armed guard?'

'DI Sanders said there should be a team downstairs soon. Just a precaution. I don't know if they'll come up to the ward. I don't know how they do these things. Maybe they're waiting to see if they pull off these arrests.'

'What arrests?'

'I'm not sure. She said they have two strong leads. She's going to call and update us as soon as anything happens.'

'Is it Laura? Have they found Laura?'

Ed hasn't told Rachel about the anniversary; that today would have been his and Laura's silver wedding anniversary. That Laura had once said they should go back to the place they met to celebrate. He feels so stupid and so guilty for not thinking of it before.

What if this really was the trigger for it all? What if Laura, in her delusions and her illness, somehow latched on to the date? What if all of this really is . . . his . . . fault?

And then he notices Rachel's expression changing. She's looking at Gemma's bed, at first frowning. Next, her whole face darkening. 'Ed. Look.'

He turns to their daughter, the headphones still in place, and something inside him shifts. Breaks. Gemma's eyes remain firmly closed. She's as still as ever. Skin pale.

But trailing across each cheekbone is a haunting but unmistakable line – the droplets catching the light from the fluorescent strip overhead.

Gemma is *crying*.

CHAPTER 60

THE PRIVATE INVESTIGATOR

Matthew and the two uniformed officers are waiting, concealed behind pillars in the central area of the cathedral called the Quire. They can't be seen from the clock area, which is off to one side, but it also means Matthew can't see what's going on.

The line's open to Wendy's phone, tucked in her top pocket, so he daren't speak, in case Laura's appeared and he's overheard. It would all have been so much easier if there had been time to plan with proper comms. Earpieces.

It's quarter to twelve. He expected Laura to turn up early. It was always a long shot but what if he's called this wrong? What if he should really be at the other cathedral – Maidstead – helping Mel check all the security? Finding Sam's wife Lily? One of the uniformed officers, an affable-looking guy, leans forward as if to speak, but Matthew puts his finger up to his lips then waves his other hand to signal that he should stay back. Keep quiet.

And then at last . . .

'Do you know what happened to the guide?' A female voice. Soft Canadian accent. He can only just make it out and has to press the phone closer to his ear, adjusting the volume to maximum.

'Off ill, apparently. I think they're probably all volunteers. Shame. I always prefer it with a guide.' Wendy sounds genuinely disappointed. Also convincing. Matthew puts his thumbs up to signal to the two uniformed officers that Laura's turned up.

He sees them exchange a nervous look and Matthew suddenly feels the full force of the risk he's taking here. There are cathedral staff and volunteers on site. They've been told to retreat to the shop area but there's still a risk. Uniformed have explained this is a key arrest but he's breached protocols. He should probably have spoken to the verger's office himself but there wasn't time.

She'd better not be armed. *If anyone gets hurt* . . .

'Just us then,' Wendy adds, clearly as a signal to Matthew. 'Expected it to be busier on a Friday. Maybe people cancelled. With the guide being ill, I mean.'

Matthew feels a tiny flicker of relief. At least no other visitors are nearby. *Good.*

'I looked it up online and they said noon's the best time for the clock but I don't quite know what to expect. Any idea?'

'I've seen it before. It's charming.' Laura's voice again. Still very quiet. Clipped too. Matthew worries that it's stress, which will make her more unpredictable.

'Oh, so not your first visit then?'

'No. I came years ago. Long time ago.'

'Oh right. Is that an American accent? Sorry to be nosy. I love an accent.'

'Canadian.'

'Oh right. I'm quite local really. From the south-west. Devon actually. Staying with a friend nearby. She's working today so I'm just killing time.'

Matthew's almost smiling at how good Wendy is.

'Actually, I've been walking miles this morning. Feet are killing me. Just need to sit down a bit. Would you mind awfully if I move your bag? Take the weight off.'

This is it. Matthew raises his arm to the two officers as a signal to stand by. He's already warned them that Laura's unstable. That they'll need to tread gently.

And then – Wendy's voice is much louder as if she's pulled the phone from her pocket. 'I have the bag. Move now. Target's isolated.'

'Go, guys.' Matthew sweeps his hand as a signal.

'Laura,' Wendy continues. 'I need you to stay calm. I'm actually an investigator and these two policemen you can see just want to have a little chat with you. No one's going to hurt you, I promise. Stay right where you are. And please raise your arms in the air for me.'

Wendy's now walked backwards and is just visible from Matthew's vantage point. She's holding Laura's bag at arm's length. Matthew moves forward himself.

'What's going on? Give my bag back! Give me my bag back!' Laura's shouting and can be heard across the cathedral as Matthew watches the two officers close in, urging her to stay calm.

We just need to talk to you, ma'am. Both arms in the air, please. That's it.

'Any weapon?' Matthew's heart's beating fast as one of the officers examines the bag and then Laura's coat pockets.

'No weapon.'

Matthew feels a wave of relief. He stares up at the magnificence of the cathedral's stonework as he dials Mel's number.

He's already thinking of the security sweep under way at the *other* cathedral. And he needs to know if they've found Sam's wife.

CHAPTER 61

THE MOTHER

I am again trawling through the laptop, trying to find anything else Gemma wrote that might be important. Help us.

I have to struggle not to torment myself; to re-read the entries that hurt so much.

> *I keep thinking about my mum and how I couldn't in a million years have this kind of conversation or this kind of relationship with her.*

'You OK? What are you looking for?' Ed looks worried.

'Just looking through photographs.' I'm not ready to share what I've found. I don't know why. Shame? Or maybe the same old, same old. Not wanting or knowing how to *talk* about things.

There's a noise outside our cubicle and I look up through the window to see a nurse talking to the guard. He nods and there's a tap on the door.

'Your sister's here to see you. Shall I let her through?'

'I don't *have* a sister.' I feel a punch to my gut and put the laptop down.

I stand. Ed stands.

'My wife doesn't have a sister, Officer.' Ed is glancing between the guard and the nurse. 'So – what does she look like, this woman? Does she have long, strawberry-blonde hair?'

I feel a wave of terror. *Laura?*

'No.' The nurse looks puzzled. 'I'm so sorry. I didn't let her through. She's out in the corridor. I followed the rules.' She looks petrified. 'She seemed very nice. Very convincing.'

'What does she *look like*?' Ed repeats.

'She has a short black crop. Like a pixie cut.'

'What age?'

'Young. Thirties.'

'Do I look as if I have a sister in her thirties?' I can't help my tone. I'm so tired of all this. Exhausted by the fear. The constant cycle of adrenaline, wondering what the hell is coming next.

I glance at Gemma, her face dried of the tears now. The headphones back in place.

When, oh when, will all this be over?

'It'll be another journalist,' Ed pipes up. 'I bet it's another bloody journalist. Why can't they just leave us alone?'

With all the coverage ramping up for the final graduation ceremony, I wonder how we're going to make it through today.

'She's still in the corridor.' The nurse is now talking directly to the guard, tipping her head towards the main door to the unit in the distance. 'Do you handle this or shall I call hospital security? I'm so, so sorry. I honestly didn't realise—'

CHAPTER 62

THE PRIVATE INVESTIGATOR

Matthew keeps looking at his watch, willing time to slow down. Mel wants him at Maidstead Cathedral as soon as possible. But it's tight. He's dropped Wendy back – they'll do a debrief later – but everything's happening all at once.

Half an hour ago, Mel called – clearly feeling the pressure. Sam's wife Lily has been picked up on the motorway so technically they're in the clear. All suspects with motives in custody. But Mel's now worrying they should have cancelled the final cathedral ceremony from the off.

I made the wrong call, didn't I? It's too much all in one day.

No, Mel. You've done great. We have them all in custody. We did it. We beat the deadline.

But we don't know which one . . .

Take a breath, Mel. And take it from me. We did OK.

It's normal to feel like this. Frustrated. Getting the suspects in custody is only ever the beginning. Very few confess. Alex is still denying any harm to Gemma. Insists he's only interested in his parental rights; swears he had nothing to do with the dolls.

Laura will need to see a doctor before she can be interviewed. Her mother in Canada has meantime confirmed more details; that Laura had been obsessing about the anniversary for months. Researching Ed and his new family on the internet. No one understood why and no one expected her to fly to the UK.

In custody, Laura keeps pleading with staff . . .

You have to help me find my husband. No one will help me. This man who took my husband; he's not who he says he is . . .

All they have beyond the arrests is a small breakthrough back at the office. The team finally have access to Gemma's social-media accounts and it looks as if Laura was the one sending her messages. *He's not who he says he is.* So that's more fuel for the interviews once they can get going.

As for Sam's wife – Lily Blake has been taken straight to hospital. She's in shock. Mel says she may just be a first-class actor but, no surprise, she claims to know nothing of her husband's shooting. For now, they can't risk putting a foot wrong. She too will need the medical all-clear re the pregnancy before any interviews.

Matthew scrapes his hand through his hair and again checks his watch. An hour and a quarter before the cathedral ceremony. He needs to hurry.

The only niggle? They haven't yet found the gun. But even that's not unusual.

Right now, Matthew wishes more than anything that he was Mel's key sergeant so he could lead on all the interviews when they do get going. With his family still down in Cornwall, he's had quite enough of waiting. The whole case is swirling around his head. He knows *exactly* what needs to be asked. Of all of them.

He puts his phone to his ear, watching a woman across the car park bashing her fist into the ticket machine. He shakes his head; *as if that's going to end well.*

'Hello, darling. You OK?'

'We're fine.' Sally sounds as if she's in the middle of something – clattering of crockery in the background. 'Sorry. Just doing the dishwasher. Any more news?'

'No change. We're going to get the ceremony out the way and then we can focus on the interviews.'

'Oh.' She pauses. 'With all the drama, I almost forgot about the wretched ceremony. Surely they're not still going ahead?' Sally's tone has changed. 'Do you really have to go? I mean – now that it's sorted. Now they're all caught.'

Matthew lets out a long, slow breath. Truth is he would prefer not to face Maidstead Cathedral again. There's been an urgent conference call – the university, the police and the local MP. It's going ahead and Mel needs him there. There have been terse messages from Amanda, who had the hump for being kept out of the loop over Sam's ID earlier. She's clearly under pressure today too. He remembers that she was among those who wanted the final graduation cancelled right at the start of this. She looked tired on the news earlier, issuing a statement paying tribute to Sam's service to the university. *It's a terrible shock and loss. There will be a commemoration in due course, but the family don't want the students let down; they've worked so hard. They want them to graduate today.*

Matthew can't think of anything worse than having to deal with the media all the time. What a job.

There was a moment when Matthew was sure the university *would* cancel. But the police hierarchy are in overdrive, issuing reassurances after the arrests to keep the tourism chiefs happy.

Meantime the poor Hartleys are having it tough. Today was always going to bring the media out in droves even before Sam's death. Rachel and Ed have had notes through the door at home. Messages on social media, begging for interviews.

One journalist even turned up at the hospital, pretending to be a relative. Mel's livid. *I want that reporter arrested. Given a scare . . .*

She was trying to breach security in a serious investigation. I've had enough.

'If you have to go to the cathedral, you'll wear your protective vest, Matthew? Like you promised.' Sally's voice again.

'Sal, I told you. It's over. You can stop worrying, love.' Matthew glances at his boot. He never told Sally or Mel that he gave Wendy his vest when they arrested Laura earlier. 'They're all in custody. We just need to figure out which one now, find the gun and build a watertight case.'

'They haven't found the gun yet?'

Matthew shuts his eyes. '*Please* don't stress. It's not unusual. Probably in a river or a bin somewhere. We'll find it.'

'Yeah, but you know me. I keep thinking what happened last time. Better safe than sorry. Wear your vest? Please?'

He doesn't answer.

Matthew checks his watch. 'Look. I'm sorry darling but I need to go.' His gaze is again drawn to the woman who's now kicking the ticket machine in frustration.

'So where are you now?'

'At the hospital. Mel's asked me to quickly check in with the Hartleys before I go to the cathedral. Courtesy update. They've been having a lot of hassle with the media. I'll ring you later. How's our lovely girl, by the way?'

'Painting seagulls. She's fine. You coming down for us soon?'

'Absolutely. As soon as I know how the interviews are shaping up. Look. I'd better go. Love you.'

'You too.'

Matthew rolls his lips together, surprised at how dry they feel. An hour and a bit until the cathedral service starts. So tight. For just a moment he thinks back to that awful day. Everyone running and screaming. Sally's face when he turned in the opposite direction. Gemma on the floor of the cathedral . . .

288

All those terrified students. *Ice cream. Ice cream.*

He can't quite believe that was just nine days ago. He takes a deep breath and is just about to head to the machine himself when his mobile rings. He expects Mel again – but it's an unknown number.

'Is that Matthew Hill?'

'I'm sorry but I can hardly hear you.'

'Sorry. Satellite phone. Borrowed from a journalist. I'm Molly Price, the university HR. I'm still on Meltona.'

The *hurricane*. He'd forgotten about that. They've had no luck reaching her all week.

There's terrible crackling on the line.

'I'm sorry. Can you speak up?' Matthew tries to adjust the volume through more interference.

And then the line goes dead.

CHAPTER 63

THE MOTHER

Ed's gone for a quick shower to freshen up before all the coverage of the ceremony. He's using the relatives' room on the floor below. Shouldn't be long.

I'm glad actually as I want to go through the laptop some more. I can't bear this feeling of helplessness. Just sitting here, waiting for the cathedral to be on the news again. I honestly can't decide what will be worse. To watch it. Or not watch it.

I try a few more essay titles. Chaucer. Shakespeare. All real. Pages and pages of it with links to research notes. And then at last I find something new. Just the title – *Poetry*. No essay question. I click open the file.

Amanda, it turns out, is not right in the head. Seriously.

I freeze. *Amanda?* Tingling in both my arms. Why on earth is Gemma writing about *Amanda*?

I scroll . . .

It's like she has this split personality . . .

. . . I wish I'd never asked for the bloody work experience now. Never persuaded her to change her mind about it; never got to know her . . .

I look at Gemma in the bed, goosebumps covering both my arms. Amanda has never mentioned working with Gemma; knowing her so *personally*.

My heart's pounding as I take my mobile from my pocket and dial DI Sanders. As the call connects, I skim more words, trying to make sense of what the hell this means. Why my daughter has this panic pouring from the page – over *Amanda*.

There's no answer. DI Sanders' phone goes straight to voicemail.

CHAPTER 64

THE PRIVATE INVESTIGATOR

It takes Matthew three attempts to reconnect to the satellite phone. A reporter answers. She's abrupt, saying she needs to file copy.

'This is an attempted murder investigation.'

That peaks her interest. At last she calls out Molly's name and the university head of HR is back on the line.

'Matthew Hill. The Gemma Hartley inquiry. You called me?'

'Oh. Yes. I had a message that I needed to speak to DI Sanders but she's not answering. They gave me your number instead. Look. We have limited time on the phone. All very basic on the ground here. I heard about Gemma Hartley but we only found out about Sam's murder from the media here this morning. So awful. And well, I'm in a bit of a panic now. The thing is, you might want to speak to our communications lead.'

'Amanda?'

'Yes. She's on gardening leave but her address is on file.'

Matthew feels something shift inside.

'Amanda's not on leave. She's really busy. Right in the thick of it. Especially today.'

'No. That can't be right.' Molly's tone changes completely. 'She *agreed*. To hand over to her deputy. We had an understanding. I've put a package together.'

'I'm not following you.'

'It's just – I've only just heard about Sam, you see.' She sounds confused now. Babbling. 'I couldn't *know*. I would have tried harder to get through before if I'd realised . . .' Again the line fades out.

'Please. You need to speak quickly. What about Amanda?'

'I'm having to let her go. I caught her taking drugs. Then found out she'd lied on her CV. Not so serious at this stage in her tenure, but we had a big disagreement. Amanda got very nasty. Very inappropriate. And then I found out the drugs issue went back years.' Another pause. 'I gave her a choice. A package to avoid anything unpleasant in the press . . . or suspension. She agreed to gardening leave until I'm back. Until I speak to the chancellor, who was away when it all blew up.'

Matthew's mind is now in overdrive, his adrenaline pumping.

'There's something else.' The line's still poor and Matthew tries to adjust his volume.

'When she first joined the university, Amanda got in a bit of a pickle personally.'

CHAPTER 65

First light today

The problem, Amanda thinks, is that people don't listen. Not properly.

Before she heads out to speak, first to Sam and then to Gemma, Amanda takes her diaries from her bedroom and puts the tall stack on the stand in the nursery.

It makes her feel good to see it. Her story. Her truth.

Whatever happens today, they will have to listen now. She thinks of all the thick, black words in the diaries and imagines her voice being heard at last. Everyone wishing they had listened to her sooner.

She's been up since four but that's not unusual. She sits in the nursery chair and takes in the elephant curtains. The cot. The mobile. The sun's just coming up and she wonders how today will go but she's not afraid; not at all. If there's any justice, if there is any such thing as karma, today is the day they will all finally see that her plan for this baby is what is best. It's what she deserves. Needs. Is owed.

She thinks of that other child – her own child who would be fifteen now. If a girl, they would be best friends. Shopping and spas and friendly fights over borrowed clothes. If a boy? A messy room. Football up too loud on the telly. She would have taught him to cook. Found common ground.

She turns her head and can imagine it exactly – the voice shouting up the stairs. You up there, Mum?

Instead she takes in the silence. How it eats right into her flesh. The emptiness – both around her and deep inside her too. Every time she puts her key in the door. She has to clench her fists to push down the bile and the rage, when she thinks of Sam, sitting with her in that clinic all those years ago. 'It's the right decision, Amanda. It's just not the right time for us to have a child.'

She thinks of him now with his pretty young wife and his pretty suburban house. How is it fair that he is the one to have the family?

No. He needs to speak to Gemma and to sort it all out. Gemma surviving is a sign that this was all meant to be. Gemma doesn't need this child; Gemma is still a child herself.

Amanda checks the time – just gone five – and feels in her pocket to smooth her fingers over the familiar white tablets in the plastic sachet. It would never have come to this if people had just listened. The doctor. Sam. Gemma. All of them . . .

But she will be heard today. However this goes.

She turns again to the diaries, neatly stacked. Corners aligned. It's all in there. She used a fountain pen once. Smart. Expensive. But it made the words too soft. Too quiet. These days she uses a thick, black felt tip – to match the voice in her head.

And if they won't listen today – Sam and Gemma? She knows what she will do; she planned it once before and she wasn't afraid then either. Because afterwards, they will have to hear her. Afterwards they will all read the thick, black words and they will see that none of this was her fault.

It will be too late and they will all be very, very sorry.

That they didn't listen sooner.

CHAPTER 66

THE MOTHER

As she steps into our cubicle, my eyes dart straight to Gemma.

'*Amanda*.' I stand up and glance at the window but there's no sign of anyone. No guard. No nurse. No Ed. 'I thought we were going to do the statement by email?' I try so hard to make my tone less surprised – steadier – but it's unnaturally high. I clear my throat, Amanda all the while watching me intently.

'Please. Don't get up, Rachel. I thought it would be easier for me to just pop by. Go over the statement in person. Have you jotted something down for me?'

I check the window again. No one; the guard must still be dealing with the journalist who tried to get through earlier.

'I'm surprised you didn't have trouble getting in. We're on a sort of lockdown.' My heart's pounding.

'Oh, it was fine. The nurse in the office saw me on the telly earlier.' She's smiling and holds up her university pass by way of illustration, before moving to the spare seat at the end of Gemma's bed.

I pull my own chair forward, closer to Gemma, and place my hand on the bedding. Gemma's diary made it clear Amanda was hounding her. But I still don't understand *why*.

'This is very good of you, Amanda.' I worry that she will see my hand trembling so pull it back into my lap. 'You must be so busy . . . with the ceremony.'

'Happy to help. I'm just so sorry you've had such a tricky time with the media.'

I look again at Gemma and realise I walked right into this. Amanda messaged earlier, asking if I wanted any help to get the media off our backs. It was before I read the laptop again. I said yes.

The television's on mute but there are pictures of everyone arriving at the cathedral. A reporter is summing up the whole, horrible story. The attack on Gemma. The professor found dead this morning. The fact that some families have decided at the eleventh hour not to attend the graduation after all.

'Shall I turn it off? The TV?' I have no idea how to play this. How to make Amanda *leave*. 'So you reckon the reporters will back off if we just make a short statement?' That's what her message said would happen.

'Yes. I do realise it's asking a lot, Mrs Hartley, but it's the strategy I always advise.'

'Rachel. Please.'

'Rachel.' She tilts her head, her eyes narrowing. 'I'll be giving another briefing to the media when I get back to the cathedral green, so I can include your statement. That should keep them happy. Keep them off your back, hopefully.'

'Thank you. Very good of you. So let's get this done then. I'm sure you're tight for time.' I glance again at the window. Still no guard. No sign of Ed.

'So have you had time to write a few words? About how Gemma's doing. The relief about the arrests. And wishing the new graduates well today?'

I reach for my iPad and notice that Amanda is staring at the end of Gemma's bed. The little hill created by the frame over her missing leg.

'Helen mentioned that she opened her eyes?'

Amanda's tone has changed and I feel bile in my throat. I clench my fist, digging the nails into my palm. I should *never* have messaged Helen.

And then my mobile rings. I move to take it from my pocket but Amanda stands.

'Don't answer that, Rachel.'

She's now staring at Gemma's face, her expression much darker. And I notice her pupils look strange. My eyes dart to the laptop. Gemma wrote about the pupils.

Amanda reaches into her bag.

'You're not to answer your phone, Rachel. You're not even to *touch* your phone. Do you understand me?'

CHAPTER 67

THE PRIVATE INVESTIGATOR

'Mel. We have a problem. Where's Amanda?'

'Amanda? I think they said the Hartleys asked to see her. Something about helping with the media. She's due back here in half an hour. Actually – hang on. There's a message on my phone from Rachel Hartley. Hold a moment. Let me listen.'

Matthew presses the lift button for the fifth floor.

'Oh Lord. Rachel's saying Amanda knew Gemma personally. Was hassling her. There's something on Gemma's laptop about it, something we *missed*.'

'I know. Mel, listen.' Matthew feels the rush of adrenaline. 'Looks like we got this wrong. There's a strong chance Amanda's our shooter.' A beat of silence. 'I just took a call too, from that head of HR. The one abroad. She finally got your message.'

'Right . . .' Mel is making the familiar segue from shock into fifth gear. 'Putting you on hold while I speak to armed response . . .'

Matthew waits and watches the lift numbers. Three. Four.

'OK. Armed team are in the grounds. On standby to move to the ward.' Mel's voice again. 'So what do we have? I need to phone Rachel Hartley back.'

'Amanda's being eased out. She's unstable. A serial drug user. And' – he pauses as the doors open on the fifth floor – 'she had an affair with Sam Blake when she first joined the university.'

Matthew steps out on to the corridor opposite the coffee machine. No one in sight.

'I need to speak to the team again. Where exactly are you?'

'Right outside the ward. I've got this.' He's staring at the double doors, his heartbeat increasing.

'No, Matt. Wait until I get armed response up there.'

'I'll speak to the nurses. If she's here already, we can't wait. I'll work with the guard on the ward.'

'He's not there. Still dealing with that reporter. *Not* on your own, Matt. It's too dangerous.'

CHAPTER 68

THE DAUGHTER – *BEFORE*

Poetry

This is getting off-the-scale ridiculous. Proper harassment. I thought I could just make it through to the graduation but I'm not sure any more. I'm wondering if I should just phone home? Or tell someone here at the university? Even the police?

I wish I'd never asked for the bloody work experience now. Never persuaded her to change her mind about it. Never got to know her . . .

Amanda, it turns out, is not right in the head. *Seriously*.

It's like she has this split personality. I mean – she seems so together on the surface. The smart suits and all the strutting about, managing photo shoots and press conferences. Always so busy, busy, busy. So 'on it'. But underneath, she's just like the rest of us. No. Way, way worse than the rest of us. She's messed up. Dilated pupils. Def on something some days.

When she changed her mind about the work experience, I was so grateful. Two whole weeks in her office. It was perfect for my CV. And she was so nice to me at first. Coffees and sandwiches at lunchtime at work. Then a drink in the bar after a really long day. Then a meal out to talk about my career. My future.

And then? After she caught me crying in the loo one day and I stupidly blurted it all out – broke down about the baby – I thought she was being so much more than a mentor. A new *friend*. The shoulder I so badly needed. Steady. Kind. So supportive.

She actually invited me round to her house, and it was such a relief to have one person on the planet to properly confide in. I couldn't believe how steady she was. I should have realised it was all fake; that none of it was to help me.

It was after I confided about the pregnancy – not knowing what to do – that she started to get really weird. Said she was retiring early. It was a big secret, she said, but it could solve *everything* for me. For both of us. She said she could help with my career. Help with the baby too. Some days it was like she was on something. Wired. When she first mentioned private adoption, I thought she meant advice. Something for me to investigate. An option for me. But that's *not* what she meant at all.

Plus she somehow guessed who the father was. Confronted me. And now she's texting me constantly. Trying to get me to change my mind. She's got this mad idea that I should let *her* have my baby. Can you believe it? A sort of 'unofficial' arrangement. She's off her head!

I'm keeping well clear but she's threatening to phone my parents. To report the affair and challenge my degree. *Do you really want everyone to know how you got your first?* As if. I spent three years slaving for it.

So. For now I'm just trying to distance myself. To get back on track. I've told her to stay away from me. That I just want to get past the graduation, and then talk to my parents.

CHAPTER 69

THE PRIVATE INVESTIGATOR

'Hello. Coffee break.' Matthew moves quickly into the cubicle, pushing the door shut with his foot behind him. Both Rachel and Amanda are seated. Body language very tense.

'The nurses mentioned on the door you were here so I got you a black, Amanda. That OK?' He holds out a cup to her and notices immediately that her pupils are dilated.

Rachel widens her eyes and glances towards a trolley next to Amanda. There's a phone on the top shelf. It vibrates with a text or message.

'I didn't know you were coming here.' Amanda stares at him and reaches for the phone, which she puts in her jacket pocket. She doesn't check the message. Is that Rachel's phone? Is that what she's signalling?

On the satellite call, Molly said Amanda had been caught using cocaine but had confessed to an addiction to sleeping tablets and other prescription drugs too. She blamed it all on the trauma over Sam. Molly also discovered she didn't even have a degree (as her CV stated) – a baseline requirement for senior staff. Alone, she said she would have overlooked it, but in context it was leverage for the severance. The drugs were the main issue.

Matthew wonders what exactly Amanda's using. He thinks of Sam's murder just a few hours earlier. He considers an immediate dive to put her in a hold, but Amanda quickly pulls her bag on to her lap and reaches into it. She meets his eye as a warning. He stills himself.

'Could you give us a minute, Matthew? We were just sorting out something private here.' Amanda's still looking at him and keeps her hand firmly inside her bag, clearly gripping something.

'Actually I've asked Amanda to leave now.' Rachel stands and moves closer to Gemma's bed. 'I'm very tired.'

'I won't stay, then. Just wanted to update that it's all going well at the cathedral.' Matthew pretends to check his watch. 'I need to get back there, actually. Can give you a lift if you like, Amanda?'

'I've got my own car.' Amanda scrapes her chair backwards towards the wall so that she can see both Matthew and Rachel Hartley too.

Matthew sips his drink. 'Where's your husband?' He keeps his voice steady as he looks at Rachel.

'Taking a shower.'

'Maybe you'd like to take a little break too. Join him? Get some rest?'

'She's going nowhere. Actually, can we change seats, Rachel?' Amanda glances between Rachel and the window on to the ward. The blinds are down but Matthew's hoping once the armed officers arrive, they'll be able to make out movements through the gaps.

'I'm fine here. I like to be next to Gemma.' Rachel's voice cracks and Matthew can see that her hand is shaking as she reaches out to take her daughter's.

'I *said* we need to change seats.' Amanda's head is jerking strangely, like a tic, and she takes her right hand, now holding a gun, from her bag and points it at Gemma.

Rachel lets out a horrible noise. Like an animal in pain. She then throws herself on to the bed, shielding Gemma's body. 'You stay away from her. You leave us alone.'

'It's going to be all right, Mrs Hartley. Let's keep everything nice and calm.' Matthew keeps his gaze fixed on Amanda, who moves into Rachel's seat in the corner. It's deliberate. She's placed herself out of line of sight through the window to the ward and hence out of line of *shot* from the ward. She must have guessed about the backup.

'Come on, Amanda. You don't want to make this any worse. You don't want to hurt anyone here.' Matthew speaks slowly but Amanda won't even look at him. It's unlikely now that armed support will be able to get a clean shot when they do turn up. So he's on his own. His mind's in overdrive, trying to work out the least dangerous of his options.

'You need to wake Gemma up.' Amanda's voice is cross suddenly, and still her head is sort of twitching. 'I told you already, Mrs Hartley, I need to talk to your daughter.'

Rachel is crying now, still lying across her daughter's form in the bed. Matthew thinks of Amelie and something shifts inside. He knows he'd do the same. Try to shield her.

'I can't wake her up. She's in a coma. What's the *matter* with you?'

'Come on, Amanda. She's right. We can't talk to Gemma today. But we can work something out. Amanda. Look at me. Talk to *me*.'

At last she turns to him, also moving the gun. Pointed now at Matthew.

'She opened her eyes. She's faking it.'

A pause. Matthew waits.

'I just want what's fair. Don't you see that?' Amanda tilts her head towards the mother and daughter huddled together on the bed. One utterly still. The other weeping. 'Look at them. I just want to know what *that's* like.' She pauses again. 'To be everything to someone.' Her tone is darker. Determined. 'I've got nothing else now. Only the baby. I just need to talk to Gemma. Make her *listen.*'

Matthew's mind is whirling, trying to figure out what the hell Amanda means about Gemma's baby. He needs to distract her. Turn her away from Gemma.

'Look. I can understand why you're so upset. About the job. After all you've done for the university.'

'You *know about that*?' Amanda lets out a little huff.

'Must be devastating.'

'I gave my whole life to that place.'

'Yes. Yes, you did.'

'It's ridiculous. You don't need a degree to do a good job.' She pauses, that chin twitch again. 'And half of the students take drugs. They don't throw *them* out.' Her tone's more distant, as if she's talking to herself. Still he needs her to look at him, not Gemma.

'So what happened with Sam, Amanda?'

She narrows her eyes and for a beat Matthew regrets the question.

'Why don't we move outside? Just you and me. And we can talk about what happened with Sam. I want to listen. I want to understand.' Matthew pauses as Amanda stares at Gemma, wrapped in her mother's arms on the bed. 'Whatever's happened, it's not Gemma's fault.'

'He spun her the very same story, you know.'

'Sam?'

'Yes. I waited for him.' Her face changes again. 'I waited for him and look what happened. I get nothing and *she* gets a baby.'

She turns the gun towards Gemma again. 'You need to wake her up. We need to talk. That baby *needs* me.'

Matthew's just trying to calculate the risk. The distance between him and Amanda across the room. If he dives, can he disarm her? Or will it trigger the shot?

But Rachel's standing up. She turns to step between Amanda and the bed. 'You can't seriously think that anyone would ever let *you* near a baby?'

'No, Rachel.' He puts up his arm, but Rachel's eyes are wide and defiant.

'You stay away from my daughter.'

And then Rachel suddenly lurches towards Amanda herself and all options are gone. Matthew dives too. There's the thunder of the gun firing. A huge punch to his chest. He can't tell where he is any more. On the ground? Is he on the ground?

His eyes are open but he can see only blackness.

There's screaming. 'You did this. You all did this.' He can't tell whose voice.

A second shot.

He blinks and blinks but still cannot see properly. Just a blur of more shapes in the room. More loud voices.

And somehow he's in another room too. So many young and frightened faces in their gowns and their mortar boards, all staring at him.

Ice cream. Ice cream.

And then it is their hall at home and Amelie is running down the stairs. *Daddy, Daddy. You need to get up.*

But he can't get up.

He can feel all the air and the blood seeping from his insides. But he can't see. He can't make Amelie hear him.

And he can't get up.

EPILOGUE

THE MOTHER

I regret the suit. Too hot. But they never get the forecast right, do they?

At least the baby looks cool. Gorgeous, actually.

I lean in to offer a finger and she grasps it in that endearing and utterly centred way, focusing her eyes with great concentration as if my finger's the most exciting thing she's seen all day. She clings tighter, tighter and then her expression starts to change and I realise what's really going on here.

'Oh no.' Gemma's tone is mortified as she leans in to watch her daughter's face also. 'She's doing a poo. Oh, Sophie, not now. *Please* – not now.'

The baby, my beautiful granddaughter – pink and plump and perfect in cream silk gown and matching bow in her hair – has decided to celebrate her first visit to church in her own inimitable style. I watch, first the pursing of the lips that to the untrained eye could be a smile, but changing – ah, yes – to that special sort of *grimace*.

'What do we do?' Gemma looks at me in a panic. 'Mum. Everyone's ready to start. What do we do?'

I move swiftly, Sophie still in my arms, to the side of the church, closer to the door that leads to the corridor. Gemma follows.

'It doesn't matter, honey. I'll ask the vicar for ten minutes. Here. You go and change her. No one will mind. There's a proper station in the ladies. I saw it earlier.'

'But the *dress*. I can't manage Sophie's dress in there.'

'Let's just whip it off here for a minute.'

'We can't do that.'

'Course we can. No one will see.' I lift Sophie under her bare arms and hold her out – legs dangling – to her mother, smiling at how surreal that word, that new label feels. *Mother. My little girl . . . a mother.* 'Take her through in her vest and I'll bring the dress in a few minutes.' I unzip the beautiful silk and between us, we slip it off, leaving Sophie in her pink, sleeveless vest and nappy – legs kicking. 'Do you want me to come with you? Help?'

'No. I'm fine. I can do it. You speak to the vicar.'

I put the dress carefully over my arm and watch Gemma head through the double doors towards the ladies in the corridor. I take in the blade – how effortlessly she now walks on her blade – and feel overwhelmed with love for her.

I think of the day she finally woke from the coma and how I so stupidly thought the whole bad dream was over. *No brain damage.* And then the *new* nightmare. All the physio. The pain. The tears. My brave, brave girl learning how to adjust her stance and her balance as her shape and her weight changed week on week through the pregnancy. Learning and relearning how to walk.

I think of her now out running while Sophie naps; how much easier she finds that blade.

I'm going to wear my blade today, not the leg. Do you think people will mind?

Of course no one will mind.

I wait for the doors to swing back into place behind her before I turn, spotting the vicar. I hold up my hand and sweep across the front of the church to share news of our little impasse. He laughs. A family man himself.

I stand alone then at the front, needing a moment. We are not especially religious. Haven't been in any kind of church since . . . Well, you know. But it's a pretty little church and Gemma so wanted this christening. This blessing. *She can make up her own mind about religion later, don't you think, Mum?*

It's a modern design – pale stone and contemporary stained-glass windows. The sun is out, casting dancing shapes of blue and green and red across the pale oak floor. That other Rachel, that Rachel before, would watch the colours and find it pretty. But this Rachel – no. This Rachel thinks only of those wretched jugs from Alex. Blue and green and red.

I smashed them all after his case – *smash, smash*. Shocked at my capacity for rage. They gave him community service, would you believe. *Community service.* The only silver lining – he's not Sophie's father. Gemma decided on a test. So we have a restraining order in place. He must never come near any of us again.

I brush the skirt of my dress and think of my counsellor. She's a great one for breathing. In through the nose and out through the mouth. *And count, Rachel.* I had expected to be past it all by now but she says I must be patient. And so I do the breathing. Four cycles and I feel a little calmer. I check my watch, wondering if they'll come.

I tap my foot and take in the little huddle of people, waiting to take up their seats. Ed chatting to my mother. He seems to feel my stare, turns and smiles. I smile back and lift the dress to signal the pause. He laughs. We're doing so much better – me and Ed. *No more secrets.*

He winks then swings his body back to my mother and I turn my gaze too. Near the font, a few of Gemma's university friends are gathered in an animated group, looking so young and fresh-skinned with their long hair and their high heels. Their high hopes.

I wonder if any of them were there. That awful day. The cathedral. *No, don't, Rachel. And breathe . . .*

I check my watch again. Were we even right to send the invitation? Probably not de rigueur at all. I mean – it's a job, isn't it? Not really personal. They didn't reply but nor did lots of others and sometimes people just forget, don't they?

Gemma so wants them here.

A couple of minutes pass and I'm just about to leave to help her out when there's the squeak of the main door. And at last there he is. Impossibly tall with his curly hair and alongside him a beautiful, slim woman and the prettiest little girl with golden curls to match her father.

I hurry through the aisle to greet them.

'*Matthew*. I'm *so* glad you came.' I want to hug him hello but realise this might be every kind of wrong. Not least because his arm is still in a sling. The last email said he'd had a second surgery on the shoulder.

'How's the arm doing?'

'Surgeon's happy. Should be right as rain. Back on the golf course in no time. I'm just wearing this to milk it.'

His wife smiles and holds out her hand. 'He doesn't even play golf. But he *is* milking it.'

'You must be Sally. I'm pleased to meet you.' I beam, worrying quietly what she really thinks of it all. Of me. Of us.

'You too, Mrs Hartley.' Her smile reaches her eyes and I'm relieved.

'Rachel, please.'

I hold on to her hand and squeeze it. I've always felt it was my fault. Matthew getting shot. Wish I could find the right words. 'We owe your husband so much. I'm really so very sorry. About the injury.'

She doesn't answer but holds the smile and squeezes my hand in return. And I realise that I cannot imagine what it's really like. To live the way he does. The way *they* do.

'Good job she nagged me to wear the vest, eh?' Matthew's winking. The story in the paper said the bulletproof vest was a last-minute thing. It was in his boot after he loaned it to a colleague. He only put it on after talking to Sally on the phone. Without it? Best not to think . . .

'You see. You should *always* listen to your wife,' I say, and we all laugh.

'Where's the baby?' The little girl looks disappointed, casting her eye around the church. 'There's no baby.'

'Comfort break. Number twos.' I grimace, lowering my voice.

'Oh dear.' Sally's now grinning. 'Remember that all too well. She's having a nappy change, Amelie.'

'Yuck!'

'I'm sparing the dress.' I lift up the folds of silk to illustrate as Amelie asks if she can light a candle and Sally nods, leading her to the side of the church where a black, wrought-iron stand of candles is casting dancing opals on the stained-glass window above.

'Seriously. Is the arm going to be OK, Matthew?'

'It is.'

'I'm so sorry. What I did. I should have left it to you. I just—' I'm thinking of that moment of madness. Diving at Amanda.

'Please. We've been through this, Rachel. It was Amanda's fault – all of it. Not yours. You were very brave.'

'Was I?' I close my eyes to the picture that still haunts my dreams the most. Matthew on the floor – shot and bleeding. And then Amanda – the gun to her own head, her eyes darting to Gemma then meeting mine one last time. *You did this. You all did this.* And then the horrible boom of the second shot, Amanda's body thrown backwards with the force.

And for the first time in that sad little cubicle, with all the blood and the mayhem as police rushed in, everyone shouting – *man down, man down* – I was glad of Gemma's coma. *Don't wake up, Gemma. Don't wake up just yet.*

'How's Gemma doing?'

It was ten more days before she opened her eyes. And at last kept them open.

'Amazing. You'll see in a minute. Actually, I'd better go. Give her a hand.'

'Of course.'

I put my hand on his good arm. And for a minute I just keep it there, eyes closed once more.

Matthew and I last talked at Amanda's inquest. Ed didn't want me to go but I had no choice – a witness summons – and, in any case, I wanted to try to understand the mania. Why on earth Amanda would do that to Gemma.

While we waited for the coroner, Matthew told me about Laura's transfer back to Canada. Some appeal deal brokered by her mother. Laura will have to stay under supervision but in a special unit, not jail. Turns out she was sending messages to Gemma as well as stalking me. She found Ed on a website through his work. Said in court that she needed to warn Gemma and me too that the man 'posing as Ed' was an imposter. *He's not who he says he is.*

She sent the note to Matthew via his daughter after reading about his work on the case. Checked his background online and got it into her head that he might be the one to finally listen to her. *You have to help me find my husband. No one will believe me.*

The sad thing is she went back to Wells Cathedral, genuinely hoping to find the 'real' Ed there again. For their anniversary.

And then the inquest.

It was held in a dark, wood-panelled room in a town hall and wasn't at all what I expected. Deep down, I suppose what I needed and wanted was a day in court for *Gemma*. A reckoning.

But that's not what I got; not what an inquest is. Both Matthew and DI Sanders tried to prepare me but I didn't truly understand until I was sitting in the room. I remember this horrible wave of realisation as the coroner explained his remit; that his job was not to rule on Amanda's crimes but on her death. Only why and how she died.

I sat there and the cruelty of it finally hit me. I wasn't there, in that dark and horrible room, as the mother of the victim. I was there as the last person to see Amanda alive.

We did at least get more of the story. The police found a nursery set up at her house. A cot with a mobile in place. A nursing chair in the corner. Elephant curtains at the window.

There were diaries too – a huge stack. Mad and angry scribblings filling page after page. Turns out Amanda had an affair with Sam when she first started at the university in her thirties. She fell pregnant but had a termination which she later deeply regretted. Sam said it was 'the wrong time'. That his wife was fragile. Not Lily; this was his *first* wife.

Amanda waited for him. Continued the affair on and off for more than a decade. She genuinely believed that, one day, he would get divorced and they would have a family of their own. But she suffered insomnia and stress and became dependent on sleeping tablets. When her doctor tried to reduce her dose, she went to dealers. And so the drugs spiral began.

When Sam *eventually* divorced, it wasn't Amanda he turned to. Instead, he broke it off with her and within two years married the much younger Lily. Amanda never got over it.

And then when Molly caught her using cocaine at work, Amanda saw it as the end. The loss of not just her job, but *everything*.

I'd not understood the link with Gemma until the inquest. Seems when Amanda found out about Gemma's pregnancy – Sam the father – she simply became fixated. And deluded. Her last chance for purpose. Happiness. She came up with this fantasy where Amanda would get her final chance to be a mother and Gemma could carry on with her life.

The coroner was told Amanda paid one of her dealers to deliver the dolls. To confuse the inquiry; to frighten the Hartleys and Matthew's family too. She got the gun from the same dealer. It matched the bullet used on Gemma. Sam too.

Amanda's diary claimed she never meant to kill Gemma; she actually planned to kill *herself* at that first graduation. A huge and bloody gesture in front of everyone from the stone balcony above the audience, supposedly to bring shame on the university for getting rid of her so cruelly. She wanted it public. A letter in her pocket pointing everyone to her diaries. *My truth.*

But when she saw Gemma, so lovely and so young in her robe down below – her whole life ahead of her – carrying the baby Amanda was now too old to have, she was in the moment overwhelmed with jealousy and rage. And made a different choice.

And Sam? Amanda's diary said she was going to Sam to press him to use his rights as the father. To persuade Gemma when she recovered to let Amanda have the baby after all.

What was so difficult is that Amanda seemed to genuinely see all this as *reasonable. Possible.*

The coroner nailed it in his summing up. 'Clearly we all know that she would never have been allowed to parent that child. This was the sad and deluded thinking of someone who'd lost all sense of the real world. We cannot know how that confrontation with Sam Blake went. Only how it so tragically ended.'

The verdict, as expected – suicide. And that was it. Over. Done. Everyone stood up as the coroner left the room but I didn't. Couldn't. I remember sitting there and feeling completely numb; that it just wasn't enough. No full stop.

I started muttering and Matthew had to take me into the corridor to find a glass of water, to calm me down.

But where's the justice, Matthew? Where's the justice for Gemma?

I promise that I do try not to dwell. The problem is it's a bit like a haunting and sometimes when the scenes all swirl in my head – just like the light through those windows in this church – I spiral; find myself muttering out loud all over again. Like some crazy woman.

'It's OK, Rachel. It's really over now.' Matthew is leaning in and I open my eyes.

'Sorry. Was I muttering?' I blush. Don't want to be this new Rachel.

'Not muttering but miles away.'

'Sorry. Sorry.'

'Don't be.' He's whispering. 'Look. It's very hard to cross paths with someone like Amanda. Someone that broken. The trick is to stop trying to make sense of it, Rachel. You have to try to let it go.'

'You sound like my counsellor.'

He laughs. I smile. Matthew was the one to recommend therapy after it worked so well for his daughter.

I take in his expression. I glance to Amelie who is on tiptoe, lighting her candle, and then back to this good man. This good father. This man who could so easily have been lost too.

'*Thank you*, Matthew.' The words sound so inadequate but he is smiling and so I finally let go of his arm, start my breathing exercises again. And make my excuses.

I hurry away to the ladies to find Gemma babbling to Sophie as she hurls the soiled nappy into the lidded, stainless-steel bin. 'Now isn't that better, young lady? You comfy now? Ready for your big entrance?'

Sophie tries to grab her mother's necklace as Gemma lifts her into her arms from the changing station.

'Give her to me while you wash your hands.'

'Thanks, Mum.'

I take Sophie and move over to a chair in the corner so that I can pop her dress back on, juggling her arms through the layers of silk and leaning back as she tries to grab my glasses. 'There. Don't you look pretty?'

I stand and look at Gemma through the mirror. My brave and beautiful girl. She dries her hands and as she turns to me, I lean forward to plant a kiss on her forehead.

For a moment she freezes. Frowning. She looks back at me through the mirror and then turns to me directly, puzzled, as if trying to figure something out.

'Do that again.'

'What?'

'Kiss me on the forehead.'

I'm thrown but happily plant a second.

'That's *it*.'

'What?'

She looks aside and then directly at me once more. '*That's* why I came back.'

'What do you mean?'

And now she's smiling, more animated, as if she's just worked out the punchline to a joke. 'You know I don't remember much from the coma. Hardly anything actually, but I do remember something now. I remember feeling you do *that*.' Speaking more quickly now.

'What?'

'Kissing me on the forehead.'

'You really felt that? In the coma?'

'I did. I just remembered that I really did. And one day—' She lets out a huff, still smiling. 'I decided to swim back to you.'

'*Swim?*' She's completely lost me now.

'Oh, never mind. It's complicated, but – that kiss. It's definitely why I came back. Why I woke up.'

I'm utterly confused but also incredibly happy to see her like this.

To imagine that she *did* hear me, or at least sense me near her some of the time. All those long days in that cubicle. This mother who messed up; who got it so very wrong but who has always loved her with every ounce of my being. And then I watch Gemma pass the kiss to her own daughter's forehead.

'Can I really do this, Mum?' She's now holding Sophie in her arms, gazing at her child, her expression and her tone changing. More intense.

She doesn't mean today. She means all of it. Gemma's signed up for teacher training – school-based so I can help with Sophie. It will be tough. We all know that. But when I think of what she's achieved already . . .

'Of course you can.' We've had the talk. About motherhood. All the mistakes I made. 'Just love her,' I add. 'No secrets. And you'll be just fine.'

Gemma smiles again. She takes a deep breath and turns finally to check her own reflection.

'And you're *sure* it's not too pink?' She is tilting her head and pulling at the neckline of her dress as Sophie tries again for the pendant. It's the dress we chose together for her graduation – in that other life. That parallel universe.

I take in the whole picture properly through the mirror. Gemma, *my* Gemma – so brave and beautiful with her blade and her baby and who to me, I swear, has never looked so lovely. This feeling more powerful than breathing – in this moment pounding all the dark scenes into dust.

'No.' I clear my throat. 'It's definitely not too pink.'

AUTHOR'S NOTE

It feels strange to admit it here, but this was a book I initially didn't want to write.

The opening scene in the cathedral came to me a few months after my elder son's glorious and very happy graduation. I was quite shaken – also cross with my brain for coming up with the dark images so soon after the contrast of our happy, happy family day.

I remember telling my husband – well, I'm *definitely* not going to write that up.

But my process has always been a strange one. My stories often feel as if they come through me rather than from me. Yes, yes, I know how ridiculous (and heaven forbid – pretentious) that sounds. I do promise that I realise deep down it's all me but maybe it's because I was a reporter for decades. Maybe my brain likes to work that way – to see these fictional stories and characters as real in the same way my news stories were real so that I can still feel in this new landscape (of make-believe) that I'm trying to do justice to real experiences. And real emotions.

Whatever the case, this story and this dark idea just wouldn't go away, however much I resisted it. In the end it felt as if Gemma and her family stubbornly camped out in my writing room, arms crossed and expressions determined – whispering more and more of the story until I gave in. It was only at the point I realised this was a mother-daughter story, that it was actually a thriller with *love* at its core, that I felt more comfortable with it.

I can only hope that you like how the story turned out all these years after the opening scene flashed into my brain. Thank you so much for reading *Her Perfect Family*. If you've enjoyed the novel, I'd hugely appreciate a review on Amazon. They really do help other readers to discover my books.

I also love to hear from readers so feel free to get in touch. You can find my website at www.teresadriscoll.com and also say hello on Twitter @TeresaDriscoll or via my Facebook author page, www.facebook.com/teresadriscollauthor, and at Instagram too @tkdriscoll_author.

Warm wishes to you all,

Teresa

ACKNOWLEDGMENTS

This is my fifth thriller – and my seventh published novel – and I learn that nothing changes. Trust me, it takes a village to make a book.

So huge thanks go to all those who have so generously played a part in helping to shape this story and send it out into the world – to my fabulous publisher Thomas & Mercer, my patient editors Jack Butler and Jane Snelgrove and my wonderful agent Madeleine Milburn and her team.

I also need to thank, as always, my gorgeous family who are so supportive, especially (with wine and chocolate!) when I hit the inevitable wobble.

And finally my heartfelt thanks go to you, my lovely readers. My stories are now translated into twenty languages and your wonderful messages from across the globe really do mean the world.

I pinch myself daily. To be doing this job – my dream since primary school – is *such* a privilege.

ABOUT THE AUTHOR

Photo © 2015 Claire Tregaskis

For more than twenty-five years as a journalist – including fifteen years as a BBC TV news presenter – Teresa Driscoll followed stories into the shadows of life. Covering crime for so long, she watched and was deeply moved by all the ripples each case caused, and the haunting impact on the families, friends and witnesses involved. It is those ripples that she explores in her darker fiction.

Teresa lives in beautiful Devon with her family. She writes women's fiction as well as thrillers, and her novels have been published in twenty languages. You can find out more about her books on her website (www.teresadriscoll.com) or by following her on Twitter (@TeresaDriscoll) or Facebook (www.facebook.com/teresadriscollauthor) or Instagram (@tkdriscoll_author).